VANESSA NELSON

ASSASSIN'S NOON
AGELESS MYSTERIES - BOOK 4

ASSASSIN'S NOON

Ageless Mysteries - Book 4

Vanessa Nelson

Copyright © 2022 Vanessa Nelson

All rights reserved. This is a work of fiction.

All characters and events in this publication are fictitious and any resemblance to any real person, living or dead, is purely coincidental.

Reproduction in whole or in part of this publication without express written consent is strictly prohibited.

For more information about Vanessa Nelson and her books, please visit: www.taellaneth.com

For John N - with grateful thanks for all your sage advice and insight.

Contents

1. CHAPTER ONE — 1
2. CHAPTER TWO — 13
3. CHAPTER THREE — 19
4. CHAPTER FOUR — 29
5. CHAPTER FIVE — 41
6. CHAPTER SIX — 48
7. CHAPTER SEVEN — 57
8. CHAPTER EIGHT — 61
9. CHAPTER NINE — 73
10. CHAPTER TEN — 79
11. CHAPTER ELEVEN — 84
12. CHAPTER TWELVE — 90
13. CHAPTER THIRTEEN — 99
14. CHAPTER FOURTEEN — 102
15. CHAPTER FIFTEEN — 112
16. CHAPTER SIXTEEN — 125
17. CHAPTER SEVENTEEN — 135
18. CHAPTER EIGHTEEN — 143
19. CHAPTER NINETEEN — 152

20.	CHAPTER TWENTY	158
21.	CHAPTER TWENTY-ONE	166
22.	CHAPTER TWENTY-TWO	171
23.	CHAPTER TWENTY-THREE	180
24.	CHAPTER TWENTY-FOUR	186
25.	CHAPTER TWENTY-FIVE	194
26.	CHAPTER TWENTY-SIX	208
27.	CHAPTER TWENTY-SEVEN	218
28.	CHAPTER TWENTY-EIGHT	227
	THANK YOU	234
	CHARACTER LIST	235
	PLACES	237
	ALSO BY THE AUTHOR	238
	ABOUT THE AUTHOR	240

Chapter One

Thea rubbed her forehead, hoping to ease the tension there, and for the words in front of her to miraculously make sense. It had been a long, tiring day looking for answers and finding nothing. Senior Sergeant Sutter had caught her attention as she arrived back at Middlefield Watch Station and asked for her help. She had hoped that she could, at least, do this one thing. But the pencil marks - thick lines and weird curls - were beyond her comprehension. She could see why Sutter had been having difficulty with the report. It was one of the worst pieces of handwriting she had ever seen. And she had worked with some of the laziest Watchmen in the city.

"No, I'm sorry," she said, handing the paper back to the Senior Sergeant. "I can't make sense of it. Have you tried Everson?" she asked, naming a junior Watchman from her previous station. One of only two Watch members stationed there to still be in service, after the former Sergeant's disgrace. Thea was the other survivor. The pair of them had been the only honest members of that station, as far as she could tell.

"Everson?" Sutter repeated. The Senior Sergeant knew every single member of the Watch across the city, so he wasn't asking about the Watchman's identity, but rather his skill set.

"Yes. He seemed to have a knack for bad handwriting," Thea explained.

"That's good to know," Sutter said. He was a compact man, the top of his head reaching Thea's shoulder, with close-cropped light hair and bright blue eyes. Apart from his neat appearance, he did not seem remarkable at first glance, but he was one of the most intelligent and organised individuals Thea had ever come across. She could almost see the bit of information being filed away in his brain.

He might nominally be second-in-command of the city's Watch, but the Watch would not function without Sutter.

"This may be a silly question, sir, but can't you just ask the Watchman?" Thea asked.

"It's an old report," Sutter said. "There's some dispute between landowners in Fallowfield that's been going on for at least a decade. I'm trying to go through the old reports and see if there's any help there. Sadly, the Watchman who took this report died a few years ago."

Intrigued, Thea was about to ask for more information, distracted by raised voices from the Watch Captain's office.

The captain's door was closed, which had been happening more often over the last couple of weeks. Ever since the Watch had sent Master Merchant Kendrick off to a black ship in disgrace.

With her sensitive hearing, she could still hear the tone and murmur of voices through the heavy wooden door, and had almost got used to the background murmur of voices. The occasional shout still got her attention. And just now, the voices had been raised loud enough to make her turn, frowning.

Thea tilted her head, trying to catch individual words, but the volume had dimmed and all she could hear was the rumble of noise. Ware Handerson, the Watch Captain, had endured visits from a wide variety of people over the past two weeks. Many merchants, usually in twos and threes, as well as tradesmen and women from the city, and even a few of the other more prominent citizens of Accanter, the ones who lived in grand houses within the Citadel perimeter and would never normally dream of setting foot in a humble Watch building.

Thea had not been party to any of the conversations, but the only thing of note that had happened was Kendrick's arrest and disgrace, so she assumed that was what had brought all the attention to the Watch Captain.

"More merchants?" she asked.

"A whole gaggle of them this time," Sutter answered, sighing. "They've been in there for a while." He rubbed his own forehead. "Thank you for your reports, by the way."

"You've read them already?" she asked, surprised. She had only left them for him the day before.

"Yes. Thank you. I've no comments," he said. "I just wanted to let you know that I'm closing the cases and putting them into the records room."

"Thank you," she said.

The reports represented two weeks' worth of work tracking down the rest of the more than one hundred people who had been recorded in Kendrick's ledger. People who had been stolen from their lives and forced into working for Kendrick and his associates. It said something for Kendrick's arrogance that he had kept meticulous records of his crimes, the ledger handed over to Thea by the former merchant's clerk.

Forty-six of the people in the ledger had been found all together and almost all of them had returned to their families. But that had still left a lot of missing people. The ledger had shown that some of the victims were at other addresses around the city, and some of them had died before anyone had known what was happening.

Thea had found almost all of them. In her own office, at the other end of the corridor, she had Kendrick's ledger sitting at the edge of her desk, along with two reports that represented people she had not been able to find. One, or both, of the reports might concern a trickster who had been hiding among Kendrick's prisoners. The creature had appeared as a frail old man on the edge of death when she had spoken to him. Thea had only discovered what he truly was after he had vanished. It was possible the trickster had managed to get caught by Kendrick and ended up on his ledger rather than another non-human, but she was not willing to take the risk. Those reports, and the ledger, would stay on her desk until she had found the answers she needed.

She had spent too much time in the past two weeks following up reports of shallow graves, speaking to bereaved families, and bringing answers where she could. Very often not the answers the families had been hoping for. It had been exhausting but necessary. And today had been another frustrating day of not finding any answers. Still, she was not giving up. Not when there were still people to find.

"You did good work," Sutter said, voice quiet.

"It shouldn't have been necessary," Thea said, the words pulled out of her.

"I know. But we don't get to choose," he said. He turned his head slightly. Unlike her, he was human, with duller hearing. But the noise from Ware's office had grown loud enough again to carry through the station. "Sounds like the argument is almost done."

Held in place by pure curiosity, Thea stayed where she was, standing with Sutter outside his office. The raised voices had died to a murmur, muffled by the heavy wood of the captain's door.

The volume rose sharply as the door opened and a group of men came out of the captain's office into the corridor. Even without Sutter's cue, the floor-length robes and rich materials told Thea that the group were all merchants.

And she knew two of them. Among the five men, two had warm dark skin and sleek black hair and faces meant for laughter. Traits they shared with their sister, Odilia Trant, who was the Watch's Mage. The brothers, Cedd and Gordie, were only a few years older than Odilia and had each recently been granted the title of Master Merchant, which Odilia was rightly proud of. Which meant that the other three men were likely also Master Merchants, all of them here representing the merchants' guild and wanting something from the Watch Captain.

"We expect action. Prompt action. At once. Immediately," one of the other three merchants said as he left the room. He was the shortest of the group, a stout, middle-aged man standing with his chest puffed out, dull brown hair blending into the shadows of the corridor. Trying to make himself look taller, and ensure he was remembered, Thea suspected, in the same way he had over-emphasised his point. He was wearing a sour expression that did not suit his slightly rounded, unremarkable face.

"If we don't see results, we will petition the Ageless for the disbandment of the Watch," another one of the merchants said, the statement shocking enough that Thea felt her jaw drop. He was a fraction taller than the first speaker, with cool bronzed skin and sleek black hair cropped close to his head. In contrast to the first speaker, this man was edged with something hard and angry. He was staring at Ware and somehow managing to give the impression of looking down his nose at the captain, despite the fact that Ware was at least a head and shoulders taller than he was.

Ware said nothing, face tight. He loomed over the merchants, broad and lean, pale skinned like most of Accanter's citizens, with grey taking over his once-dark hair. He wore his uniform without any of the airs and graces of the merchants around him. He was also, unlike the merchants, not human but Ageless-born. Thea wondered if any of the merchants knew, or cared.

The third stranger said nothing, which somehow drew Thea's attention more than the fury of the other two. He was a slender man, reasonably tall for a human, with dark red hair and freckles dusted across his pale skin. He was standing with his arms folded in the sleeves of his robes, a common stance for merchants. And staying quiet. Watching. Taking everything in. Exercising restraint. Thea's skin prickled with unease. There might be four other Master Merchants, but she had an instinct that this man was the one to watch.

The merchants might think they had worried Ware, but Thea knew the Watch Captain better than they did. His jaw was clenched, a touch of white showing around his mouth. He was not worried. He was furious. And holding on to his temper with difficulty. Which made Thea wonder just what else had been said in the room before the merchants emerged. The threat to disband the Watch was bad enough. The Watch might be made up of different stations and hundreds of members across the city, but Ware was both its head and its heart. He had worked hard to reform it since he took it over, turning it into an honest force for order across the city. Thea wondered if the merchants knew, or cared, how much work Ware had done to reform the previously corrupt Watch, or the impact that had had on the citizens of the city. Ordinary folk in Accanter knew that they could take their troubles to the Watch and be heard.

"We should go," Cedd, the oldest of Odilia's brothers said. "The *Crescent Moon* is due at dock this afternoon."

The three merchants that Thea did not know glared at Cedd, then reluctantly agreed. The first speaker, the short one with the brown hair, sent another frown at Ware.

"Do not ignore us. Remember our demands," the merchant said before turning with the others and filing down the stairs.

Ware remained standing in his office door, head tilted as he listened to the sound of the merchants leaving. The merchants' guild had moved their headquarters to a purpose-built building only two streets away, so there were no carriages waiting for them. The merchants would walk the short distance to their offices. And doubtless start all manner of gossip if they kept talking in the same loud, angry voices as they had used in Ware's office.

"My office," Ware said.

He had seen Sutter and Thea. Of course he had, Thea realised. He had served in the Archon's army, Conscripted into service, and even though his service had cost him an eye, he was still sharply observant.

"Give me a moment," Sutter said, and ducked back into his office, the unreadable parchment in his hands.

Thea made her way to the captain's office, finding him staring out of the window, which had been opened to let in a gust of air.

"A difficult afternoon, sir?" Thea asked.

Ware glanced over his shoulder, mouth quirking in what might have been a smile.

"An understatement if ever I heard one." He sighed, then drew in a long breath from the open window before coming back to his desk and opening a drawer. "I have something for you." He pulled a small object from the desk and held it out to her. It was a Watch badge, but not like any she had seen before.

The Watchmen wore plain tin badges. Watch Officers had bronzed badges, with the Sergeants and Senior Sergeant having a bit of edging around them to show their higher rank. Ware's own badge was a polished bit of silver.

The badge Ware was holding out to her was half bronze and half silver, split diagonally across its length.

"That's a new design," she commented, taking it from him. The metal warmed to her hand, a trace of magic sliding across her skin. All Watch badges had a bit of magic in them, courtesy of Odilia. Thea stared at the smooth, perfect surface, unable to see a join between the two different metals.

"We had to come up with something for your new rank," Ware said. His earlier fury had gone, replaced by quiet amusement.

Her new rank. She stared at the badge on the palm of her hand. The simple folded-over metal that would fit onto the notch at her lapel. It was almost impossibly heavy in her hand, carrying the weight of Ware's expectations, and yet she would not turn it away. She was an Investigator now. The only one in the Watch. It had seemed an excellent idea when she had been told about it. She would be nominally stationed here, with Sutter and Ware, but free to work anywhere across the city. It meant that none of the Watch Sergeants would have to house her in their station, wondering if she might turn on them as she had on her old Sergeant.

But it also set her apart from the others. Like having an office on the same floor as Ware and Sutter, physically apart from the main floor of the station where most of the station's members did their work.

And here was this badge, which was another potent symbol of her different status.

And those were just the obvious, outward changes. There were more changes that very few people knew about. The secretive group that Ware belonged to, which wanted her help. She was curious to know if they really were as unbiased and interested in the truth as they had claimed. And the recent discovery of her true nature, which she didn't want to think about. Not now and not ever.

"Can I have my old badge back?" Ware asked, still amused.

Thea looked up, startled, her free hand automatically going to the old, worn Watch Officer's badge she was wearing. Ware had given it to her as a temporary measure when her own badge had been stolen. And she had never thought too much about where it had come from.

"This was yours, sir?" she asked, taking it off and handing it across to him.

"Yes. It saw me through a few adventures," he answered, glancing down at it with a fond smile on his mouth before he put it away in the drawer. "And I'm sure you'll see plenty of adventures with yours, too."

"Sir," Thea acknowledged. She put the new badge onto her lapel. It fit perfectly. Of course it did. Odilia's work was always excellent.

"You wanted to see us?" Sutter asked from the doorway.

"I did." Ware sighed, and took his seat, reaching into another drawer of his desk and bringing out a familiar bottle and three glasses. "No, you're going to need this," he said, when Sutter lifted his hand to refuse the liquor.

Sutter and Thea settled in chairs opposite the desk and accepted glasses of the amber liquid. It wouldn't have much impact on either Ware or Thea, but Sutter was human and the drink was potent. Thea cradled her glass, wondering what news was so bad that Ware thought they would need a drink to weather it.

Ware rubbed his hand across his eye. It was the false eye, and it was always a bad sign when it was bothering him. He glanced aside, as if he was wondering if escape through the window was possible.

"The merchants' guild wants me to drop the charges against Kendrick," he began without warning.

"They can't be serious," Thea said, the words exploding out of her. "Do they know what he did?" The reports she had provided for Sutter were the least of it. She could still remember the horror of discovering the secret room at the back of the weaver's factory, with narrow bunk beds full of exhausted workers forced to work for Kendrick. And those were the ones who had survived. Many had not. There was more than one family across the city mourning a loss just now. They might have answers, and know what had happened to their family member, but it did not make up for the loss. Not even a little bit, in Thea's eyes.

Kendrick had taken people from their ordinary lives, just grabbed them up and forced them to work for him. Thea could also remember, as clearly as if he was in front of her, the disgust on his face. He had seen his kidnapped victims as things to be used. Not people.

Stopping Kendrick and freeing the people left alive had been the least she could do. The very least. It had given her some satisfaction to know he couldn't hurt anyone else.

The thought that Accanter's merchants wanted the criminal freed was enough to turn her stomach.

"Yes," Ware said, swallowing the contents of his glass in one gulp and pouring himself another.

"They don't care?" Sutter asked, holding his own glass with a white-knuckled grip.

Ware didn't answer at once, staring into his drink. Thea had seen him look that tired only once before. When they had found the forty-six people that Kendrick had been holding. There were no prisons in Accanter. Or so they had thought.

"They don't think we had the right," Ware said at length, voice harsh. "He was a Master Merchant."

Thea drew in a sharp breath. "What do they think should have been done instead? A fine?"

Ware's mouth turned down, giving her the answer.

"No, really?" Thea said, her stomach twisting. "One of Accanter's citizens captured and held over a hundred people across the city, and they think he should just pay a fine?" Her voice had risen to an undignified squeal by the end. She drew a breath, remembering the other thing about Kendrick's captives. All of them had been non-human. And all the Master Merchants standing outside Ware's office earlier were human. It was possible that they didn't care as much about other races. The thought made her stomach turn and she clamped her jaw shut, not wanting the taste of the words in her mouth.

"Not to mention the magic," Sutter said, voice as low and hard as Ware's had been. The Senior Sergeant swallowed the contents of his glass with one gulp, coughing, and held out his glass for more. Ware refilled it without speaking.

Thea set her still-full glass on the edge of Ware's desk so that she could grip the arms of her chair. The wood creaked under her fingers and she relaxed her grip a fraction, taking a long, deep breath.

"But you didn't agree," she said, realisation creeping over her. "You didn't agree to release Kendrick. And so they threatened to disband the Watch," she concluded. Leaving the ordinary citizens of Accanter with nowhere to go for help.

"They did," Ware said, and swallowed another drink. He set his empty glass down on the desk and eyed the bottle. Another shot would have no effect on him, Thea knew. It was the principle of the matter. Even though it was late into the afternoon, it would set a poor example to the rest of the station if the captain was smelling of alcohol.

"Does this happen often?" Thea asked, brow wrinkling. "People threatening to disband the Watch, I mean. There have been quite a lot of angry people in the building over the past two weeks," she added by way of explanation.

"We usually get threatened with closure about once a year," Sutter said, shaking his head. "But it's never serious."

"The citizens who live in the Citadel perimeter don't like paying fines," Ware said, face relaxing into what might have been an attempt at a smile. He leant back in his chair, the wood creaking ominously around him.

"But this is different," Thea said slowly. "So, you think the merchants' guild are serious? Or do they have the ability to disband the Watch?"

"They can't do it on their own," Sutter answered, so promptly that Thea knew he'd looked into the matter at least once before. "Only the Citadel itself can disband the Watch."

The great fortress that loomed over the city, the home of the land's ruling elite. The Ageless. Every major city across the empire had a Citadel. This one was different, though, because in this Citadel the Archon, the ruler of them all, had chosen to make her home.

"We are permitted to operate by the grace of the Archon," Ware said, his voice flat. Impossible to tell what he was thinking.

Thea ducked her head to hide her expression. The Archon didn't care about the citizens of Accanter. Not one bit. What she did care about was that the citizens of her empire obeyed her and her laws, however outrageous they were. The Archon seemed to believe that the citizens of her empire were there to provide her with taxes and warm bodies to fight her never-ending wars. Edris already ruled most of the known worlds, but was not satisfied with what she had.

Still, having the Watch responsible for the city outside the Citadel's perimeter was one less task for the Archon's soldiers and the Ageless. So the Archon and the Ageless seemed to regard the Watch as useful, and left them alone for the most part.

"The merchants don't tend to deal well with the Ageless," she said, picking up her drink and taking a sip. The amber liquid slid down her throat, warming her. "How likely is it that the Ageless will even listen to them?"

"Normally I would say not very likely," Ware said. "But they seem more determined this time. I've never had five Master Merchants in my office before," he added, and poured himself another drink.

"What happened to Kendrick's property?" Thea asked, curious.

Ware's good eye brightened for the first time since she had come into the room, and a genuine smile crossed his face.

"She's smart," he said to Sutter.

"We knew that already," the Senior Sergeant said, smiling in turn. He looked across at Thea. "The Citadel has decreed that as Kendrick had no heirs, his property falls to the Ageless. Unless the Archon decides otherwise."

"Oh, my," Thea said, and finished the rest of her drink. "No wonder the merchants are furious."

Master Merchant Kendrick had owned a great deal of property across the city, and at least two trading ships that Thea knew of. Thea had no very clear idea of what would normally happen if a merchant was expelled from the guild, but she had a suspicion that at least some of the former merchant's property would normally be split among the other merchants.

But the Ageless had taken that option away, along with the vast wealth that Kendrick had accumulated through his life.

"Indeed," Ware agreed with her, a broad grin spreading over his face. "Ahem. I mean, it's terrible for them," he said, not even trying to be serious.

"So, let me see. They think that if Kendrick is reinstated, and pays a fine for the things he did, then, what? They will be able to expel him from the guild and claim his property?" Thea speculated, thinking aloud.

"Something like that," Ware agreed.

"They don't know Kendrick at all, do they?" she said, turning her empty glass in her hands. "There is not a chance that he would surrender his position."

"Indeed." Ware rubbed his eyebrow over his false eye again. "And we can't risk Kendrick raising another army."

"Yes," Sutter agreed, shifting his position in the chair. He'd been injured by Kendrick's armed guards, shot with a crossbow bolt. And, as a human, he probably wasn't fully healed yet.

Thea flinched at the memory of the armed men that Kendrick had assembled, and who had attacked the Watch. Bladed weapons were forbidden in the city, one of the absolute laws set down by the Ageless which they rigidly enforced. Even the Watch could not carry weapons. And yet, Kendrick had managed to hire a large number of mercenaries. That was not the only forbidden thing he had done. She remembered the corrupt magic he had used. She blinked. The Watch might have an unlikely ally in keeping Kendrick away. The Ageless.

"How likely is it that the Citadel would set Kendrick free? I mean, even if you dropped the charges, he still used magic." And not just magic, but borrowed magic, which seemed like something the Ageless would not take kindly to. He had somehow drawn one of the highest-ranking mages in the city into his scheme. Sisley, who had been apprenticed to the Citadel's seniormost mage, had been helping Kendrick. The Ageless had taken Sisley away. And no one had seen her master, Mage Waters, for some time. As far as Thea knew, the Ageless were still looking for Waters.

Ware's face lightened into another genuine smile. "I don't think the merchants have worked that one out yet," he said, looking as if he was trying not to laugh.

Thea turned her own laugh into a not-very-convincing cough, sobering as she realised that, even if the Citadel and the Ageless might refuse to release Kendrick, there was no guarantee that the Ageless would allow the Watch to continue.

She had an unexpected moment of nostalgia for her old station, where her greatest worry had been the corrupt and lazy Sergeant. It had not been pleasant, but she had understood perfectly where she stood and what she was. It had been so much simpler then. Now she was weighted with concern about the potential disbandment of the entire Watch not to mention the potential release of one of the worst criminals she had ever encountered.

Chapter Two

The thought that the Master Merchants of the city had demanded Kendrick's release weighed on Thea's mind overnight, and was still troubling her in the morning as she walked through the city.

Kendrick had been clever, in some ways, in limiting his kidnapping to non-humans in a city that was mostly populated by humans. Perhaps he had calculated that the mostly human population would turn a blind eye. As revolting as the idea was to Thea, she knew there was a real division and suspicion in the city.

And that was just between the human and non-human populations. The Ageless-born were in a category all of their own. It might only take one Ageless parent to make another Ageless, but most of the children were born without wings, Ageless-born, with no legal rights or citizenship until their twenty-fifth birthdays. Thea had believed that was her, living under the constant threat of Conscription, terrified that she was going to be found and dragged away into the service of the Ageless. Very, very few Ageless-born survived their Conscripted service.

She shook off bad memories and her own recent discovery. She didn't want to think about that.

Even if the city's people despised the Ageless-born and were often suspicious of the non-humans, she remembered the many, many people who had turned out to help when Kendrick's awful conduct had been exposed. Ordinary city folk giving what they could in food, clothing and shelter. And some merchants, too, volunteering their vehicles to help transport the victims back to their families. Not everyone in the city was narrow minded.

But everyone in the city was under the rule of the Archon and the Ageless, and Thea was reminded of that as she took a long, restless walk around the city in the morning.

There must have been another ship in overnight. There were several ragged, hollow-eyed people on the streets near the docks. A few of them wore tatters of their uniforms, and most of them were injured in some way. More victims of the Archon's never-ending wars. The Archon's army was always hungry for new recruits, but had no use or interest in the soldiers once they could no longer fight.

Thea watched as a man wearing an old uniform jacket, one arm strapped across his chest and half his face raw with healing wounds, tentatively greeted an older woman who was crying as she hugged him. His mother, Thea would guess, and although she clearly loved her son, there was pain in her face as well. Thea understood the bittersweet reunion. The Archon's empire, and Accanter, were hard places to live for anyone not in perfect health. With so many people seeking employment across the city, employers could pick who they wanted to work for them. And those devastated by war were not the first choice.

The mother tucked her hand under her son's good arm and led him away, still crying. Thea could only hope that the family had enough resources to provide for the son. The city was a place of great opportunity for anyone willing and able to work hard, physical jobs. It was unforgiving for everyone else. Even for those people, like the son, who had served in the Archon's wars.

Thea could not help glancing over her shoulder at the Ageless Citadel, perched on the edge of the cliffs that loomed over the city. It was impossible to ignore, clearly visible from everywhere in the city. A potent reminder, as if any of the city's residents needed one, of who was in charge. There were specks of white in the air around the rising towers of the buildings. They looked like birds, but Thea, and every other resident of Accanter, knew what they were. The Ageless in flight.

She dragged her eyes away. The arrogance of the Ageless was one problem she could not fix.

Worry about the Watch and Kendrick now twisted with disgust at a reminder of the Archon's disregard for her citizens, Thea turned another corner and found herself on the path back to Middlefield Watch Station. She was still restless, but she should go back to her desk, or ask Sutter if there was something she could do. Perhaps he needed help with the land dispute that he'd mentioned the day before.

She had just reached Sutter's doorway when footsteps on the stairs behind her drew her attention. The newcomer carried with them the trace of frost she associated with one of the Ageless and she turned, not wanting her back to whoever it was. She was somehow not surprised to recognise the figure coming up the stairs wearing the black uniform of one of the Archon's army. The design stitched in silver thread across his heart showed a pair of wings, telling everyone that he was Ageless, even if he was wearing his human face just now.

Commander Reardon. Ageless warrior, in charge of one of the garrisons at the Citadel. And her father. She got her height and her dark hair from him, in sharp contrast to her petite, blond mother. In his human *aspect* he appeared to be somewhere between thirty and forty years old, showing little signs of age on his lightly tanned skin, but the Ageless did not show their years and Thea suspected he was closer to a century old. Relatively young in Ageless terms.

Old enough to have been marked, though. He had a scar on his temple, which was highly unusual for one of the Ageless as it was difficult to permanently mark them. She was sure there was a story behind that scar.

She had never found time to ask him about it, and would not do so now. He did not look as if he was in a good mood, brows drawn together, although he was still holding his human *aspect*, and there was no evidence of his wings.

Seeing him so unexpectedly chased away the worry and restlessness and replaced it with a mix of feelings she did not have time to fully work through. Her first instinct, borne of years of warnings from her mother, was to turn and leave. She wanted nothing to do with the Ageless. And yet. She did not think he meant her harm, not deliberately. So she stayed where she was, and a moment later was glad she had done so.

Reardon was followed by a far more welcome figure, wearing the dark robes of a Mage. Niath. Her middle did a weird, not unpleasant, turn, seeing Niath again. It had been a week or so since they had last crossed paths and she had missed his company. They didn't always agree, but she found she enjoyed their debates and not knowing what he might say next. The mage appeared to be a human in his early thirties, with his bronzed skin, short black hair and bright blue eyes. But he, like Thea and so many others, wore his human *aspect* as a disguise, hiding his true nature.

Reardon lifted a hand, beckoning Thea and Sutter forward, but did not check his stride, heading for Ware's open office door.

Her irritation at being summoned so casually smothered by curiosity, Thea exchanged glances with Sutter and by mutual agreement they also headed for Ware's office.

The captain was standing behind his desk when they reached the door, facing Reardon with square shoulders and a grim expression.

"What can the Watch do for you, Commander?" Ware asked.

"There's been a death," Reardon said. "It needs investigating."

"Where?" the captain asked.

"The Summer House," Reardon said.

Thea's brows lifted. There were a few grand houses outside the city limits. All of them surrounded by high walls and vast stretches of land, often with memorable names that bore no relation to the houses themselves. The Summer House was one. She had never been to any of the houses, but had heard whispered tales about them and the fabulous wealth that they held.

"That's outside the Watch's jurisdiction," Ware said, frowning. The Citadel permitted the Watch to operate within the city's limits. And no further. "And we have plenty of work to do within the city."

Reardon's face tightened further until Thea could almost see the sharper angles of his Ageless *aspect* through the softer human contours.

"The dead man is Master Merchant Bordan Hannaford. I understand he was here yesterday." The Ageless warrior locked eyes with the Watch Captain.

Ware's brows had lifted and he seemed startled. "You are remarkably well informed, Commander."

"One of the city's wealthiest citizens is dead," Reardon said, the words bitten out. "I would have thought that is of concern to the Watch."

The two men stared at each other, sending prickles of unease across Thea's skin. Ware had not agreed to the Commander's request. And Reardon was not backing down. All of which made Thea wonder just what else was going on.

"Why do you want us to investigate?" Thea asked.

"The circumstances of the death are ... strange," Reardon answered, surprising her. She had not really expected him to respond.

"In what way?" Thea asked, frowning.

"I would rather not say," the Ageless said, turning back to Ware. "I don't want to prejudice your investigation."

Thea's eyes travelled past Reardon to Niath, standing in his customary pose with his hands behind his back. He caught her eyes and nodded a greeting.

"You suspect something magical, though," she said, "or you wouldn't have brought Mage Niath."

Reardon's lips pressed together in what looked like irritation. Not used to being questioned, she thought.

"I volunteered," Niath said unexpectedly, a hint of mischief crossing his face. "There's not much to do at the Citadel just now."

"You and Mage Niath have worked well together in the past," Reardon said to Thea, surprising her again. "If Captain Handerson can spare you," he added, looking back at Ware.

Ware was still standing, expression grim. Doubtless considering the implications of the death of a Master Merchant. One who had been very prominent in the guild. And who had threatened him with the disbandment of the Watch only the day before.

"Do we know when he died?" Thea asked.

"Around noon," Reardon answered. Thea's brows lifted. That was not that long ago. He shook his head before she could ask any more questions. "I would rather not say anything else."

"Very well," Ware said, voice heavy. "Commander, I assume we will have the full cooperation of the Citadel if we meet any resistance?"

Thea's brows lifted, wondering just what kind of resistance Ware was expecting.

"Of course," Reardon said, as if he had expected the question.

"Thea, will you take the lead on this? I'll send for Iason and Dina. We'll need to arrange transport for you. It's too far to go on foot."

"I have horses for Thea and me," Niath said, "and Commander Reardon has brought a carriage for the physician and examiner. We assumed that they would want to bring some equipment."

Ware's lips twitched, as if he was suppressing a smile. "So you anticipated our cooperation."

"We hoped," Niath said, inclining his head slightly. "And it sounds like an intriguing mystery," he added.

"If you leave now, you should reach the house before nightfall," Reardon said to Thea. "I'll meet you there."

He turned on his heel and stalked away.

"I wonder how he found out about the death," Sutter said. He had been standing quietly, observing the conversations.

"A good question. Thea, make sure to ask him," Ware said, taking a seat at his desk.

"You're not coming with us, sir?" Thea asked, surprised.

"No. I suspect I will have the merchants' guild in here again soon," Ware said, rubbing his forehead over his false eye. "And as much as I would be happy not to speak to them, I need to be here."

"Sir," Thea acknowledged. She turned to Niath. "Shall we go?"

Chapter Three

Thea had rarely been out of the city, and normally would have been distracted by her surroundings. There was no time to look around this time, though, as Niath set a fast pace. The journey to The Summer House tested even the horses' endurance, all three horses blowing hard when they got there. Niath's groom, Sam, promised to look after them, assuring Thea they had taken no harm. It was good for them to get a good run now and then, he added.

With that reassurance, and no longer distracted by having to keep her seat on a fast-moving horse, Thea was able to turn her attention to the scene in front of her.

They had arrived at high stone walls with heavy metal gates, guarded by a pair of what looked like house servants dressed in dark trousers and purple shirts. The purple must be the house's colour, Thea realised, seeing a thick ribbon of that colour threaded through the gates.

The servants had let them through the gates without a word, avoiding eye contact.

As they passed through the gates, a frisson of magic slid over Thea's skin. Someone had put strong protections on the walls of this property, and not that long ago judging by the strength of the magic. She glanced across at Niath and found him looking back at the walls, brows raised.

But then the house came into view and she forgot about the magic for a moment, too interested in the scene before her.

It was easy to see where the house's name had come from. It was built of pale, red sandstone that glowed like a summer sunset, soft and bright even in the fading daylight. The house was enormous, about the same size as Brightfield House, the old, proud house that was now the base of operations for the Watch's mortuary and scientific examinations.

The Summer House was set among mature trees and what looked like a wild garden, but which Thea was quite sure was carefully planted. A river ran in front of the house. No, not a river. The water curved around the house. A moat. Thea's brows lifted, and she blinked. But no, she had not imagined it. The house sat within its own moat.

She had only seen a moat once before, when she and her mother had still lived at Kellto. They had been to visit one of her mother's old teachers, in a fortified house with its own walls and moat.

With the moat stirring up memories, she looked at the house again. It fit with what little she had seen of Bordan Hannaford. He had been an almost ordinary looking man in a position of power, and the house in front of her was proof of the wealth and influence he had.

But, like Master Hannaford's plain appearance, the house was not just the grand residence it had seemed to be at first glance. What had seemed a splendid, beautifully crafted building now took on a different aspect. She could see by the turns of the walls that the people inside the house would have a complete view of the surrounding lands. No one would be able to sneak up on the inhabitants. And there was a hint of what might have been a walkway on parts of the roof. A perfect spot for archers to nest and fire down on anyone approaching with hostile intent.

There was an open stretch of packed earth ahead of them, and a wooden walkway that would take them across the moat into the building itself. Just around the corner of the house, Thea could see the outlines of more buildings among the trees. Doubtless the stables and other outbuildings necessary for such a grand building.

She got off Hern's back and took a moment to stretch, easing out her sore muscles, before stepping forward, towards the house. It seemed even larger now that she was on the ground.

There was another pair of servants standing at either side of the house's open door on the other side of the walkway and even as she looked, a third person emerged between them, crossing the walkway with rapid strides. She was dressed like the others, in dark trousers with a purple shirt, but there was a silver brooch on her shoulder and the faint clink of keys when she walked. Perhaps the house's steward.

As she came closer, Thea's attention sharpened. The woman walked with absolute confidence, sure of her surroundings, and with the sort of measured, controlled movement that Thea had noticed before among the Archon's soldiers. She was tall enough to be Ageless-born, and her movement suggested that she might have had weapons training. Interesting.

The woman came to a halt a few paces away. She had thick, cropped dark hair and pale skin similar to Thea's, her face made up of strong, definite angles, her dark eyes reddened. And she was definitely Ageless-born. Thea could not help wondering if the woman's mother had, like so many others, been tricked by an Ageless pretending to be human. The Ageless seemed to enjoy disguising themselves as simply human and mingling with human women, careless of any wingless offspring that they might leave behind.

"You must be Investigator March and Mage Niath," the woman said, her voice harsh. "I am Fionn. I'm the steward here. It's this way," she said, and turned.

"A moment, please," Thea said.

The woman stopped, shoulders square, and turned back, lips pressed together. Impatient or annoyed at the delay. Thea didn't know her well enough to tell.

"What?" Fionn asked.

"The dead man was the owner?" Thea asked.

"Master Merchant Hannaford. Yes."

"And is Master Hannaford's family also in the house?" Thea asked. Dealing with grieving relatives of the dead was one of the least favourite tasks of any member of the Watch, but it was very necessary.

"The master had no family," Fionn answered flatly.

Thea blinked, remembering the scale and size of the house and the grounds around it. It was enormous for just one person. However, the merchant had doubtless been more than wealthy enough to keep the property and the numbers of household staff that would be needed to maintain it.

"And how long has he owned this house?" she asked.

"Twenty years, perhaps more."

"And have you been here all that time?" Thea asked. Beside her, she could sense Niath, quiet but listening intently. Perhaps wondering what information Thea was seeking. She wasn't quite sure. Not yet.

"Yes. I started as one of the house servants. I've been Steward for a decade," Fionn said, chin lifting slightly. Proud of her achievement.

"He must have trusted you," Thea remarked.

Fionn said nothing, just swallowed, her eyes brighter.

"Who found him?"

"One of the kitchen staff. He was late for his midday meal, so Thomas went looking for him. I assume you'll want to speak to Thomas. I've asked him to wait in the dining room."

"Thank you. So, Thomas went looking for him. Until then, no one had noticed anything wrong?" Thea asked.

"No," Fionn said, with evident impatience. "Don't you want to see for yourself?"

"I do. Thank you," Thea said. The itch to ask more questions was still present. There was something important trying to get her attention. Something she needed to know.

Fionn turned and led the way across the wooden walkway without another word, her footfalls making almost no sound against the planks.

Thea paused halfway across as another ripple of magic crossed her skin. Another layer of defence around the house, set into the moat beneath her feet. She glanced at Niath and he nodded. He had felt it, too.

Not wanting to alert Fionn, or make her any more hostile, Thea continued, following the Steward as she led her unwanted visitors through the impressive, arched doorway and into a reception hallway that was twice the size of a Watch station's main room. Without pausing, Fionn continued into the house, leading them along a wide, wood-panelled corridor that was shadowed in the fading light.

She stopped at a door that looked just like the other ones they had passed. Made of the same wood as the panelling in the corridor, at first the only way Thea could tell it was a door was by the handle. Then she noticed that the handle was out of place, the metal latch and locking mechanism pulled out of line with the rest of the door. She turned to Fionn, lifting her brows.

"Thomas had difficulty getting into the room," Fionn said, face tight.

"What do you mean?" Thea asked, confused.

"There was a key in the other side of the lock," Fionna said.

"You mean the door was locked from the inside when Thomas came looking for the master?" Thea clarified, eyeing the door handle. It did not look particularly damaged. Testament to the solid craftsmanship of the building, and also to Thomas' strength in managing to pull out the lock.

"Yes. He thought he was over-reacting by breaking the lock to get in," Fionn said, voice harsh. "But then Thomas found the master. He's still in there. Commander Reardon said not to touch anything. So we haven't." Fionn hesitated. "It's getting dark. Do you need lights?"

"No need," Niath said. "Thank you."

"I'll leave you to it," Fionn said, and took a step back.

"A moment. Commander Reardon said he would meet us here. And we're expecting Physician Pallas and Chief Examiner Soter as well. They shouldn't be too long," Thea said.

Fionn's face tightened, and Thea could almost read her disgust at the idea of more visitors.

"Fine. I will show them here when they arrive," she said, turned on her heel, and stalked away down the corridor, footsteps making as little sound here as they had on the walkway outside.

Thea's eyes narrowed. The woman had definitely had some kind of training. An odd requirement for a house steward.

Still, there was another mystery closer to hand, and one she had been asked to look at.

She glanced at the door in front of her, then at Niath. "Shall we?"

Niath provided lights for them, little sparks of magic that floated into the air of the room, giving them more than enough light to see.

It was a study, with more wooden panelling on the walls that weren't covered in shelves. The shelves were stuffed full of books and ledgers and parchments. It might look disordered, but Thea had the sense that it was perfectly organised.

There were a few chairs in the room, gathered around an open fireplace, and another pair set opposite one of the largest desks she had ever seen.

Behind the desk was another chair. This one occupied.

Master Merchant Bordan Hannaford was leaning back in his chair, eyes staring up at the ceiling. Thea remembered him standing outside Ware's office the day before. A short, stout man with his chest puffed up, over-emphasising his words. He had demanded action. Expecting results from Ware.

He was not expecting anything anymore. He was dead. That much was obvious from his complete stillness. And the very large knife that was lodged into his chest, thrust slightly upwards where his heart should be.

Thea's brows lifted. Reardon's reluctance to talk much about the death had suggested a far greater mystery.

"So, he was stabbed," she said, looking across at Niath.

"It appears so," he said, frowning.

"What?"

"Well, it's odd. He's sitting just behind the desk. And the knife has gone straight into him. How did his killer get that angle?" Niath asked.

"Good question," Thea said, turning back to the dead man. She realised as she did so that neither she nor Niath had moved from the threshold of the room. "Keeping out of the way for Dina to do her work?" she asked Niath.

"Indeed. The examiner is very good at her job. And I do not want to annoy her," the mage said, mouth quirking in a smile.

"Agreed," Thea said.

Now that she had time to look at the scene again, she could see more oddities. As Niath had pointed out, the dead man was sitting close to his desk. For someone to have put the knife in at that angle, they would have needed to be right in front of him. It was possible that the body had been moved after death, but nothing else in the room seemed to have been disturbed. The papers on the desk were tidy, there were no signs of a struggle elsewhere. The windows were closed and there didn't seem to be any other doors to the room.

"So someone managed to get in here, kill him, and get out without disturbing anything," Thea said. "Interesting."

"Isn't it?" Niath said, eyes bright.

"Has anyone used magic in the room?" she asked.

"It's difficult to tell. This whole house is saturated with old spells."

"I sensed the ones on the walls and in the moat. There are more?" Thea asked.

"Yes. The walls and moat are active spells. Very well-crafted defences. Designed to alert someone in the house when the lines are crossed. The spells in here are mostly old. Some cleaning spells. Someone has used a light spell in here before. But they are all fairly old. And there are some other spells I can't interpret yet," Niath added.

"The defence spells," Thea said slowly. "Designed to alert someone in the house. Would that person have to be a mage?"

"Not necessarily. You can craft the spells to sound an alarm of some kind that anyone can hear." Niath looked around the room again, then back at her. "But the spells were quite new, so a mage has been here fairly recently."

Before Thea could ask anything else, there was a knock at the door behind them. She turned in time to see the door open, Fionn's face replaced a moment later by Dina peering into the room.

"Thea. Niath. Good to see you. What have you touched?" Dina said by way of greeting.

"Nothing," Thea said, biting her lip to hide an inappropriate smile. "We just stepped inside the room. We've not gone beyond this point."

"Good, good," Dina said. "Now, do step out again."

Thea and Niath obliged, finding Iason standing behind Dina, the taller examiner almost completely blocking his view of the room.

The pair were a study in contrasts. Iason Pallas was a short, slender man, always impeccably dressed in dark, three-piece suits with white shirts, his black hair and beard neatly trimmed. Dina Soter was the same height as Thea, and permanently tousled, from her short, curling red hair to her plain working clothes.

"Good day to you, Thea. Niath," Iason said, staying where he was as Dina took a step into the room.

"Physician," Niath said.

Thea's attention had been distracted by another person walking down the corridor towards them. Reardon had arrived. The corridor was becoming too crowded for Thea's liking, the walls closing in around her, breath and pulse quickening. She put her hands behind her back and clenched her fingers together, the discomfort distracting her for a moment to let her draw a breath and tell herself that the walls were not closing in. Nor was the ceiling getting closer. There were just too many people around her. That was all.

"Commander," Fionn said. She also folded her hands behind her and then took a step back, so that she was closer to the wall. Perhaps she didn't like crowds, either. It was common enough among the Ageless-born.

"Fionn," Reardon said, and looked past the steward to Thea. "What have you learned?"

"Very little so far. Fionn, I have some questions for you, while the physician and examiner are making their preliminary assessment," Thea said, taking her notebook out and moving further down the corridor to where she could still see into the room but Iason and Dina had space to work.

The steward followed her, along with Reardon and Niath.

Fionn stood with her back to the wall again, and lifted her chin, waiting for Thea's questions. Not openly hostile. Not quite. And her eyes were still reddened from crying.

"You said that one of the house servants found him," Thea said. "Did anyone move Master Hannaford after you found him?"

"No. Thomas found the master just as you see him," Fionn said, swallowing. "And no, we didn't hear or see anything unusual before then."

Thea nodded, making a note. "Who has been in the room today?"

"One of the staff would have cleaned the room at first light," Fionn said, frowning slightly. "I can find out who. And after that, no one but the master until Thomas found him."

"Was that the usual pattern?" Thea asked.

"Yes. The master didn't like anyone else going into the room without him. Even the staff." Fionn hesitated, then went on. "But he didn't normally lock the door when he was inside. Just when the room was empty."

Thea nodded, filing the information away. The merchant's protectiveness of the room made a certain sort of sense. It had looked, from her one glance, as if Bordan Hannaford had kept all of his business records in that room. He would not have wanted those available to just anyone.

"The mage tells me that there are magical defences around the property," Thea said. "Who set those?"

Fionn's face changed, an expression of distaste clear before she smoothed her features again. She did not like whoever set the magic. Interesting. "The master had arrangements with a mage. Jilt Fisk."

"You don't like him much," Reardon said, startling Thea. He and Niath had managed to make themselves still and quiet and she had almost forgotten they were there, focusing on Fionn.

"No, I don't," Fionn said. "He's arrogant and keeps harassing the female servants."

"Does he indeed?" Thea murmured, making another note. She had come across a few bullies like that in her time. "I will look forward to meeting him," she said, glancing up and meeting Fionn's eyes. "I'm sure that you manage to keep him in check."

A flicker of surprise and a tiny smile crossed the steward's face. "I do," she confirmed.

"When was Mage Fisk here last?" Thea asked.

"Three days ago. He visits every month, at least once."

"Is anyone else in the house a mage?" Niath asked.

"No."

"So, how were the alarms sounded?" Niath asked.

"If the alarm is triggered, there's a loud noise," Fionn said, grimacing in memory. "We have some counter-spells downstairs to silence them. I can show you if you need to see them," she said, with evident reluctance. Not wanting strangers trampling over the house, or some other reason. Thea couldn't tell.

"And none of the alarms were sounded today?" Thea asked. "Before Master Hannaford was found dead, I mean."

"No. Nothing."

"So, the only people in the house were Master Hannaford and the household staff?" Thea asked.

"Yes." Fionn's face tightened. She understood the implication of that perfectly well. If no one had come or gone from the house, then whoever had killed Bordan Hannaford was still in the building.

"And what about afterwards. Someone left the house to alert the Citadel?" Thea asked. It seemed the only logical way that Reardon could have found out about the death. Even though she had no idea why the steward would have alerted the Citadel and not the merchants' guild or the Watch.

"No," Fionn said, her face tightening again. "I sent a distress message to Mage Fisk. He left us a communication spell to summon help if we ever needed it." From the pinching of her face, Fionn had not liked having to use that spell. Not one bit. Whether it was because she had to rely on the mage, or because she had to ask for outside help, Thea could not tell.

"The mage alerted the gate guards at the Citadel," Reardon said, "and they told me something was wrong. I came here to see for myself."

"That was very generous of you," Thea said. The words were sharper than she had intended, but she still could not understand what interest the Citadel would have in a merchant's death.

"Not at all," Reardon said, as if she had paid him a compliment. "The neighbouring houses are occupied by Ageless, and I wanted to make sure there was no danger. When I saw the body, I knew this was not a simple matter."

That explained his presence, at least to Thea's satisfaction. The Ageless were protective of their spaces. Even though the grand houses in this area were set far apart, having a murder in the neighbourhood was bound to raise some concerns.

"We haven't had any contact with the other houses," Fionn said, her face still tight. She was Ageless-born, managing a grand house for a human merchant. Thea suspected that there was very little communication with the other houses. "Not the master and not any of the staff."

"Please ensure that no one leaves until I've spoken to them," Thea said. She glanced over her shoulder to see Iason and Dina conferring next to the desk in the study. "If you'll excuse me for a minute," she said and made her way along to the door of the study. "What news?"

Chapter Four

"Well, he's definitely dead," Dina said. It wasn't meant as a joke, Thea saw, but a statement of fact. "Beyond that, we can't tell you what happened. Not yet."

"I will need to examine him further," Iason added, "but it does look as if the knife was the cause of death. Dina and I were just trying to work out how he was stabbed."

"The steward has confirmed that he wasn't moved," Thea said. "He's exactly as they found him."

"That's what we suspected," Iason said, glancing across at her, a crease between his brows. "And it's puzzling."

"It's as if he just sat there and let someone shove a knife into his chest," Dina said. "That's bad enough, but even worse, there's no angle for the blow from anywhere around him."

"Could someone have stood behind him?" Thea asked.

"No. The angle and force needed for that knife would be impossible from behind," Iason said, quite certain.

"The only way to get a knife in like that is to stab directly into the chest. From the front," Dina said, equally certain. "And there's not enough room between him and the desk."

"Standing on the desk?" Thea asked, the words sounding ridiculous in her own ears. Still, she felt she had to ask.

"We considered that," Iason said.

"But the papers on the desk haven't been disturbed," Dina said, "and anyone standing on the desk would have left footprints, or some disturbance when they jumped down."

Thea frowned at the dead man, who was still staring up at the ceiling, his head tilted back. She looked up, following the line of his unseeing gaze. There was a wood panelled ceiling high overhead. Nothing more. Certainly no answers as to how the merchant had been killed.

"From above?" she asked, the words out before she thought about the implications of that. The only beings who could attack from above were the Ageless.

"We considered that, too," Iason said. "If there had been an Ageless in here, the downbeat from their wings would have cleared the desk."

And no Ageless would have bothered to tidy up after themselves, Thea knew. If the killer had been Ageless, the room would have been a mess. She nodded, conscious of Reardon not that far away. "So, not Ageless then." She tried to hide her relief. She could not do anything about the Ageless. They were outside her jurisdiction. Even if they had been in the city, there was nothing she could have done. Ageless did what they wanted, and there were no consequences for them. "Is it strange that he is looking up?" she asked Iason.

The physician's brows lifted a fraction and he turned back to the body, moving to walk around the desk, inspecting the dead man from different angles.

Thea waited. He was taking her question seriously, which she had not expected.

"I think it was the force of the blow. It takes a great deal of strength to break through the chest like that," Iason said at length. "His head would have snapped forward and then back."

"So he was not posed?" Thea asked.

"I cannot tell." Iason was frowning again, and looked across at Dina. "It's possible he was staged."

"I'll check his clothing for other fibres," Dina said, sounding as if she was looking forward to the task. "If someone did stage this, they did an excellent job."

A prickle ran across Thea's skin as she looked around the room again. A seemingly impossible killing, in a room that bore no sign of disturbance. Whoever had done this had been careful not to leave any clue or trace that might lead back to them.

Apart from the knife, there was nothing that seemed out of place in the room, although she made a mental note to ask Fionn to confirm that.

"What can you tell me about the knife just now?" she asked, addressing the question impartially between Iason and Dina.

"It's a fighting dagger," Reardon said unexpectedly. She looked across. He was standing just inside the door, hands tucked behind him, an odd mirror of Niath's posture, where the mage was standing on the other side of the open door. "We use them in training and combat. It takes some skill to learn them."

Thea nodded, ducking her head to hide her expression. She had trained with fighting daggers, among other illicit weapons. They looked as if they should be easy to use, but Reardon was right that it took skill to use them. The weight and balance of the weapon were odd. Not her weapon of choice, but handy to conceal within clothing and brutally effective at close quarters.

"There's nothing personal on it that I can see," Iason added, "but Dina and I will look more closely when we get to Brightfield House."

Thea thanked him, and made another mental note. This time to ask Fionn if any of the staff had weapons training.

"A number of the staff here will know how to use the daggers," Reardon said, surprising her again. "Fionn and a few others were Conscripts in the Archon's army."

Thea's brows shot up. "They have weapons in the house?" she asked.

"Several, I should think," Reardon said, sounding almost amused.

Thea clamped her mouth shut before she could say anything hasty. Within the city limits, one of the Archon's laws was that citizens were forbidden from carrying weapons. She had assumed that the ban would apply here, too. It seemed not.

Dina had no such hesitation. "You mean that any one of the staff here have the skill to do this? And you're only mentioning this now?"

"Not all of them," Reardon said, frowning slightly. "And it may not be relevant."

"May not be-" Dina bit off her words and glared at the Ageless.

"We'll need to question the entire staff anyway," Thea said. "And search the house. It seems as if no one could have got into or out of the grounds during the day." She remembered the size of the building and wished they were closer to the city. It would take her all night to search the place thoroughly. Assuming that the steward allowed her access in the first place.

"We'll get Master Hannaford back to the mortuary," Iason said. "It's already getting late. Unless you need us for anything else, Thea?"

"No, thank you," Thea said. "Will you be able to examine him tomorrow?"

"Yes. If you come by in the afternoon, we should have something more to tell you," the physician said.

"Then let's get on with a search and speaking to the staff," Thea said, trying not to glare at Reardon as she turned towards the door. "Unless there's anything else you'd like to tell us first, Commander?"

"No. I don't want to prejudice your investigation," Reardon said. Which meant, to Thea's ears, that there was plenty more he could tell them, but he was not going to.

Thea lost her battle in trying not to glare and stalked past him into the corridor without a word, Niath following her. Fionn was not that far away, with a slender young man who swallowed nervously as Thea approached.

Thea paused in her stride, took a breath, calmed herself, and nodded to the pair. "You must be Thomas. Will you tell me what you saw earlier?"

Thomas could add nothing to the information that Fionn had already provided. Despite his appearance, Thea realised quickly that Thomas was also Ageless-born, which explained how he had managed to pull the lock out of the door.

Once she had spoken to Thomas, the steward flatly refused when Thea asked to search the house. It was her master's property, and she was protective of his privacy even in death. And Thea had no grounds to insist. They were far outside the city limits and the jurisdiction of the Watch. And Reardon had disappeared. He had left with the examiner and physician, Fionn said. Apparently, he thought he should escort the pair, and the body, back to the city.

Thea wished that Reardon had stayed. She wanted to glare at him some more. And get him to order Fionn to allow a search. The steward might obstruct a member of the Watch, but Thea suspected she would stand aside for one of the Ageless.

After some discussion, Fionn reluctantly agreed to let Niath use his magic to detect how many people were in the building, and then confirmed the number reported by Niath as all being household staff. All accounted for.

With a fortified house, surrounded by magic, and with many members of staff trained in using weapons, there should have been little mystery as to who had killed Bordan Hannaford. It should have been one of the staff.

And yet, despite a long night of questioning every member of the household, with Niath putting in the occasional query as well, when dawn arrived, Thea was no closer to an answer than she had been when they had first arrived and seen the body.

Fionn and several of the other household members readily admitted to being trained in weaponry, and although she would not give them free run of the house, the steward seemed to realise that the weapons were relevant. She showed Thea and Niath to the house's armoury, a small, windowless room packed from floor to ceiling with enough weapons to keep a small army supplied. Thea had never seen so many weapons gathered together in her life, her skin crawling at being in the presence of the potential for so much harm.

They were outside the city limits, though. From Reardon's reaction, and the contents of the armoury, it seemed that the prohibition that the Archon had placed on weapons only extended to Accanter. Thea suspected that if the Archon saw this room, she would be quick to forbid these weapons, too. But, for now, they were legal.

None of their weapons were missing, Fionn said. The knife that had killed the master had not come from within the house. At least not the weapons that the house's steward knew about.

There had also been no disturbance in the magic around the house. All the staff carried a token which let them pass through the magic without raising any alarm. Thea had a moment of hope, wondering if one of the tokens had gone missing, which was dashed by Fionn shaking her head. All the tokens were accounted for.

The steward had personally checked them. And in the short time she had known Fionn, Thea was confident that the steward had done her job thoroughly.

With every possible avenue of questioning closing faster than she could keep track, Thea was in no very good mood when the first rays of daylight crept through the windows.

They were in the house's dining room, settled at one end of a table which could easily seat thirty people. Her hand was cramped from taking notes, her eyes gritty from lack of sleep, her stomach hollow from too long without food or drink.

Niath was a couple of chairs away from her. He had asked the occasional question, but had mostly been quiet. He was paying attention, though. The few questions he had asked had been pointed, picking up gaps in the stories that various members of staff had told them.

The household staff did not want them here. That much was clear. Some of them had not cared much about their master, but they did not like being questioned, having to account for their day.

As the door closed behind the last member of staff, Thea sat back in her chair, glaring at the sunlight she could see.

Before she could say anything, the door opened and Fionn appeared. The steward did not appear to have slept, either. She was carrying a large tray.

"I had the kitchen make you a meal. I'm sorry I didn't think of it sooner."

The steward set the tray down on the table and Thea's brows lifted. Someone, perhaps Fionn or perhaps the short, stout woman who was in charge of the house's kitchens, had correctly judged the appetite of a weary Watch Investigator and Citadel Mage. The tray was loaded with food, a tall pitcher of what looked like fruit juice and glasses half full of water.

"If you need anything else, let me know," Fionn said, and took a step back.

"A moment," Thea said, her voice hoarse with a night of talking. "The mage. What's his name? Jilt Fisk. I'd like to speak to him."

Fionn's mouth lifted at the corners. "I thought you might. He should be here when you've finished your breakfast."

"He's coming here?" Thea asked, startled.

"Well, I sent four people to get him," Fionn said. She was definitely smiling. "So I expect him soon."

The steward left the room with a definite spring in her stride, far more cheerful than she had been at any point since Thea had met her. It might be petty, sending people to scoop up the mage and bring him back here, but if he caused as much trouble as Fionn had suggested, Thea did not blame the steward for her satisfaction.

The clink of cutlery called her attention back into the room and she found that Niath had set places for each of them, across the table from each other. He topped up the glasses with the fruit juice that Fionn had brought.

"Have you dealt with this mage before?" Thea asked, taking her place behind a large plate of food.

"No. But if he is the one who did the work here, he is good at his job," Niath said.

The room was silent for a while as they both emptied their plates, then there was no more time for conversation as a knock sounded at the door and Fionn came in again.

"The mage is here. I'll take the tray away and send him in," she said, and collected everything with quiet efficiency.

"Thank you for the meal. It was delicious," Thea said.

"I'm glad you enjoyed it," Fionn said. It sounded like an automatic, polite response. Then she hesitated in front of the door and glanced back. "Good luck with the mage."

Thea's brows lifted and she exchanged glances with Niath as the door shut behind Fionn.

They did not have long to wait. The door burst open again, so violently that it slammed back against the wooden panelling, and a tall, slender man in the dark robes of a mage stalked into the room. He had the pale, cool skin of someone from north of Accanter, with close-cropped fair hair almost blending into his scalp.

"How dare you?" he said, piercing, pale eyes coming to rest on Thea. "You have no authority over me. I'll have your badge for this."

"You must be Mage Fisk," Thea said, getting to her feet without any hurry. "It's good to meet you. Won't you come and sit down?"

"No. I will not sit down. I fulfilled my contract. I alerted the Citadel to the distress call. That should be the end of the matter. I demand an explanation as to why I was dragged from my home in the middle of the night. None of the servants here or that woman will tell me. Why am I here? On whose orders?"

"I am Watch Investigator Thea March. This is Mage Niath. You are here because there has been a death in this building, and we are investigating the truth of it," Thea told him, voice cool.

"Niath?" Mage Fisk stared across the room at Niath, who was standing near the windows, hands behind his back. "I've heard stories about you."

"Oh, really?" Niath said, with every appearance of curiosity. "Do tell me more?"

"Perhaps later. For now, mage, come and sit down," Thea said.

"Wait. A death? You said a death? Who is dead?" Mage Fisk demanded.

"Master Merchant Hannaford," Thea said.

That diverted the mage from his indignation. He went still, blinking in what looked like genuine shock, as if he could not believe what he had heard, before he flicked a hand, dismissing the idea.

"No. Impossible. He is protected on these grounds."

"By your spells, yes," Niath said. "But someone got through those spells and killed him."

"No, that's impossible," Mage Fisk said, a great deal of his self-assurance fading. "There's no way that an intruder could have got through the spells."

Thea gestured to one of the chairs at the table. The mage's eyes followed her gesture. He looked at the chair for a moment, almost as if he had never seen one before, then moved, slowly and carefully, across the room to take a seat, gathering his robes around him as if searching for comfort or reassurance. She glanced over at Niath and lifted her brows, inviting him to continue the questions.

Niath looked surprised, but came towards the table, took a seat and frowned at the other mage.

"Tell me about the structure of your spells," Niath asked.

Fisk stared at the other mage for a long moment, expression hardening. Perhaps believing that Niath was challenging him. Perhaps he just didn't like discussing his work.

"I started with a standard warding sequence," Fisk said at length, voice flat. "Using the Perry principles."

"They are a solid start," Niath agreed, "but your spells are far more sophisticated. Did you layer in something else? A Gaderian sequence, perhaps?"

Fisk blinked, the hard expression disappearing and being replaced with something altogether more human. Thea had seen similar expressions on Dina and Iason's faces when they were deep into discussing their favourite topics, and settled herself more comfortably. It seemed that Niath had found the key to getting Fisk to talk. And talk he did.

Thea listened, both fascinated and utterly confused, as the two mages discussed technical details of how the spells were constructed and the safeguards that Fisk had built into them to ensure that no one could cross them without sounding an alarm, unless they had one of the tokens he had also created.

She might not understand much of the things that were being discussed, but she understood enough to know that Fisk had been thorough in his work. He might be an unpleasant human being, but his work seemed competent. He was able to answer all of the questions Niath put to him without hesitation.

At length, when the sun was almost at its highest point outside, the two mages sat back from each other.

"It should not have been possible for Master Hannaford to be killed within these walls," Niath told Thea.

"But he was killed. And we need to find out how," Thea said, a chill trailing over her skin. The room around them seemed perfectly ordinary, nothing out of place. And yet a few rooms away an impossible murder had taken place.

"Don't you mean why?" Mage Fisk asked. He had spoken to Niath as an equal, trading information. He looked down his nose at Thea, lip curling.

"That, too," Thea agreed, holding on to her temper with difficulty. "Will you come to the room with us and see if anything has been disturbed?" she asked. She was reluctant to spend any more time with the mage, but he had been responsible for the spells around the house. He should be able to tell if there was anything out of the ordinary.

"Yes." The mage got to his feet, waiting with evident impatience while Thea closed her notebook and got up.

"It's this way," Thea said.

"I know the way," Fisk said, stalking out of the room.

Thea had a certain grim satisfaction in watching Mage Fisk go from arrogant and sure of himself to frowning and doubtful as he checked and rechecked the spells in the room and could find nothing wrong. He could not explain how someone had got into the room and killed Master Merchant Hannaford. And it made him increasingly nervous.

He ended up standing behind the chair that the merchant had been found in, staring at the room with a tight, haunted expression.

"What's wrong?" Thea asked. None of her senses were telling her that there was any danger, but the mage was deeply disturbed.

"I provide security spells for several prominent people," Mage Fisk said, and swallowed. "This should not have happened."

Thea's brows lifted. No wonder the mage was worried. One of the people who had used his services was dead and apparently the mage's spells had not prevented that. It would not be long before word spread among his other clients. The mage could find himself out of work very quickly. And, judging by the quality of his robes, he was used to fine living.

"There's no breach in the spells that I can sense," Niath told Thea. "Nothing to explain how someone managed to kill the merchant."

"There has to be something," Fisk said, paler than before. "There has to be. There is nothing wrong with my spells."

"I did not say there was," Niath said, more gently than Thea would have done. "But the man is still dead."

"Is there any magic that would let someone disguise themselves and get past the spells?" Thea asked, not looking at Niath.

She sensed rather than saw his attention fix on her for a moment. Unlike Fisk, Niath was not human but hiandar, one of the night kind. And he possessed the ability to make himself unseen, even to people walking close by. Thea had experienced it first hand.

"No," Fisk said, curt and dismissive. "Don't be ridiculous. Some of the night kind can apparently blend into shadow, but they can't walk through walls or get past boundary spells."

"I see," Thea said. She was standing with her hands folded behind her back and her fingers curled into fists. She did not like Mage Fisk. Not one bit. But he seemed to be honest, about his magic at least. "So, no magic that can explain this?"

"Not that I know of," Fisk said, not looking at her.

"Very well," Thea said, and moved towards the door.

"What, that's it?" Fisk said. "You're just going to leave?"

"Mage, we have been up all night questioning the household staff and now you. We need to get back to the city to find out what the physician has learned, and start making other enquiries."

"Oh. So you're not finished with the investigation, then," Fisk said.

"No. The investigation has barely started. We may need to speak to you again, though," Thea said.

"Hopefully you'll be more discreet about it than that damned woman."

"You mean Steward Fionn?" Thea asked, turning to face the mage.

"Yes. Who else? She had me dragged here."

"A man is dead," Thea said, voice clipped. "He was killed while surrounded by your magic. Magic that was supposed to protect him. If you like, next time we need to speak to you I can send Watchmen to your house instead?"

Fisk flinched. Clearly liking that idea even less than the steward sending more household staff. "No. If you need to speak to me, contact my staff. They can arrange something." He brushed a hand down his robes in what looked like a habitual gesture to smooth the cloth, and stalked out of the room, brushing past Thea.

"You don't like him much," Niath said when Fisk had left. He sounded cheerful.

"No. He's arrogant and thinking only of himself."

"Well, his entire business may be destroyed if people start thinking that his magic is no good," Niath said, sounding even more cheerful.

"You didn't like him either," Thea said, turning to the mage.

He grinned. "No. Not at all. He gives mages a bad name. Oh, his work is competent enough, but there's no need for the robe twitching."

Thea choked on a laugh and shook her head. She took a final look around the room. It was still a mystery as to how the merchant had been killed. And she had no idea why. Not yet.

"What's wrong?" Niath asked.

"Someone went to a great deal of trouble to kill Master Hannaford in a seemingly impossible way," Thea said. She felt even more confused than she had been when she had first walked into the room, and with no clear route forward to answers. "Two mages, the city's best physician and examiner haven't been able to figure out how."

"You will work it out," Niath said, with complete assurance.

"You think so?" Thea asked, glancing at him. She wanted him to say yes, wanted his reassurance. She must be far more tired than she had realised.

"Of course. You are an excellent investigator," Niath said, as if stating a basic fact, like the sun was out.

Heat bloomed under Thea's skin and she ducked her head. "Thank you," she said, feeling a little lighter. "If Fionn will not let us search, we should head back to the city," she added.

"Yes. Perhaps Dina or Iason will have more to tell us," Niath said. "And we can get more information from Commander Reardon."

Thea made a face as they left the room. "I wouldn't count on that. I don't think he gives up his secrets easily." Even as she said that she realised she was still irritated that he had dragged them into this enquiry and left them. It might be interesting to see how much information she could get out of him.

Chapter Five

While Niath went to find Sam and organise the horses, she gave instructions to Fionn that nothing was to be touched until the investigation was done. Fionn protested, wanting to at least tidy up the study and clear away the papers. Thea refused. She was too heavy-headed to think clearly at that point, but had a nagging feeling that there was something she had missed, and she did not want to risk losing it.

By the time Sam and Niath were outside with the horses, ready to travel, Fionn had reluctantly agreed to keep the study, and the house, exactly as it was.

With that promise in mind, Thea got back on the horse and rode out with Sam and Niath, the effects of working through the night catching up with her, and with a visit to Iason and Dina still ahead of her when she wanted nothing more than a warm bed and several hours' sleep. She had a childish hope that her mind would come up with some brilliant idea or solution to the mystery and she would wake up the next morning with answers clear in her mind.

The horse she was riding didn't need anything from her, content to trot along at a steady pace, quickly passing through the boundary of the house's grounds and heading back towards Accanter.

It was strange being out of the city, with no houses crowding around her and no Citadel looming overhead. Instead, there was the road ahead of them, the surrounding land allowed to run wild with thickets of mature trees and open stretches of waist-high grasses mixed with wildflowers and the occasional patch of tangled shrubs.

On another day, Thea might have spent more time looking around her. Today, with the smooth gait of the horse, air brushing against her cheek, and nothing to do, Thea half dozed in the saddle, turning over the events of the previous day in her mind. The discovery of the body. Reardon's reluctance to give them any information. The impossible way that the merchant had been killed. Niath's confidence that she would find out what had happened.

"We're being followed."

Niath's voice cut through her wish for sleep. She sat up in the saddle and looked around. Nothing. At this point on their journey the road they were following was bounded with open fields to one side and the edge of a thick patch of trees to the other side, a wide strip of grass between the road and the trees.

"Where? Who?"

"Somewhere to our right," Niath answered. The side with the trees, Thea realised. He sounded abstracted, as if most of his concentration was elsewhere. "And someone with magic. They are trying to hide themselves."

"The merchant's killer?" Thea speculated. "It would be very convenient if they would turn themselves in."

"No. But I think I recognise the magic," Niath said, something in his tone sending shivers down Thea's spine. "Come in closer to me. You, too. Sam," he said over his shoulder.

Thea nudged her horse closer to Niath's even as Sam closed the small gap from the rear.

When she was close enough that her knee was almost touching Niath's, his magic slid over her. Warm and compelling, it made her want to draw even closer. No other magic had that effect on her, but she could always tell when Niath was using his power.

"I've put up a boundary around us," Niath said. He still sounded as if he was focusing on something else.

"Can you tell how many people?" Thea asked.

"One or two," Niath said, voice flat. "No more than that."

"Using magic," Thea said slowly. "Someone we've encountered before?" she asked, trying to remember the people they had met who had magic. It was quite a short list. The Citadel Mages, Waters and Sisley. A pair of shadowed figures who had attacked them with an ancient magical weapon used against the Ageless. Former Master Merchant Kendrick, who had used borrowed magic.

But Sisley and Kendrick were in custody. Waters was missing. And the two shadowed figures had vanished. Or so she had thought.

Before she could ask Niath for more details, or what he suspected, movement to the side drew her attention. A dark-robed figure had emerged from the trees close to the road and was standing, waiting for them to notice him.

"Is that Mage Waters?" she asked.

"It looks like it," Niath said, voice grim.

Thea was about to ask him who else it could be, when she remembered the other creature they had encountered recently. A trickster, who could assume whatever form they chose. So it might not be Mage Waters standing next to the road.

"Sam, keep the horses here, will you?" Niath asked, and slid to the ground before stalking towards the dark-robed mage, his magic fading as he moved away.

Thea managed a far less graceful dismount, her body stiff and heavy, and followed Niath.

"Were you followed?" Mage Waters demanded as soon as they were within human hearing.

"Followed? By who? From where?" Niath asked, stopping.

Thea halted, too, at Niath's shoulder, and drew in a sharp breath, shocked at the changes in the man. He was thinner than she remembered, his angular face even more drawn, eyes darting from side to side, the wisps of white hair across his head standing up in all directions. The beautifully crafted robes he wore were stained and had a few tears that she could see. He was a far different man than the one she remembered meeting, briefly, in Ware's office when she had been a Watch Officer carrying out her first murder investigation. The seniormost Citadel Mage, he had been assured and confident, carrying his cold, old power around him like a cloak. He seemed to have aged, and could not stay still, fingers moving in odd patterns, head turning this way and that as if searching for something.

He reminded Thea of some of the soldiers returning from the Archon's wars. Their bodies might be whole, but their minds were hollowed out from the horrors they had seen. Thea had always found them difficult to be around, a sharp and terrible reminder of the price people paid for the Archon's ambitions to rule the entire world.

She had to force herself to hold her ground and not to turn away from Waters, but to keep looking at him, seeing what he had become.

"You know. You must know," Waters said, turning back to Niath and meeting the younger man's eyes for a moment.

"Sir, no, I don't. You seem unwell. Come, we can get you to the city. You can rest," Niath said, voice gentle.

"No. Can't go to the city. They're there."

"Who is, sir?" Thea asked, pushing down her own unease, matching Niath's gentle tone.

"They. Them. The ones." Waters' voice rose in pitch and his whole body trembled. "I helped them, you see. I helped them. Didn't know what they were doing. Didn't know. I didn't know. You have to believe me. I didn't. But it was bad. Bad bad bad."

He took a step forward and his knees gave out, sending him to the ground in a tumble of stained and smelly cloth.

Thea took a step forward, stopped by Niath's hand on her arm. There was a bit of force behind the mage's grip she had not been expecting.

"What is it?" she asked, glancing at him.

"I'm not sure."

"Is it the trickster?"

"No. Not that. But he's not himself. The magic around him is wrong." Niath was frowning as he stared at the mage.

Waters was kneeling on the ground, hands clasped around his middle, rocking back and forth, lips moving but no sound emerging.

"He seems very different," Thea commented. "When I met him, his magic was cold. Old. But quite powerful. I can't sense it anymore." She had never heard of anyone losing their magic before. Had not even realised it was possible. And he had been one of the most powerful mages in the city.

"Interesting," Niath said, looking from her to the mage. "He does seem diminished."

"Do you think Sisley did this to him?" Thea asked. Apprentice Sisley had been found trying to make a blood sacrifice of one of Kendrick's captives, intending to pass the power she harvested onto the former master merchant. As far as Thea knew, Sisley was still being held by the Ageless. As the former apprentice to the Citadel's seniormost mage, Sisley had enjoyed unfettered access to the Citadel, and to the Ageless. The Ageless would want answers.

Niath didn't answer at once, still frowning at the mage kneeling on the ground.

"We can't leave him here," Thea said. "He looks like he's been sleeping rough for weeks."

"He doesn't want to come with us," Niath said.

It didn't mean much, Thea knew. Between them, she and Niath would have no difficulty in overpowering the human, and forcing him to come with them.

The idea made her skin crawl. She had too many memories of the desperate people who had been held captive by Kendrick to want to compel Waters to come with her now.

"Sir," she said, taking another step closer and crouching down so that she could look into his face. "Do you remember me?"

"Watch Officer Thea March," the mage said. His lip curled slightly, as if in distaste, the shadow of his former self peering through. It seemed he had disliked her as much as she had disliked him.

"That's right. Can you tell me what you're afraid of?" she asked.

He stared back at her, body trembling, hands trembling as he laced his fingers together and then broke them apart over and over. Closer to him, Thea could see the pulse beating hard at his throat and caught a smell of something foul around him. Not just the odour of an unwashed body living rough for weeks. Something that smelled dead and rotten.

His lips peeled back from his teeth, showing yellowing stains, and his lips moved. Trying to speak, no sound coming out.

"What is it?" Thea asked. She had an impulse to step forward, easily curbed as another waft of that foul smell drifted to her.

"Dead dead dead." Waters' voice was barely above a whisper, words ill-formed. "You're dead."

He looked up at her and his face changed, expression sharpening, lips curling, eyes focusing on her. The terrified old man faded, replaced by something much more dangerous. The smell around him grew.

Thea got to her feet and took a careful step back.

"There's something wrong," she said to Niath.

He moved with her and they took another two steps away from Waters.

"Can you smell that?" she asked.

"No. What?"

"It smells like something dead and rotting," she said, glancing aside from the kneeling mage at Niath's sharp intake of breath. "What?"

"That's it. That's what's different. He's used blood magic."

"Like Sisley was using?" Thea asked, turning her eyes back to the mage. Waters was still kneeling, but he had stopped twitching. Instead, he was too still, his unblinking gaze focused on her and Niath.

"No. Sisley was giving power to Kendrick. I think Waters has taken the power for himself," Niath said. He muttered something under his breath. A spell of some kind. Thea felt his magic around them, warm and familiar.

"That sounds bad," she said.

"It is. It can be like a drug at first. But it drives people mad eventually," Niath said.

"Well, he does not seem himself." Thea stared at the mage. The hard, lethal edge had faded and he had started trembling again. "He's dangerous, isn't he?"

"Very," Niath said, voice flat. "And you're right, we can't leave him here. Do you have your rope?"

"Of course."

"May I have it? It's safer for me to get close to him," Niath said.

Thea handed a coil of Watch rope over to Niath without hesitation and stayed where she was as Niath made his way, slowly and carefully, to the kneeling mage. Niath looped the rope around Waters' wrists and spoke another spell, another wave of his power sliding over Thea's skin.

"That should hold him. We need to get him into the Citadel," Niath said. He put a hand under Waters' elbow. "Come on, sir," he said.

The mage rose to his feet, trembling again, expression slack, lips moving. He moved with Niath without resistance, eyes landing on Thea when they drew closer. Waters giggled, an odd, high-pitched sound that made Thea's skin crawl.

"Dead dead dead," Waters said, in a happy, childish voice.

"I'll send Sam ahead," Niath said, keeping the mage walking towards the road. "We'll walk with him. I'm not putting him on a horse."

"No," Thea agreed, following the odd pair.

Sam wasn't happy about being sent away, but went, pressing his horse to a flat-out gallop along the road so that he faded even from Thea's sight very quickly.

Which left her and Niath and the old mage in the middle of the road, the remaining two horses showing white at their eyes, heads up, nostrils flaring as they focused on the old man. The horses refused to go anywhere near the former mage which, she thought, just proved that they had a good deal of sense.

Unable to ride the rest of the way, and unable to talk freely with a half-mad mage for company, it was going to be a long journey back to Accanter.

Chapter Six

Thea had the horses' reins in one hand, walking a clear dozen paces behind Niath and Waters. Even after a while of walking, the horses refused to get any closer. Probably showing better sense than her or Niath. Providing she kept them a safe distance back, though, the horses were happy to plod along behind her. Niath had suggested she could ride if she wanted, but Thea had refused. She had no illusions about her riding skill. The horses were close to panic, and if they ran, she would be on the ground in a heartbeat. So she was walking, murmuring soothing words to the horses from time to time, and keeping an eye on the mages ahead of her.

Niath was keeping as far away from Waters as he could and still keep hold of the end of the rope. The old mage did not seem to want to run or resist, but from time to time Thea still caught the foul smell from him, and remembered the way his face and posture had changed from a fearful, trembling old man to a cold, sharp predator in human form. She wasn't sure which was the real Waters, not yet, and it seemed that Niath shared her doubts.

They were still a long way from the city, particularly on foot. Thea estimated that it would be a long time past nightfall before they reached the city limits. She hoped that Sam would be bringing back transport for the mage to speed their journey along a bit. And possibly some food. The breakfast that Fionn had provided for them was a long distant memory.

She could ask Niath if he had some food with him. He usually carried some.

But that would mean getting closer to Waters, and she did not want to do that.

Even as she daydreamed about the oatcakes or small, decadent cakes that Niath sometimes carried, a prickle ran up her spine from between her shoulder blades, coming to rest at the nape of her neck. It felt as if someone was watching her. She slowed her pace a fraction and looked around.

At first, she could see nothing. Then she spotted an odd movement in the trees to the side.

"Niath," she called. The word sounded wrong in her ears. Flat and lifeless. As if she was speaking into a pillow, the sound muffled and swallowed by feathers.

The mages kept walking, as if they had not heard her.

"Niath!"

No response at all. And the movement in the trees had resolved into shapes. Two people. Perhaps more. And they were definitely following her group.

She drew out her Watch whistle and blew, hard.

The magically powered sound cut through the air.

Niath stopped at once, turning, brows lifting. His lips moved.

"I can't hear you," Thea said, putting the whistle away. The words were still wrong, muffled somehow. She pointed instead, towards the trees.

As Niath turned towards the trees, a blot of darkness shot into the air.

Thea screamed a warning. There was no need. Niath had seen the danger.

Magic flared around him in a cascade of brilliant light, and the weapon fell to the ground, the thump too loud against Thea's ears.

"*Fyr na dathan*," Niath said grimly, stalking back along the roadway to Thea, his magic spilling out around him. Waters was following him, the old mage tripping on his robes as he tried to look into the trees rather than where he was going.

Before Thea could say anything, another blot of dark shot out from the trees.

Niath flung up a hand, sending magic out to meet it, and another cascade of light split the afternoon.

Fyr na dathan. Fire of the gods. A magical weapon used against the Ageless.

Shock held her still for too long a moment as she remembered, all too clearly, the effect of that magic weapon. Years of training came to her aid. More than one of her instructors had told her that being still was the quickest way to get killed. Breath and sound came back in a rush, her heart beat loud and fast. She needed space to move. She quickly turned and threw the reins over the horses' heads so that they wouldn't tangle in their legs, then held a hand out to Niath. "Sword, please," she said, voice higher than normal.

Niath kept his eyes on the trees as he reached into his robes and pulled out a familiar fruit knife. It shimmered with magic, transforming into a sword that fitted Thea's hand as if it had been made for her.

And just in time.

The pair of shadows that had been hiding among the trees burst out into the open. Two men, clad from head to toe in dark clothing, their faces covered. Each of them carrying a sword. And each of them masters with the weapon.

They had met before. Twice. The first time, they had nearly killed Niath with the magical weapon, and Thea had been unable to stop them from escaping. The second time, they had been in the company of a supposed goddess and had vanished with her.

She set her jaw. They would not escape this time.

"Stop them!" Waters called.

Thea spared a glance for the old mage. He was staring at the two shadows running towards them.

"Is he speaking to us or them?" Thea asked.

"I don't know," Niath said. He dropped the end of the rope he had been holding. "Stay here and stay out of the way," he told the mage, taking a step forward.

Thea moved with Niath, skin prickling at having Waters at her back. But right now the greatest threat was in front of them.

There was no more time to think or worry about the mage. The two shadows were on them. Thea engaged the closest one, her beautiful, magically made sword meeting the attacker's blade with a ring that made her ears hurt. The other sword gleamed in a way that suggested it, too, had magic woven into its length.

And the man wielding it was a master. He moved with her, anticipating her attempt to separate him from his companion and draw him away from Niath and Waters, flicking his sword forward in an attack that almost sliced into her arm. She managed to bring her blade around in time, turning her hips, slicing back and catching his blade with a force that rang up her arm into her shoulder. The impact sent him stumbling back, tripping over something on the ground, and she followed, stamping on his sword so he couldn't raise it against her, reversing her own sword and thumping him on the head with the weighted pommel.

There was no time to see if she had knocked him out. A brush of air against her cheek was all the warning she had that the other man was there, his blade seeking her throat. She moved back, stumbling in her turn, falling the way she had been trained to, rolling back up to stand, sword ready, facing her attacker.

He had not expected her to recover so quickly, she saw. He was out of position. She took advantage, pressing forward, reversing her sword again and cracking him across the ribs. He stumbled back, a muffled cry of pain escaping, but righted himself as quickly as she had, bringing his weapon up.

He was injured, though, and she was not.

"Thea, down," Niath called.

She dropped to the ground without question and a bolt of magic flew over her, thudding into the man, sending him into the air and several body lengths back towards the trees. Thea winced as the man hit the ground. He would most likely have at least one broken bone.

"Oh, that worked well," Niath said, sounding pleased. He marched past her towards the fallen man.

"Was that *fyr na dathan*?" Thea asked, scrambling to her feet and following him.

"It was. I hope they liked having their own weapon used against them," Niath said, reaching the man's side.

"Careful," Thea warned, even as the man surged to his feet, blade up, as if he was not injured at all.

Somehow Niath avoided being skewered with the blade, stepping aside more quickly than any human would have managed.

Thea moved in front of Niath, blocking the man's next attack with her blade, the force of the block echoing through her body.

"Thea," Niath said, in a low, urgent tone.

"What?" she asked through gritted teeth, trying to hold the block against the masked warrior.

"There are more of them this time," Niath said.

Thea spared a glance behind the man and saw he was right. There were more shapes moving among the trees. Another four, perhaps. And she and Niath were much closer to the trees than they had been.

"Back," she said to Niath. The man in front of her pressed his attack and she saw that his free arm was hanging by his side, not moving. He was injured.

It was impossible to tell from the way he fought, though. There was a charred ring on his chest where Niath's magic had struck him, and one arm was useless, but he was pressing his attack against Thea with single-minded determination, and she was barely holding her own against him.

There was no possible way that she and Niath could hold against any more attackers. Not if they were all like this one. She kept edging backwards, further away from the trees and the other shadows. Still, her arm was tiring and it was getting more difficult to hold her sword.

Even as her heart sank, Waters giggled again.

"Oh, pretty pretty."

"What?" Thea asked, keeping her attention back to the man in front of her, trusting Niath to work out what the mad mage was referring to.

"In the sky. Ageless," Niath said. "At least two of them. Coming this way and fast."

Thea would never have believed she could be relieved or pleased to hear that Ageless were on their way. Until now. When she was faced with overwhelming odds of highly trained and experienced foes, who could use magic.

Their attackers had seen the Ageless, too, and surged forward out of the trees, trying to overwhelm them.

"Down!" Niath called, and Thea dropped to the ground again, narrowly avoiding a vicious sweep of her attacker's sword.

Niath's magic flew over her head and slammed into the nearest two of the new attackers, sending them flying back into the air.

Thea scrambled to her feet, head spinning for a moment, but she kept her sword up, ready to defend against the next attack. The man who had been fighting her was standing a pace or two away, finally showing signs of weakness. Both arms were by his sides and he was breathing hard.

But there were two new attackers still standing. Uninjured, and armed. One flung up a hand and threw magic towards Niath.

Niath blocked the magic and sent more of the *fyr na dathan* back to the attacker, flinging him back towards the trees.

The other man was nowhere to be seen. Not in front of them, anyway.

Thea whirled, sword up, and spotted the final attacker running towards Waters, who was staring up at the sky. The attacker had a sword ready to use, blade gleaming.

"Waters! Move!" she yelled, starting to run towards the mage.

He didn't seem to hear her.

Thea pushed herself as fast as she could move, far faster than any human, closing the distance to the would-be assassin. She was going to be too late. Far too late. It was too great a distance to close.

She heard a cry behind her. Niath.

Magic flew past her, aimed for the attacker. It missed.

The shadowed man drew back his sword arm, preparing to strike.

And was knocked off his feet, along with Waters, by a powerful downdraft of wings, the attacker smothered a moment later by a pair of blinding white wings.

The Ageless had arrived.

Thea stumbled to a halt, swaying, sword held ready. Waters was safe.

But that left Niath. And she had run away from him.

She turned and had to step sideways to catch her balance.

Niath was right behind her, his human *aspect* faded, stripped away into the angular planes and black eyes of a hiandar.

"They weren't after us," he said, stopping beside her. "They were after Waters."

"It seems so," Thea said, trying to catch her breath. She was lightheaded, stomach hollow and twisting inside. Trusting the Ageless behind her to look after the single attacker, she looked past Niath's shoulder and blinked. "Where did they go?"

The mage turned and she saw his shoulders and back stiffen. He muttered a curse that lifted her brows.

The ground in front of them was clear. There was no sign of the other masked men who had attacked them. There was some evidence of a fight in trampled grasses and a broken branch or two where the edge of the magical weapon had struck. But nothing else.

Thea spat out a curse of her own, drawing a sideways look from Niath, his face returned to its human *aspect*. He looked as if he was trying not to laugh.

"Why were you being attacked by the warriors of Alayla?" a familiar voice asked from somewhere behind her.

She turned to find Commander Reardon standing, his wings tucked behind his back, holding the still-masked attacker with one hand. His face was still in its Ageless *aspect*, made of sharp angles and black eyes, skin almost as pale as his wings, the silvered scar at his temple standing out.

"Warriors of Alayla?" she repeated, brows lifting. She glanced at Niath. "I didn't know such a thing existed. Although it does explain a few things."

"This is a warrior of Alayla," Reardon said, giving the man in his hold a brief shake. The man's head flopped. Unconscious. Or possibly dead. "And you still haven't answered my question."

Thea was tempted to say something rude, but swallowed the words and shook her head instead. "I don't know. We were riding along, back to the city. We came across Mage Waters, and then the warriors turned up."

"I haven't seen the warriors for a long time." The new voice came from somewhere behind Reardon and sent a shock wave through Thea. She knew that voice. She remembered it, vivid and real, from the worst day of her life. Along with the scent of cinnamon.

She took a step sideways so she could see around Reardon, and stopped again. It was him.

Another Ageless, this one with cool-toned, dark skin and a kinder face, even in his Ageless *aspect*. He had his wings tucked behind him, but she remembered them spread out around him, his voice soft and soothing as he carried her in his arms down to the ground where Theo's body lay.

"Really?" Niath asked, cutting through Thea's memories with his usual boundless curiosity. "This is the second time we've met them."

"What?" Reardon demanded. "When did you encounter them before?"

"The masked men that used the *fyr na dathan* then disappeared. These are the same fellows," Niath said, waving a hand, not in the least intimidated by Reardon's scowl. "Why is he still masked?"

"Because it's not a mask," Reardon answered. "They use some kind of magic to fuse their clothes to them, including the masks."

"Does that mean they can't eat or drink?" Thea asked, remembering the warrior with his injured arm, and the others knocked over by Niath's magic. Rest, food and drink had always been necessary ingredients for recovery in her experience.

"We don't know. We've never had one of them long enough to tell," Reardon said, face and voice grim. "What do you think?" he asked over his shoulder.

It was almost shocking to see the confident, assured Commander of the Archon's garrison ask for another's opinion, and with evident respect. Reardon was treating the newcomer as an equal.

The other Ageless moved closer to Reardon and inspected the limp man.

"I think he's still alive," he said, voice dry, "which is more than we've been able to achieve before. They usually kill themselves rather than be caught," he explained as an aside to Thea and Niath. "Oh, my manners. I am Trymian. You must be Niath. But I don't know you, young lady."

"Watch Investigator Thea March," Thea said, face and lips stiff. He didn't know her. Of course he didn't. He could not possibly connect a skinny nine-year-old girl he had rescued half a world away with the grown woman in front of him. She had carried a different name then, one which she had not thought of in years.

"Trymian," Niath said slowly, his eyes brightening. "The greatest Ageless scholar since Gaderian himself? It's an honour to meet you, sir. Is it true that you have studied all the ancient texts on magic and have most of them in your library?" Thea had never seen Niath so excited.

Trymian laughed, his Ageless *aspect* fading until he was returned to his human appearance, achingly familiar to Thea even after the years since she had last seen him. He had a face meant for life and laughter. He was the only Ageless who had always made her feel safe. He might be powerful, but she had never once worried that he would harm her.

And she had seen a similar face recently, she realised. The pretend bookseller in Accanter, Mort. The one who had a basement full of disguises and who was, along with Ware and Niath, part of a secret organisation seeking the truth. Mort looked like a younger version of Trymian. They were too alike to be anything other than father and son.

She ducked her eyes away, hoping her surprise hadn't been noticed.

Before Trymian could answer Niath's question, Mage Waters stumbled forward, hand held out.

"I know you," he said, staring at Reardon. "I know you, don't I?"

"Yes, you do," Reardon said, half-turning to face the mage, still holding the unconscious man in the air. The extra weight did not seem to be bothering the Ageless. "I'm Reardon."

"Yes, yes, yes. A dangerous one, you are," Waters said. His voice was high-pitched again, face slack, fingers trembling as he raised a hand to point to the Commander. "You carry death with you."

Reardon, still in his Ageless *aspect*, did not look amused. Before he could react or say anything, the limp man in his hold abruptly came to life, drawing a long, slender dagger from somewhere about his person and leaping forward, striking out with one smooth slice that cut through Waters' neck. The warrior was not done. The sweep of his blade continued, the blade reversing in its path until it lodged securely somewhere in the warrior's chest. He went limp again, and this time Thea knew, without having to be told, that he was dead.

Chapter Seven

The murder and suicide were over before she had been able to do more than raise her sword. And Reardon was still holding on to the warrior's arm.

Reardon dropped the dead warrior with a curse, his wings flicking open and then closed with an almost audible snap, face tightening. There was a fine mist of blood spray across his face.

"They were after the mage?" Trymian asked, turning to Thea and Niath. "Why?"

"No idea," Niath said, spreading his hands. His eyes had shaded towards his hiandar *aspect*, perhaps shocked by the violence he had seen, his human side reasserting itself as he took a long breath. "Thea?"

She frowned down at the dead mage. There was a large and growing pool of blood around him, his already pale skin fading further in death.

"Thea?" Reardon prompted. He was almost back to his human *aspect*, too, his wings gone. As she glanced up at him, he drew a white square of cloth from a pocket and wiped his face, grimacing as the cloth turned red with the mage's blood. "What do you know?" he asked.

"I don't know anything," she said, and realised she was still holding the sword. She held it out to Niath. "Would you mind?"

"Not at all," he answered, and took the sword, turning it back into a fruit knife and hiding it away in his robes.

"Well, you suspect something," Reardon prompted, not impressed with the delay.

"Mage Waters was half mad when we found him. It looks as if he's been living rough for a while. He was mostly incoherent. But he said he helped them. And that he hadn't known what they were doing, but it was bad." Her nose wrinkled, hearing the words spoken aloud. The mage hadn't told them much. Not really. "He didn't say who they were," she added, before Reardon could ask.

"He's been using blood magic," Niath added. "He stank of it."

"His own blood?" Trymian asked, with the same sort of boundless curiosity that Niath displayed.

"I don't know," Niath said honestly.

"Waters referred to *they*," Reardon said, staring down at the dead mage. "You have some ideas?" he asked Thea.

"Well," Thea began, and swayed on her feet, lightheaded again. She set her teeth together and braced herself, locking her knees. "We know that the Hand of the goddess had access to magic. And someone had to have worked the spells that brought Alayla into existence."

"The Citadel's senior mage using blood magic? The Hand of the goddess? Alayla in existence?" Trymian asked, brows lifting. His eyes were bright with interest as he looked at Reardon. "You've been holding out on me, young man. I had no idea that things were so interesting in this city or I would have paid the Citadel a visit long before now."

Thea watched, fascinated, as Reardon's face tightened and he hesitated. In the short time she had known him, she knew that he rarely hesitated.

"It's not something I want widely known," he said to Trymian at length.

"Really? And yet this young Watch Investigator and mage seem very familiar with the matters," Trymian pointed out.

"They've been involved in most of the incidents," Reardon said, sending a sideways look at Thea. "They seem to have a knack for finding trouble."

"Thank you," Niath said, as if he had been paid a great compliment.

"I don't think it's a good thing," Reardon said, brows lowering.

"No, you wouldn't," Niath said, looking as if he was trying not to smile.

"So, you were saying something about bringing Alayla into existence?" Trymian said, turning back to Thea.

"I was. But, sir, do you mind if we discuss this another time? We're still some way from the city and I'd like to get the bodies to the mortuary for inspection," Thea said, not looking at Reardon, anticipating that he would not like the idea.

"Good," he said, surprising her. "There should be a cart along in a minute. That will get the bodies back to the physician. I will be there when he examines them."

Thea opened her mouth to protest, then thought better of it and closed her jaw with a snap that jarred her teeth together. He was letting them take the bodies to the mortuary, under Iason and Dina's care, and not insisting that they went to the Citadel and out of Thea's reach instead. That was a win, in her view. And she knew the physician well enough to know he would not let the presence of an Ageless warrior put him off his work.

"Physician Pallas said he would examine Master Hannaford today, too," Thea commented, "so we may get some news of him as well."

"Who's he?" Trymian asked. "A member of the Hand, perhaps?"

"I don't think so, sir," Thea said. "He was a master merchant. He was killed in his study yesterday around noon. Niath and I were just coming back from his house to the city when we found Mage Waters."

"Another body?" Trymian's brows lifted. "Connected, do you think?"

"I don't know," Thea said slowly, looking down at the masked corpse. "But we haven't been able to work out how Master Hannaford was killed. It's possible that magic was involved. Can you tell me, sir, do the warriors of Alayla all use magic?"

"Most do," Trymian answered readily, eyes brightening. He had been a wonderful teacher, Thea remembered. All the children had loved his lessons. He had made them all feel as if they were special, and no question had been too small for his attention. "They use written spells. We think that they might tattoo them onto their skin."

"Really?" Thea asked, interested.

"Yes. Although, that is mostly guesswork as we've never been able to examine one properly," Trymian said, staring down at the corpse. "I wonder if we'll have better luck with this one."

"We won't know until we try," Reardon said, surprising Thea again. Experimenting did not seem like something the Commander would have much time for.

"The cart's getting near," Niath said. He was standing near Thea in his favourite pose, hands folded behind his back, staring along the road in the direction of the city. "We should be back to the mortuary by nightfall," he added.

"Good," Thea said, taking a step towards her horse and having to catch herself before she fell. She muttered a curse, heat flooding her face.

"Here," Niath said, handing her a familiar-looking cloth-wrapped bundle. "We've been working for two days without a rest," he said to the Ageless.

"And then fighting warriors of Alayla," Trymian finished, putting one hand on his heart. "And now we have kept you both talking when we could have been resting." It was as close to an apology as Thea had ever heard from any Ageless.

Thea ducked her head, uncomfortable with the sympathy, and bit into the oatcake Niath had provided. Her whole body was leaden with fatigue, the small bit of energy from the oatcake enough, she hoped, to make it back onto her horse and into the city without falling off.

"I will arrange a guard for the bodies," Reardon said, frowning. "The physician may examine them in the morning."

"Daylight would be better, actually," Trymian agreed.

They were being considerate of her weakness, Thea realised, her cheeks and ears burning, skin itching in discomfort. She wanted to protest, to say that she would manage to attend the mortuary this evening, but the words stuck in her throat. It would be a lie. She would not manage. She had pushed herself to the limit, with the overnight questions and the brutal fight with the warriors. Her mother and her trainers had warned her that actual combat was far more exhausting than training. And they had all been right. She was capable of endurance in her weapons practice, but not in a real fight, it seemed.

Still, she had survived. That was something.

"I'll need to get a message to Captain Handerson as well," she said, when the oatcake was gone.

"Very well," Reardon said, as if granting her permission.

Her embarrassment faded into irritation and she turned her shoulder, as if the cart approaching them was far more interesting than an arrogant Ageless warrior.

Chapter Eight

Thea arrived at the mortuary in the early morning, surprised and pleased to find that she had arrived before Niath, Reardon and Trymian. Ware and Sutter were already there, conferring with Iason and Dina in low tones in the mortuary.

The mortuary was full of morning light, bright and sunny in contrast to the grim business that went on in the room. There was a quartet of Archon soldiers at the door, which she had never seen before, but they simply stood still while she walked between them. She wondered for a moment why they were outside the room rather than watching the corpse they had been sent to guard, but it did not seem a sensible question to ask.

Each of Iason's three tables was full, the sheets that covered the bodies turned down so that the heads were visible. Bordan Hannaford. Waters. And the masked head of the warrior of Alayla.

"Good morning, everyone," Thea said as she came through the door. A night's rest had helped a lot. She had fallen into bed and slept without dreams until Gilbert the cat had woken her at dawn, insisting that she let him outside.

"Thea. I hear that there was a fight yesterday," Ware said. He was still looking tired, with tension across his shoulders. She wondered how many visits from local dignitaries he had endured since word of Master Hannaford's death had spread.

"Warriors of Alayla, no less," Dina said. She nodded to Iason's writing table. "I found reference to them in the library here. Thought you might want to take a look."

"Yes, please," Thea said, and took a step towards the writing table. "If that's alright?"

"Yes, of course. We've seen the passage already," Ware said.

Thea found a heavy, old book propped open on the writing table, one of the pages depicting what looked like a fearsome battle, with a lot of weapons that seemed too big for the small figures to wield. The other page was headed, in old script, "Warriors of Alayla." The words below were handwritten in big, blocky text, and essentially warned the reader to be wary of the warriors as they were fearsome, fanatically loyal fighters.

By the time she had finished reading, footsteps outside the room heralded the arrival of Reardon, Trymian and Niath.

Trymian's introduction to the others was cut short by Reardon scowling at the guards at the door. "Why are you out here? You're supposed to be watching the body."

"Sir," one of the quartet said. "We made that point."

"They did. Several times," Dina said, with false cheer. "But if you think I'm going to let some clumsy, over-muscled soldier trample all over our evidence, you are mistaken."

Reardon's brows lifted and he blinked. Thea hid a smile, and suspected a few others in the room were doing the same. They had all, at one point or another, been on the receiving end of Dina's temper. From the way the soldiers shuffled their feet, as if wanting to move further away from the door, Dina had not held back her opinions when chasing them out of the room.

"They are here for your safety, too," Reardon said, voice mild.

"Oh, is that so?" Dina asked, eyes glinting. "Please tell me how a dead body is dangerous? We've had hundreds here over the years."

"This one has magic," Reardon said, deadly serious.

"Dina, Commander," Iason said, taking a step forward. "May I begin? It's going to be a long day, I think."

"Of course, physician," Reardon said, positioning himself at the other end of the table from Dina, and far enough back that he wouldn't get in Iason's way as the physician drew the sheet off the masked warrior then made a slow, careful circuit of the table, his hands tucked behind his back as if avoiding the temptation to touch anything.

Everyone else spaced themselves around the corpse, careful to stand out of Iason's light, Thea finding a place near Niath.

"Mage Niath, would you monitor the body in case there is any dangerous magic?" Iason asked, coming to a halt at the corpse's head.

"Of course," Niath said.

"I will do so as well," Trymian said. He was standing near Reardon and had been so quiet it was easy to forget he was Ageless. "I have experience with these warriors, physician," he explained. "And know some of their tricks."

Iason nodded, and lifted his hands, reaching for the masked head. Thea's brows lifted as she realised he was wearing gloves. He was always meticulous with cleanliness in the mortuary, helped by cleaning spells from Odilia, but she did not remember seeing him wearing those heavy gloves before.

She could feel her muscles tense as the physician moved, slowly and carefully, putting his hands on either side of the dead man's head, exploring the shape of his skull.

"Interesting," Iason said after a moment. "This covering, whatever it is, is some kind of fabric, and there is movement between it and the skin beneath. May I have a scalpel, Dina?"

The examiner handed over one of the instruments Iason had lined up on a tray at the side of the room, and stayed by Iason's side, watching as the physician made a small, careful incision at the side of the head.

Thea found herself leaning closer, wanting a better look, as the physician carefully cut around the side of the head. He handed the scalpel back to Dina and then gently peeled back the dark mask.

"Watch out!" Niath and Trymian called at the same time.

Dina grabbed Iason around the waist, hauling the smaller man away from the body, even as Trymian and Reardon surged forward, hands out.

The air crackled with magic, sending static across Thea's skin, and the body on the table exploded outward in a shower of black, jagged fragments.

Thea ducked, flinging an arm up across her face, waiting for the shower of whatever-it-was to descend on her.

The shower never came.

She peered through her fingers, then lowered her arm.

The fragments were held, suspended in the air, all around the table, the air around them fizzing with the frost of Ageless magic.

Reardon and Trymian were standing on either side of the table, their hands raised. They glanced at each other and nodded, acknowledging a job well done.

"You knew this would happen?" Thea asked, staring at the pair.

"It's happened before. But no one has ever got as far as your physician," Trymian said. "Is everyone alright?"

Thea looked around the room to find that, apart from the suspended explosion, everything seemed completely normal. The others in the room were staring at where the body had been with similar, stunned expressions.

"That is very impressive magic," Niath said, taking a step closer. "What spell is that?"

"I should be happy to teach you," Trymian said. "Another time, perhaps."

"Yes, of course," Niath said. "Thea, look at this. The entire body exploded. There's nothing left."

"I can see that," Thea said, not moving from her position near the wall. "Those fragments look sharp," she commented.

"They are. They have sliced through people in the past," Trymian said. He glanced across at Thea, then looked at the others. "It's quite safe to approach, if you want. The magic will hold for a long while yet."

Given that assurance, everyone in the room moved closer to the suspended fragments.

"Did you see anything before the body exploded?" Thea asked Iason.

"Very little. I had a brief glimpse of dark skin with tattoos that seemed to shimmer, and then Niath and Trymian called their warning," Iason said. He looked as disturbed as Thea had ever seen him, clothes rumpled from Dina's handling. He pulled off his gloves with steady movements, though, and smoothed down his waistcoat. "Can we take one of the fragments to study?" he asked Trymian.

"Study? That's an interesting idea," Trymian said. "We can try, although they tend to dissolve quickly once they are out of the magic."

"Dissolve into what?" Dina asked, eyes sharp.

"No one has studied that," Trymian admitted.

Dina sniffed. "Amateurs," she said, and gathered a heavy glass jar and pair of long-nosed tweezers from the instrument tray that scalpel had been on. "I assume I can just take one?" she asked Trymian.

"Indeed. I can add some of the holding spell to the jar, if that helps," he suggested.

"That would help, yes," Dina said, peering at the scattered cloud of fragments in front of her. She selected one, by some criteria Thea could not even begin to guess at, and drew it, slowly and carefully, out of the cloud of fragments before dropping it into the jar. The fragment stayed floating in the middle of the jar as Dina added a thick wooden lid before holding it up to the light. "It is truly black. It doesn't seem to reflect any light at all. Maybe I should collect another one, too," she said, turning back to the cloud.

"I do not think that would be wise," Trymian said.

Dina's chin lifted, and she looked as if she would argue.

"Are they dangerous? Even one or two of them alone?" Thea asked. Her heart was still beating a little too fast, with the lethal cloud of fragments less than an arm's length away.

"Without careful handling, yes," Trymian said. He held up a hand before Dina could protest. "I am sure you would take all possible precautions, madam examiner, but they have a mind of their own. Difficult enough to keep track of one, let alone more."

Dina sniffed again, clearly unconvinced, but did not try and argue, somewhat to Thea's surprise. However, the examiner had just been given a new puzzle to solve, and one which no one else had studied. Knowing Dina as she did, Thea suspected it would be a while before anyone saw her once she got the fragment back to her workroom in the basement of the building.

"Well, there's nothing more that I can do for this man," Iason said, eyeing the jagged cloud in front of him. "Will this hold steady for a while?" he asked the Ageless.

Reardon and Trymian exchanged glances.

"For as long as we can hold the magic," Trymian said. "Which should be several hours. We would propose destroying it before then, though."

"The destruction might cause some disruption," Reardon added.

"In that case, I had best get on with the others," Iason said, moving to the next table along where Mage Water's parchment-pale skin almost blended into the sheet covering him.

The physician hesitated before he reached for the sheet. "Are there any dangerous magics on Mage Waters?"

"Not anymore," Niath said, moving to stand at the foot of the table. "He had blood magic on him when he was alive, but it's faded. I can clean him for you, if you like? Just of magic," he added.

"That would be welcome, thank you," Iason said, and took a step back while Niath spoke a spell.

Niath's magic, warm and vividly alive, filled the room. "He's safe for you to handle now," he told Iason.

After the explosion of the first body, the examination of the second was almost dull. Iason found old scars and partly healed wounds on Waters' arms. Niath suggested that those might be from blood-letting, the mage using his own blood for the magic. That drew frowns, but reluctant agreement from Trymian and Reardon.

The mage had been in poor physical health before his throat was cut, with small scrapes and bruises across his legs that Iason speculated came from trampling through undergrowth and living rough. He had been thin almost to the point of starvation, too. But there was no mystery as to the cause of his death. And no clues anywhere else on his person or in his clothes about who he had been afraid of.

"We've been looking for him," Reardon said, the offer of information unexpected enough that Thea wondered if she had heard him right. He didn't notice her stare, his eyes on the dead mage, once again covered up to his chin in Iason's sheets. "We wanted to ask him how much he knew about what Sisley was up to," he added, naming Waters' apprentice.

Thea's mind took her back to the warehouse full of desperate people and Sisley performing a vicious ritual to draw more power for Kendrick. The apprentice had been a more than willing accomplice in Kendrick's ambition.

"How long was he missing?" Trymian asked.

"At least two weeks. Maybe a little more." Reardon's jaw tightened. "When we realised Sisley had been helping Kendrick, we also realised we hadn't seen Waters for a few days."

Thea's brows lifted. Even after the events of the morning, that was shocking news. Waters and Sisley were two of the few humans with unfettered access to the Citadel, and all the Ageless. The Citadel where Edris lived, and where there were rooms full of Ageless treasures, both of gold and of knowledge. "The Citadel lost track of its seniormost mage and his apprentice?" she asked, unable to keep the disbelief out of her voice.

Reardon glanced across at her, his face shifting fractionally from his human *aspect*, showing the sharp bones of his Ageless nature for a brief moment. He was frowning, thoroughly displeased at something. Although she did not think he was annoyed with her.

"Indeed," he said, answering her. "And Waters had managed to hide himself quite well," he added. "We've been looking in the city and in the surrounding areas. Human magic is usually easy to detect."

"The Watch have been keeping an eye out as well," Ware said, further surprising Thea. "No, we didn't give direct orders," he added, under Reardon's frowning glance, "but we asked the patrols to report anything unusual. There's been no sighting of the mage."

Reardon was still frowning, clearly dissatisfied with something.

"Presumably you were looking for the mage that you knew," Trymian said, "not someone who was using blood magic. That makes a difference."

Thea did not pretend to understand magic, but it made sense to her. She remembered the last time she had seen Sisley, and how changed she had been by the magic she had been using for Kendrick.

Reardon looked up, attention on the older Ageless, and his face relaxed a little. "That's true."

"I don't understand what he was doing out there," Thea said. "He doesn't seem to have been well-equipped to live on the land."

"That particular bit of land is uninhabited, and mostly covered in forest," Reardon said, surprising her with the ready information. "The trees provide a barrier between the city and the nearest houses, and there's nothing of interest there."

"A perfect place to hide, then," Trymian finished, nodding. "Or it's also possible he was trying to get to one of the houses and got lost."

"The Summer House was the only one I saw," Thea said.

"There are other houses. But usually only flown to," Reardon said, face closing in again.

Ageless houses, he meant. Thea remembered that most of the properties around the Summer House were occupied by Ageless. Naturally, the Ageless would not want anything as ordinary as a road leading up to one of their homes. She could not help wondering how the household staff managed to get supplies to the buildings, but kept that as a question for another day.

"Well, he can't tell us why he was there," Dina pointed out, as practical as ever. She was still holding the glass jar with the bit of darkness in it, as if she didn't want to let go of her new project.

Brought back from idle speculation, Thea looked at the last body in the room. "Did you learn anything more about Master Hannaford, sir?" she asked Iason.

"A little." Iason moved to stand by the final table and gave them all a brief update on Master Hannaford. The cause of death had indeed been the knife. And it had been inserted head-on, so the merchant had been facing his killer. Iason could not explain why the man had simply sat there and allowed himself to be killed, but that was what seemed to have happened. There were two things of note apart from that. The merchant had a scar along one of his forearms that looked recent, although it had healed. It had been a deliberate cut of some kind, and reminded Thea of the scars on Waters' arms, although the one on Master Hannaford was much longer. And when Iason had undressed the man, he had found a key on a chain around his neck.

Iason handed the key over to Thea. She turned it over in her hand. It was about the length of her palm, and an unusual design.

"I don't remember seeing a lock in his study that this would fit," she commented. "But I can check again."

"He also had an office at the merchants' guild building," Ware said. "There might be something there."

"Do you think the merchants' guild will let me in?" Thea asked.

Ware's mouth lifted in a sour smile. "They have made it clear that they expect his death to be our top priority. If they want it solved, they should allow you access."

"The remaining Master Merchants were in our offices at first light," Sutter said. He paused, lips pressed into a flat line. "Apparently, they didn't think we were doing enough to investigate Master Hannaford's death."

"I see," Thea said, tucking the key away in a pocket. "Well, I'd like to speak to them as well so I can ask to see his office when I go there." She turned to Iason. "Is there anything else of note to report, sir?"

"Not just now." Iason glanced along the mortuary to where the fragments of the warrior were still suspended in the air. "However, I would like my mortuary back."

"Of course," Trymian said. "We'll need to clear the room first. Anything you don't want damaged."

Thea saw Iason's eyes widen in dismay as he looked around at the cabinets and shelves and trays of instruments.

"We'll help you," she said, the offer out before she thought about it, and that she was offering not only her own services but her superior officer and two Ageless.

"Of course we will," Trymian said, as if he had not noticed anything wrong with her offer. "The more hands, the shorter time it will take."

"And those boys outside can use their muscles for something useful for a change," Dina said. Thea bit her lip to hide a smile. She had all but forgotten the Archon soldiers still standing in the corridor.

Reardon's face tightened, but he gestured for the soldiers to come into the room and lend a hand.

Trymian turned to Iason. "Is there anything particularly volatile we should take care with?" he asked.

"That cabinet over there," Iason said, pointing to the larger of the cabinets, a solid-looking construction. "I store chemicals in there. They are all flammable."

"Would it be easier to shield the cabinet?" Niath asked.

Thea responded to Dina's beckoning gesture, going over to help the examiner lift and then move the writing desk out of the mortuary into the hallway, losing track of whatever discussions Niath and Trymian were engaged in. It sounded a little bit like the technical discussion that Niath had had with Jilt Fisk the day before.

With Niath and Trymian engaged in setting up whatever magical defences they could around the cabinet Iason had pointed out, the rest of them helped Iason move everything else out of the room, including the other two bodies, the table tops lifting off into serviceable stretchers. The Archon soldiers, and Reardon, all lent their strength with no complaint and the room was cleared far more quickly than Thea would have believed possible.

Once that was done, Thea went back into the doorway of the mortuary. Niath and Trymian were standing at either end of the table with the fragments above it. The afternoon sun was absorbed into the shards, rather than reflecting off them.

"Wait out here," Reardon said, and stepped past Thea, closing the door behind him so that Thea had to take a step back to avoid the heavy wood.

"What now?" Iason wondered.

"I don't think we'll have long to wait," Ware said.

"You've seen this done before, sir?" Thea asked.

"Not this precisely, but I have seen the Ageless destroy things after battle," Ware answered, face tight.

Before Thea could form a suitable response, there was a dull thud from the room behind her and a wave of magic crawled over her skin. Not the warm, compelling sensation of Niath's magic, but something much older and colder that made her want to turn and run away. Far away. She held her ground, drawing a breath, and then wished she hadn't as she caught the faintest trace of the foulness that Mage Waters had carried with him. She had not noticed the stench in the mortuary, but the room was always furnished with candles and cleaning magic. The corridor they were gathered in was not.

Another thump sounded through the door, followed by the welcome sensation of Niath's magic on her skin, chasing away the chill of the old magic and Mage Waters' smell.

"I think they may be done," she said, but did not move to open the door.

"Well, I guess we need to put everything back, then," Dina said. She sounded almost cheerful at the prospect. "Assuming the Ageless and their soldiers will stay around to lend a hand, of course," she added, sounding even more cheerful.

Thea bit the inside of her lip to hide a smile. The examiner, like many Ageless-born, had no real love for the Ageless. It must please her to see them employed in menial tasks. It had surprised Thea that Reardon had been so willing to assist. But then again, perhaps he had not wanted to leave Trymian alone with the remains of the warrior that had so nearly proved lethal.

The door of the mortuary opened and Niath appeared along with a cloud of pale grey smoke and an odour that caught the back of Thea's throat and made her cough.

"Do the windows open, physician?" Niath asked, sounding hoarse. "The room is safe, but the smoke is foul."

"Yes," Iason said, and dug into a pocket, producing a long, slender key. "Here." He handed the key to the mage.

"Won't be a moment," Niath said, and ducked back into the room, closing the door behind him.

Thea could track the sound of the windows being opened and the tread of footsteps on the floor, turning to face the door again just before it opened and Reardon appeared.

"The room is safe again," he said, "and nothing in your cabinets was disturbed, physician," he told Iason. "This all needs to go back into place?" he asked, eyeing the abundance of things gathered in the wide corridor.

"All of it," Iason confirmed. "Thank you," he added, picking up the nearest object, which was one of the tall candle holders. "I think if we set the candles first, it will help clear the air," he suggested.

"Good idea," Thea said, and picked up the nearest candle holder. There had been two at each table, she remembered, and saw the others gathering the rest of the candles.

The mortuary echoed to their footsteps as they went inside, the smoke almost cleared from the air, all the windows flung open. The only sign of disturbance was a scattering of pitch dark ash over the third table, where the fragments had been.

"Oh, I want some of that," Dina said, putting her candle holder down. "Don't get rid of it just yet."

Thea worked with the others while Dina found another glass jar and gathered a large scoop of the dark ash. It slithered into the jar and she put a stopper on it as quickly as possible, staring at the ash as it swirled around the jar.

"It is still moving," she said after a moment, frowning.

"Allow me," Trymian said, holding out his hand for the jar. Dina hesitated, but handed the thing over. The Ageless took the jar in both hands, staring down into the swirling ash. Thea's skin prickled with the sensation of magic being used, and the ash stilled, as if cut off from life. "There. There's no more magic in it. But I would still be careful." He hesitated in his turn, holding the jar back out to Dina. "I would like to be there when you examine this and the fragment."

Dina looked torn between wanting to accept his help and reluctance. Thea could understand. The examiner's work space was her own domain, and Thea had the impression that she did not like other people being there, let alone a strange Ageless. Somehow, common sense won.

"That would be most helpful," Dina said. "Shall we get started?"

"Now?" Trymian asked, brows lifting.

"The room is almost back to normal. I assume that Niath and Commander Reardon, or the soldiers outside, can deal with the ash," Dina said, the last words spoken over her shoulder as she left the room with light, brisk strides.

Trymian shook his head slightly, and turned to Niath. "If you need anything, you know where to find me."

"Sir," Niath answered, inclining his head, a touch of longing on his face as he watched Trymian follow Dina.

"You could always go with them," Thea suggested. They might all look very different, but Dina, Trymian and Niath shared a never-ending curiosity and love of learning.

Slightly to her surprise, Niath did not hesitate. He shook his head. "There's work to do here, and then we're going to see the merchants, aren't we?"

Thea agreed, wondering what more revelations might be in store for her at the merchants' guild. She could only hope that there would be no more explosions that day.

Chapter Nine

It was late afternoon, almost evening, by the time the mortuary was back in order to Iason's satisfaction. To Thea's surprise, Ware, Sutter and Reardon all stayed and worked alongside her and Niath, uncomplaining, as they adjusted the layout of the mortuary under Iason's direction. Niath and Reardon did something, she was not sure what, and the black ash disappeared as if it had never been there. All the same, she saw Iason's gaze turning to the empty table from time to time, doubtless remembering the body that had been there.

Despite the hour, and the hollow in her stomach, Thea decided she could not put off visiting the merchants' guild until the next day. The return of the warriors of Alayla and Waters' death might not have anything to do with Bordan Hannaford, but the merchants had threatened to disband the Watch if they didn't see results. And from the exhaustion on Ware's face, he was still under a great deal of pressure. So she wanted to do what she could to keep the investigation moving, and let the merchants know that work was being done.

She and Niath made their way across the city to the grand, purpose-built guild hall that sat a few streets away from the Middlefield Watch Station. Their route took them past the Harrow bakery which, thankfully, was still open, selling its wares to weary people on their way home from a long day working. There were a few tables outside the bakery, designed for people to stand at and eat, and Thea and Niath paused there before continuing on their way.

The merchants' guild was still bustling with activity, despite the hour. There were lanterns on either side of the entrance steps, casting more than enough light for human eyes to make their way up the steps.

The doors were two storeys high, standing open in welcome, made of stained glass and dark wood, the glass panels depicting too many things for Thea to take in all at once, but she thought that the images were mostly of trading ships.

The entrance hall was even taller than the doors, its vaulted ceiling high above, lit with more lanterns, the ceiling panels between the wooden vaults painted with more images.

To one side of the hallway, looking tiny in comparison to the setting, was a beautifully crafted desk made of at least three different types of wood, with a dark-clothed clerk settled behind it, a large ledger in front of her.

"Good evening, officer, mage. What can the guild do for you?" the woman asked. If she had not been sitting in the entrance hall, Thea might have walked past the clerk without noticing her. The woman was meticulously neat, her dark hair pulled back into a tight knot at the back of her head, her face unremarkable. The sort of quiet, efficient worker that merchants seemed to favour.

"We're here to see the Master Merchants," Thea said. "I assume they are still in the building?"

"Master Gadsden and Master Paulin are in," the clerk confirmed, getting to her feet. "If you'll follow me."

Thea tried not to stare too much at her surroundings as the clerk led them through a set of doors into a large room more ornate than anything she had seen on her brief, rare visits to the Citadel. There was a pair of double doors at the other end of the room and the clerk opened one of them, sticking her head inside and saying something before she turned back to Thea and Niath and beckoned for them to go through the doors.

Thea and Niath went through the doors and found themselves in an even more opulent room. There was gold leaf on the panelling on the walls, another painted ceiling overhead, and pale, rare marble under their feet.

In the centre of the room was a long table that reminded Thea of the one at Master Hannaford's house. This one was easily the same length, but set for only a dozen people, the armed chair at the far end draped with a black cloth of mourning.

There were two other people in the room, both men that Thea recognised from outside Ware's office. The medium-height man with bronze skin and close-cropped black hair and the tall, slender man with pale skin, vivid freckles and red hair. The two were standing close together at the side of the room, apparently looking through a huge ledger that had been set on a reading stand. They both turned and faced Thea and Niath shoulder to shoulder.

"Master Merchant Paulin and Master Merchant Gadsden? I'm Watch Investigator Thea March. This is Mage Niath. I'm looking into the death of Master Merchant Hannaford. I'd like to ask you some questions," Thea said, stopping halfway down the length of the table and folding her hands behind her back. Niath stopped beside her and adopted the same pose.

"An awful business," the tall, red-headed man said. "Truly awful. Dalston and I were just looking over the ships that Bordan had due in and trying to work out how to deal with the cargo." He had an almost accent-less voice, expressing his dismay without much emotion behind it.

"Indeed," the other man said. Dalston Paulin. Thea remembered him threatening Ware. And seeming quite serious in his words.

He and the other Master Merchants had wanted the disgraced Kendrick to be brought back, to pay a fine and to be allowed to carry on his business, Thea remembered. And they had threatened Ware with the disbandment of the Watch if he did not make it happen.

"How can we help you, Investigator March?" the red-headed man asked, in the same calm, accent-less voice as before. Roe Gadsden. Thea remembered him as a silent observer in the brief scene she had witnessed, standing by and watching while Paulin threatened Ware.

"When did you last see Master Merchant Hannaford?" Thea asked, drawing out her notebook and opening it to a blank page, pencil poised. The waiting pencil had prompted more than one person to speak over the years.

"The day before he died," Paulin answered, with evident reluctance. He might have answered her question, but the hard, angry edge that Thea had noticed before was still there. "We were at the Watch Station. The one a few streets away. We came back here. We spoke for a while, then we all left, went to our homes."

"I didn't realise that Bordan had travelled out to the Summer House until we got word of his death," Gadsden added. "There are rooms in this building which he sometimes used rather than travelling out of the city."

"He didn't have a house in the city?" Thea asked, brows lifting.

"Well," Gadsden said, then stopped and looked at Paulin.

"He did. But his wife lived there. They lived separate lives," Paulin said, face pinching. It wasn't clear what he disapproved of. The separate lives, or that the wife had the house while Master Hannaford lived out of the city.

"This is the first I've heard that he was married," Thea commented, making a note. "Was it a long-standing marriage?"

Paulin made a noise somewhere between a snort and a laugh. "You'll need to ask her." He gave Thea the address. She didn't recognise the street or the house name. "It's inside the perimeter," he added, and her confusion cleared. So, Master Merchant Hannaford had owned a house within the Citadel's perimeter but, rather than staying there, he had split his time between rooms in the merchants' guild and the Summer House. Thea found herself very curious indeed to meet a wife who might have driven a powerful, wealthy man out of his home. And wondered, too, why the efficient Fionn had not mentioned a wife in any of their discussions, leaving Thea instead with the definite understanding that the Master Merchant had not had any living relatives.

"Very well," Thea said. "I assume, then, that any property Master Merchant Hannaford had will go to his wife?"

Gadsden and Paulin stared back at her, the two very different men looking very similar for a moment.

"We're not legal experts," Paulin said, in a voice as cold as Accanter's brief, harsh winters, "but that seems a fair assumption."

Thea made a note. "What can you tell me about Master Merchant Hannaford's business dealings?"

Both merchants stiffened, and pointedly did not look at each other, instead keeping their eyes fixed on Thea. It was an odd reaction and sharpened her interest. This pair of merchants had been among those trying to insist that Kendrick should simply pay a fine. She could not help wondering whether they, too, had secrets they did not want brought to light.

"What do you mean?" Paulin asked.

"I am not a merchant," Thea pointed out, "but it seems to me that any successful merchant might have enemies. Business rivals, for example."

"Oh. Well. I suppose we're all rivals, in a sense," Gadsden said. "Although we do tend to specialise in different goods and different trading routes where we can."

"Bordan was tough but fair," Paulin said, sounding as if it was grudging and hard-won respect. "He had been a Master Merchant longer than anyone else, and held his position when others didn't."

Thea wanted to ask about the others, who had not managed to hold their position, but held that back for now. These men had treated Ware's office as if it was their own, and were now standing in their own territory, confident and assured of their positions. She was very aware of being a guest in this building. She couldn't remember the last time any member of the Watch had been allowed inside. The two merchants in front of her seemed very sensitive to any discussions about their and the guild's business. Besides, they had given her more information than she had expected, and if she pressed them too hard about guild business, they might turn the discussion to Kendrick. A subject she wished to avoid, knowing that her own opinion would not be popular with them. She still needed their cooperation. For now.

"Did he have much property, apart from the house in the city and the Summer House?" Thea asked. The only master merchant she had had any close dealings with was Kendrick, and he seemed to have owned half the commercial buildings in Accanter.

"No, not him. He had money. A lot of it," Paulin said, shaking his head. "But property? No. Not in Accanter, anyway."

"Elsewhere, perhaps?" Thea asked, something in his tone prompting the question.

"Perhaps. I couldn't say. My business is here," Paulin said, voice flat.

"Bordan was from here, but he'd travelled along the coast," Gadsden said. "It's possible he had property elsewhere."

"So, where did he store his goods?" Thea asked.

"The guild owns several warehouses," Gadsden explained. He glanced aside to Paulin. "Investigator, if there's nothing more, then I would like to get back to my family. It's been a long day."

"Just one more question. Did Master Hannaford have an office or study in this building?"

"He did, yes. We all do. Do you want to see it?" Gadsden asked, brows lifting. "He didn't keep much in there."

"I would like to see it, yes," Thea confirmed, putting her notebook away. "Will you show me, or should I ask the clerk at the door?"

"I'll take you," Paulin said, sounding less than pleased. "His office is next to mine, and I need to go back there anyway."

"Thank you," Thea said, and nodded to Gadsden. "Thank you, sir, for your time."

"I hope you find whoever did this," Gadsden responded, the first sign of real emotion crossing his face. It looked like anger and grief combined. "Bordan is a sad loss to the guild."

"I will do my best," Thea promised.

Gadsden nodded, a grudging acceptance of her word, and Thea and Niath followed Paulin out of the room. One short conversation with a pair of merchants and Thea had discovered that the dead man had a wife, and perhaps a number of disgruntled rival merchants who had been stripped of their title of Master Merchant. She could not help wondering what other secrets she might uncover as she looked into Bordan Hannaford's death.

Chapter Ten

There were no secrets in Master Hannaford's office. A few papers, some pens, and a brand new blank ledger were set out on his desk, as if ready for him to come and sit down to work. And nothing else. No personal items, no correspondence. It was a meticulously tidy space, and Thea could not help wondering if Bordan had left it this way, or if one of the other merchants had tidied up.

She remembered the study at the Summer House, and the shelves full of ledgers and parchment, the desk scattered with papers. Remembered, too, the ordinary-looking man who had risen to the highest rank in his guild. The Summer House fit better with her impression of him, with the evidence of his work all around his working space. The bare shelves and almost empty desk at the merchants' guild did not feel as if they belonged to the same person.

There was also nothing in the room that looked like it would fit the key that Iason had found around the dead man's neck.

By then it was late into the evening, and she hid a yawn as she and Niath left the guild building.

"Sorry," she said, face warming up.

"It's been a long day," Niath said.

"And a frustrating one in many ways," Thea added. She paused at the foot of the building's steps, mind turning over what they had learned, and what she might do next. "I'd like to visit Mistress Hannaford. It's odd that the steward didn't mention her."

"I thought so, too," Niath agreed.

They arranged a time and place to meet and Thea headed home, glad to have a little time and space alone with her thoughts and glad, too, to be moving, walking along streets that were familiar, with the occasional burst of noise as she passed a tavern, the scents of beer and food curling into her, reminding her that it had been a long day and she had not eaten much.

She arrived home to find her mother settled at the kitchen table, her own ledgers open in front of her, several of them piled haphazardly on top of each other, a mug half-full of what looked like cold tea at her elbow. Thea hesitated in the doorway, hit by a mix of conflicting memory and feeling. Her mother and this house, particularly the kitchen, had always been places of safety and refuge. She knew she would always be welcome wherever her mother was. That had not changed. But her unquestioning faith in her mother had been shaken. Her mother had lied. Caroline March had known who had killed Thea's twin, and had not told Thea.

Thea was struck by the now-familiar push and pull of anger at her mother's deception and guilt at her own deception. She had not told her mother everything, either. The now-familiar itch set off at her shoulder blades and she changed the direction of her thoughts, away from those unwanted wings. It was getting easier to ignore them with practice. And they had not reappeared since she and Niath had been thrown to their deaths a little over two weeks ago.

Mage's traps, and wings and magic had no place here in this kitchen with its mismatched furniture and long history. She and her mother had spent hours here over the years, talking or settled in companionable silence.

Tonight, it did not feel quite like home. Did not feel like the place of safety she had always believed it to be.

Still, this was her mother. Who had moved them halfway across the world and had worked hard to keep them safe.

The room might feel different now, with the air full of secrets, but it and the house around it was still a place Thea knew she would always be welcome, no matter what had happened, no matter what had been said or done.

Thea's pause and conflict had taken a moment only, over in the time it took for Caroline March to look up and smile at her daughter, her blonde hair gleaming in the faint light, still neat and in place, unlike Thea's unruly hair which tended to escape its pins at the slightest chance. "You're late."

"I know," Thea said, and crossed to her mother's side to give her a hug. She was careful, as always, with her greater strength against her mother's delicate human body. "A new case. Is there some stew or something?"

"I made chicken pie earlier," her mother said, and tilted her head towards the stove. "There's a plate for you."

"Oh, thank you," Thea said, seeing the covered plate. "Do you want some more tea?"

"That would be lovely, yes," her mother answered, stretching her arms out then rolling her shoulders. "I've been so busy in the shop I'm behind on my book keeping."

"Ugh. Paperwork," Thea said, wrinkling her nose. There was a lot of paperwork involved in working for the Watch. And she hadn't even started writing up the events of the day. She busied herself with the familiar task of filling the kettle, setting it on the stove and readying the teapot, picking at her food while the tea brewed.

When Thea was settled at the table, both of them with fresh mugs of tea, she sat back for a moment, fork in one hand.

"Trymian is in the city," she told her mother with no preamble. "He's been here for at least a couple of days."

"Here?" her mother asked, brows lifting. Then she smiled. "It would be so good to see him again. It's been too long."

"Yes," Thea agreed. She remembered Trymian being one of the rare visitors to their quarters when Theo was alive. Thea could only remember a handful of visits, but he had always been someone that her mother had clearly liked and respected. The pair of them had engaged in fierce debates, often ending in laughter, while Theo and Thea had played games of their own. More than once a much younger Thea had wondered what it would be like to have Trymian as her father rather than an absent and unknown warrior Ageless.

"How did you come across him?" her mother asked, breaking through Thea's remembrance.

"Through the case. He and Reardon turned up," Thea said, not meeting her mother's eyes, ignoring the stab of guilt. She did not tell her mother everything about her cases, or the dangers she faced. Her mother worried enough.

"He and Reardon?" her mother said, brow lifting. "I didn't realise that they knew each other."

"I'm not sure for how long, but Reardon seemed to respect him," Thea commented.

"Did he know who you were? Trymian, I mean," her mother asked, smile fading.

"I don't think he recognised me, or knew who I was. I assume that Reardon hasn't told him," Thea said, and bent to her plate. She didn't have much appetite now, but knew she needed to eat.

"Probably not, no," her mother agreed. "Reardon was always very private. And when we were in Kellto, Trymian never asked." Her mother's face tightened, old pain and grief surfacing for a moment. Kellto was the Citadel where Theo had died. They had been comfortable there, if not exactly happy, until that awful day of falling falling falling, and her mother's rage and grief. Her mother shook her head. "I suppose if Trymian is going to be here for a while, Reardon might tell him. Or he might find out." From the tone of her mother's voice and expression, she was not sure how to feel about that.

"I don't know if that's a good thing or a bad thing," Thea admitted.

"Oh? I thought you liked Trymian."

"I did. And I probably still will. But he's Ageless," Thea said, sitting back from her half-empty plate. "And we've been avoiding the Ageless."

"So we have," her mother said, a curious expression on her face. It looked like something between regret and guilt, although Thea could not imagine what her mother had to feel guilty about.

Regret, she could understand. Their lives might have been very different if Theo had not been killed. But she and Theo had been born without wings, and would still have grown up as Ageless-born among the Ageless. And the Ageless despised their wingless offspring.

Her chest tightened as she wondered if Theo would also have grown up to develop wings. She could easily imagine her bright, mischievous twin among the Ageless. He had never let anyone intimidate him and had the intelligence to match even the adults around them.

And if he had lived, Thea could not imagine what their lives would have become. Still in the Citadel at Kellto, she supposed. There was always work to be done around the Ageless.

And if they had stayed, if Theo had lived, she would never have discovered how much she enjoyed solving puzzles. She would never have seen the breadth of life that existed in Accanter. Would never have had to pick up a weapon.

She missed her brother every day. Wished he was still here. But had to admit, in the quiet of her mind, that this life she had suited her far better than the constraints of being a servant in a Citadel.

Chapter Eleven

The house and grounds were not what Thea had expected. Learning that Master Hannaford had an estranged wife who lived within the Citadel perimeter, she had formed a hazy idea of a luxury home, with his wife living an extravagant lifestyle. Within the Citadel perimeter there were a lot of grand houses with rooftop terraces and wide balconies to accommodate visits from the Ageless. Those houses also had large, walled grounds around them, and there were rumours of private guards as there was no Watch to keep order, and the Ageless were not that interested in helping the population stay safe.

The property she and Niath arrived at shook Thea out of her lazy, half-formed assumptions before she had even met the lady of the house. The grey stone walls were high and well-maintained, but the gates were made of plain wood and opened by a casually dressed young man with a patch over one eye. When Thea asked for Mistress Hannaford, he pointed behind him, along a driveway of packed earth, towards a grey stone house that could barely be seen through the trees.

The house itself was only two storeys high, and not that much larger than the house that Thea shared with her mother. The roof was pitched, formed of slate, with no landing places that Thea could see for any visiting Ageless. In fact, as she looked around the grounds, she saw nowhere obvious for the householders to welcome any Ageless. The grounds were almost wild, packed full of mature trees and shrubs, with what looked like an orchard off to one side, a few people carrying baskets moving among the trees.

The door of the house was made of the same plain wood as the gates, and opened as they approached to reveal a tall woman with black hair in a simple braid hanging down in front of one shoulder. She was dressed in plain trousers and a tunic, and lifted her brows slightly as Thea and Niath got off their horses.

"Have you come to tell me Bordan is dead? You've wasted a trip," the woman said.

"Mistress Hannaford?" Thea asked, blinking. There was nothing about this woman to show that she was one of the wealthiest citizens of Accanter.

"That's me." The woman folded her arms across her stomach.

Thea moved a little closer and saw signs of strain on the woman's face, and a slight reddening to her eyes. She was putting on a fierce front, but grieving, too. "I'm very sorry. We didn't know that Master Hannaford was married, otherwise I would have been here sooner," Thea said.

Mistress Hannaford stared back at her, jaw set, and Thea suffered another shock. She knew that face, that bone structure. She had last seen it on a master merchant who had been holding non-humans enslaved. She blinked.

"I'm sorry for staring," Thea said, "but you look familiar."

"You must mean my brother. Kendrick." The woman's eyes narrowed and she eyed Thea up and down. "Wait. Are you the one that caught him? Thea March?"

"I am," Thea said, stomach tightening. Impossible to tell how the woman felt about her brother.

To Thea's further surprise, the woman unfolded her arms and walked forward, catching Thea in a fierce, hard hug.

"Thank you," the woman said, stepping back, her eyes over-bright. "Thank you for stopping him at last."

"You're not what I expected," Thea said, the words out before she knew what she was saying. "I'm sorry," she said again, heat flaring under her skin.

The woman laughed and shook her head, and all resemblance to Kendrick vanished. The former merchant had been cold and arrogant. The laughter, with its genuine warmth, was not something that the merchant would ever have managed.

"Please, call me Megan. Won't you come in? I suspect you may have questions for me."

"Thank you," Thea said, and glanced at Niath before following Megan inside.

Niath's eyes were bright with curiosity and he smiled slightly as he met Thea's gaze. "She's not what I expected, either," he said as he fell into step beside her.

Inside, the house was almost austere. There were no sculptures or other pieces of artwork around the modest entrance hall, and Megan led them along a faintly dusty wooden floor until they reached a bright, sunny kitchen that reminded Thea forcibly of Niath's kitchen. It was a room meant for work, with no fuss about it. There was a table that would comfortably seat a dozen people, and one side of the room was taken up with a lengthy worktop covered with trays of baked goods. The baked goods were nothing like Niath's, though. These were fanciful, dainty creations. Little bits of flair and colour with what looked like webs of spun sugar, smooth icing and bits of froth as decoration.

There were two people at the other side of the kitchen, pouring ingredients into a mixing bowl. One of the people had a sleeve that ended at the elbow, and Thea could see the end of a wooden leg in place of a foot on the other one.

"Mick. Si. Why don't you take a break?" Megan suggested. The two people, like enough to be brother and sister, nodded and left through the back door. "Take a seat," Megan said. "I'll put the kettle on."

Thea took a seat at the table, Niath a couple of chairs away, and watched out of the corner of her eye while Mistress Hannaford moved with confidence around her kitchen, brewing tea and bringing mismatched mugs to the table along with a plate of small cakes. She took her place on the other side of the table from Thea and Niath and lifted her brows. "What, you've never seen anyone make tea before?" she asked, mouth quirking up in a smile that lit her face with warmth.

Thea felt her face heat up again.

"I recognise these cakes," Niath said, picking one up. It was small enough to fit in the palm of his hand, dressed with pale pink icing. "You do catering for some of your neighbours."

Megan's eyes sparkled and her lips twitched again. "Indeed. It's my one talent. I can't make small talk or dance to save myself, but I can bake. These frilly little things are very popular. And if I provide the food, then no one wants me at the parties."

Thea frowned slightly. She could see the logic of that. Social standing seemed to be very important in this part of the city. But Megan sounded quite cheerful about being a social outcast.

"How long were you and Master Hannaford married?" she asked, resisting the lure of the pretty cakes. For the moment.

"Oh. A while. Ten years. More."

Thea's brows lifted again. "You must have been very young," she said, caught off guard.

"I was." The woman grimaced, her humour fading. "You might say Bordan rescued me. Kendrick was going to marry me off to one of his business partners. Bordan offered a higher price."

"Price?" Thea repeated.

"My brother had ambitions. I'm sure you noticed that. He thought he could sell me to one of the high-class families and better himself."

Thea was glad she hadn't taken a cake as her stomach turned. She could all-too-easily imagine Kendrick selling his sister if he thought it would bring him some advantage.

"But Master Hannaford lived elsewhere," Thea said. It was bordering on a rude question, but she was curious and it might prove relevant to the merchant's death.

Megan's face creased into distaste for a moment. "Yes. I think he had an idea that I would be like my brother and able to help him with fancy parties and the sort of politicking he loved. But I've no interest in it. So we lived separately."

"But still married?" Thea prompted.

"Oh, yes. Bordan had too much pride to let anyone think he'd failed. He probably told his friends all sorts of stories. But the fact is, we didn't suit at all well."

Thea turned that over in her mind. Megan sounded almost dispassionate about her late husband. Hardly likely to scheme and plot to visit his house outside the city and stab him to death.

"When was the last time you saw your husband?" Niath asked, surprising Thea. He normally left the questions for her.

He seemed to have hit on a sore spot, though. Megan's nose wrinkled in distaste again.

"A few days ago. He came to see me here," she said, and looked around the room as if wondering if he was going to come through one of the doors. "He wanted my support. Did you know he was trying to get the Watch Captain to pardon Kendrick?" Megan shook her head, lips pressed together, and went on before Thea or Niath could answer. "He seemed to think that me being

Kendrick's sister, my word might carry more weight with the captain. I refused. Told him that Kendrick is exactly where he needs to be. We argued."

From Megan's white knuckles and tension in her body, Thea guessed it had been a fearsome argument. As well as the anger, though, the lady seemed afraid, which caught Thea's attention.

"Did he threaten you?" Thea asked.

Megan looked up, startling blue eyes holding Thea's for a moment. "You're perceptive, aren't you? Yes. He did. He threatened to sell the house. Said he'd been supporting me for long enough. And my pet projects. Said he wasn't prepared to pay for them anymore."

"Pet projects?" Niath prompted, a moment before Thea could.

"The other people who live here. They have nowhere else to go," Megan said.

Thea remembered the eye patch, and missing arm, and wooden leg, and suspected that if she were to speak to everyone else who lived or worked around this house, she would find that none of them had the whole, supposedly perfect bodies so prized by the Ageless and employers across the city. She remembered seeing the returning soldier greeting his mother, the reunion tentative and bittersweet. This city had a seemingly endless supply of able-bodied and willing workers. Anyone carrying a long-term injury or missing limb would most likely not be hired.

"So it wasn't just you he threatened," Thea summarised, "but the other people here, too."

And that gave the estranged wife a solid motive to kill her husband, Thea realised, heart sinking. She didn't want to believe it. Despite being Kendrick's sister, she liked Megan Hannaford.

But even with the strong motive, Thea still could not imagine this woman sneaking into the Summer House and killing the merchant. Any more than Thea could imagine Ware Handerson doing the same.

"He thought so, at any rate," Megan said, the tension vanishing into a small smile that was full of satisfaction. "I told him I didn't need his money. He might have paid for the house, but our neighbours here pay well for my silly cakes, as he liked to call them. I've got more than enough to keep the house and feed all of us."

Thea found herself smiling back, mentally crossing Megan off her list of suspects, her smile widening as Thea imagined the late merchant's reaction to being told his wife didn't need him, or his money.

It still left Thea with the problem of finding out who had wanted Bordan Hannaford dead, and how the killing had been done.

Chapter Twelve

It was early afternoon by the time Thea and Niath returned to Middlefield Watch Station. Thea had given in to temptation and tried some of Megan's cakes and had then wanted to eat the lot. They had been delicious, and as light and frilly as they looked. A few blocks away from Megan's house, Thea had realised she was hungry for proper food. Niath had needed no persuading to stop at the Harrow bakery on the way back to the station, and Thea was still finding crumbs on her uniform when they went up the station steps.

The doorway ahead of them was filled with Ware and Sutter, both wearing frowns.

"Something wrong, sir?" Thea asked.

"Another death. Come on, it's not far," Ware said, and strode ahead of them, turning around the side of the station.

The words *another death* ran around Thea's head and she tried to work out what Ware had meant as she and Niath fell into step behind the pair of Watch members. Another death connected to Master Hannaford? Surely not another impossible death? Apprehension rose and she exchanged a brief glance with Niath as they turned another corner and found themselves heading for the merchants' guild.

Ware went up the steps with swift, impatient strides and paused in the entrance hall, Thea, Sutter and Niath all stopping around him.

Rather than the quiet and efficient clerk who had greeted them last time, Master Merchant Gadsden was in the entrance way. The cool reserve he had shown before was gone, his face tight and pale. He glared at the four of them.

"This is unacceptable, Captain," he said, voice trembling faintly. From the expression and the tense way he was standing, Thea realised he was struggling to contain his fury. And he had chosen to direct the fury at the Watch. It seemed an odd reaction. "Completely unacceptable. I demand action. At once."

"Show us," Ware said.

Gadsden turned on his heel and stalked away into the building. They followed a route familiar to Thea from her previous visit, going through the grand room next to the entrance hall and then up the stairs to the upper floors where the Master Merchants' offices were.

Cedd and Gordie Trant were standing outside an open door, closer together than they normally stood, faces and bodies tense as Thea's group approached.

"There," Gadsden said, pointing into the room. "Unacceptable," he said again, still with rage shaking his voice.

"Will you and the Merchants Trant wait somewhere else for us?" Ware asked. "We could be some time, and we'll have questions for you."

"And we will have questions for you, too," Gadsden said, and flicked his hand at the Trant brothers. "Come. We'll go to the meeting room."

Only when the merchants had gone did Ware turn and look into the room. He blew out a breath, shaking his head. "This is not good."

Thea's curiosity overrode her manners, and she moved closer to Ware's side so that she could see into the room.

It was a merchant's office, a large, elaborately carved desk set facing the door. Master Merchant Paulin was sitting behind the desk, eyes towards the ceiling, a large knife pointing out of his chest.

Shock of recognition held her still, both at the identity of the victim and the way he had been killed. "Another death, indeed," Thea said slowly, eyes travelling around the room, hoping for some clue as to who had done this and finding nothing. She looked back at the dead man, remembering the hard, angry edge he had carried in life, and wondered how anyone had got close enough to him to kill him.

"Iason and Dina will be here soon," Sutter said, before she could ask.

"Is this the way Master Hannaford was killed?" Ware asked, glancing at Thea.

"It looks like it, yes, sir," Thea answered. "Do we know who found him?"

"No." Ware's jaw tightened. "Just one of the questions I have for the other merchants."

"The door lock is broken," Sutter said, pointing. "We'll need to check, but it looks as if whoever found him had to break the door to get in."

"Also consistent with Master Hannaford," Thea said, before Ware or Sutter could ask. "He was locked in his study. The person who found him also had to break the lock to get in."

"There's a trace of magic in the room," Niath said. "May I go closer?" he asked, glancing at Ware.

"Yes. We need to know what it is. I'll explain to Dina," Ware added as Niath hesitated a moment more.

On that reassurance, Niath moved into the room, standing just inside the doorway, effectively blocking everyone else's view of the scene. He bowed his head and Thea felt his magic curl into the air. A slow, gentle unfolding.

As Niath's magic spread, her skin prickled. She had not been aware of any other magic before he worked his own spell, but there was something else there. Another trace of magic, this one carrying the frost she associated with the Ageless.

Even as she realised that, Niath took a step out of the room and glanced at her before turning to Ware. "There was an Ageless in this room in the last day or so. I'm not sure who, but the trace of their presence is unmistakable."

Ware nodded, face still tight. Thea remembered the merchants' threat to shut down the Watch, and Ware and Sutter telling her that the only ones with power to do so were the Ageless. The Ageless had power to do anything they wanted.

"There was no obvious trace at Master Hannaford's death," Niath added, as if anticipating Ware's question. "But then, Commander Reardon was there, so he might have masked the signs."

"Last day or so," Thea repeated. "So, perhaps not connected with the death at all?" she asked, hearing the hope in her voice. The presence of an Ageless opened up another round of possible suspects. Ones she could not question, or even get close to.

Niath moved away from the door, opening up the view into the room again. "I can't be sure," he answered her. "The Ageless tend to have a forcible presence that takes a while to fade. They might have been here when the merchant died, or it could have been two days ago."

Thea nodded, the little bit of hope dying out. She would still need to consider whether one of the Ageless had been involved, after all.

She tried to distract herself by looking at the scene again. It was remarkably similar to the previous death, down to Master Paulin looking up at the ceiling. She followed his line of sight but, as with Master Hannaford, there was nothing in particular to see.

Footsteps behind them announced the arrival of Iason and Dina, the physician ahead of the examiner for once. He nodded to them and took a first look into the room, Dina peering over his shoulder.

"Has anyone been inside?" Dina asked.

"None of us," Ware said. "Mage Niath stood in the doorway as he sensed magic, but we haven't been into the room itself."

"Magic?" Dina asked, turning to Niath. "What sort?"

"The presence of one of the Ageless," Niath told her.

Dina's nose wrinkled in distaste and she opened her mouth to say something.

"But no active spells?" Iason asked, before Dina could say whatever intemperate thing was on her mind.

"No," Niath confirmed. "There's no active magic, or spellwork, in the room."

"Good," the physician said, and crossed the threshold, going to stand to one side of the desk. "This is remarkably similar to Bordan Hannaford's death. Dina?"

"Yes, I agree," she said, moving to stand behind the physician, careful to follow the path he had taken. She looked back. "Who broke the door?"

"We think one of the staff here, trying to get into the room," Thea said, "but we got here only a few minutes before you. We haven't had time to find out yet. Is the key still in the lock?"

Dina took a careful step to one side so that she could see the other side of the door and scowled, giving Thea her answer before the examiner spoke. "Yes. The key is in the lock on this side."

"We'll need to see who had keys," Sutter commented.

"Well, we'll be a while," Dina added, glancing over her shoulder to the others. "Plenty of time for you to go ask your questions."

"Indeed," Thea acknowledged, trying not to smile, and turned to Ware. "Sir, are you taking the lead on this matter?"

"No," Ware said, without hesitation. "You're already working on the Hannaford case, and this seems related. I'll come and observe, though. Sutter, will you stay here and make sure Iason and Dina aren't disturbed?"

Thea's brows lifted. It was the sort of posting that a junior Watchman might be assigned, not one of the most senior officers in the Watch. After a pause, she could see Ware's reasoning. This was the merchants' guild, which was already hostile to the Watch. The merchants might not let another member of the Watch into the building. Sutter did not protest or argue, simply nodded his agreement, accepting the task where any number of Sergeants might have argued. It was one of the things that made him so good at his job, Thea realised. He did what needed to be done.

"Master Gadsden said something about a meeting room. Do you know where that is?" Ware asked Thea.

She lifted her brows.

"No, I have not been invited into this building before," Ware said, a slight smile lifting his lips. "The merchants dislike any interference in their business."

"Sir," Thea acknowledged. "It's this way," she said, and turned, heading down the corridor, Niath and Ware with her.

The meeting room where she and Niath had met Roe Gadsden and Dalston Paulin before was full of vivid daylight, and almost as empty as her previous visit. Master Merchant Gadsden was pacing one side of the room. Cedd and Gordie Trant were standing at the other side, in similar poses, arms across their fronts, hands tucked into the wide sleeves that merchants favoured.

The table surface gleamed in the daylight, clear apart from a bottle and a few glasses at one end.

As Thea, Ware, and Niath came into the room, Gadsden stopped his pacing.

"Well?" he demanded.

"Sir, I have some questions for you." Thea came to a halt not far from Gordie, and folded her hands behind her.

"What about finding who did this?" Gadsden demanded.

"Your answers will help me do that," Thea said, holding on to her patience. The rage she had sensed earlier was still there, tamped down a little but still simmering under the surface.

"She's taking the lead?" Gadsden asked, staring at Ware.

"Investigator March was already working on the death of Master Hannaford," Ware said, in a mild voice that made Thea immediately wary. The Watch Captain was many things. Mild was not one of them.

"What, you're too good for this?" Gadsden asked, sneering.

The personal insult made Thea blink. She had not realised there was any connection between the merchant and the captain.

"By no means. But Thea is already working on the matter, and is an excellent investigator. She has an impressive track record of solving difficult cases," Ware said, still in that mild voice. "Thea, you have questions?"

"Sir," Thea nodded, and turned to Gadsden. "Who found Master Paulin?"

"I did," Cedd answered, coming to stand near Gadsden, facing Thea. "We were due to go to the docks. He was late."

"Can you tell me what happened, please?" Thea asked, taking out her notebook and pencil.

Cedd nodded and described finding the door locked, and Paulin not answering. There hadn't been anyone else around, and the merchants all kept their own office keys. He had seen Paulin earlier in the day, and the other merchant was not one to miss an appointment. Worried, Cedd had managed to break the lock and found the merchant dead. He had sent the clerk for the Watch and then gone to find anyone else in the building.

Thea listened and took notes of what Cedd relayed, and also Gadsden's clear annoyance at how the younger merchant had dealt with the matter. Thea considered Cedd's actions to have been sensible, but the other merchant evidently disagreed. She could not help wondering how Gadsden would have preferred to deal with the matter.

"Who else was in the building at the time?" Thea asked, when Cedd fell silent.

"Just us, I think," Cedd answered, brow creasing. He turned to his brother. "Anyone else?"

"No members of staff?" Thea prompted.

"Oh, no, there would have been some, yes," Cedd answered. "The clerk. And there's a kitchen with a few people and some maids, I think. Roe?"

"We have a staff of eight," the older merchant said, his voice dry, as though amused by Cedd's lack of knowledge. "There are two clerks who usually work alternate days here and at the docks. Then there is a cook and two kitchen assistants and the rest are general staff. They do whatever is needed to keep the place in good order."

"So there may have been what - seven? - members of staff here earlier?" Thea asked.

"Perhaps. The staff come and go through the day as their tasks require. The kitchen staff go to market most days," Roe said. "But none of them would have had business at the offices," he added.

"Thank you," Thea said. "I'll need to speak to the staff," she added, "but apart from them, it was just the three of you in the building as well as Master Paulin?"

"That's correct, as far as we know," Gadsden said. "The building is open to all members of the guild. But I didn't see anyone else."

"Where were you, sir?" Thea asked.

Gadsden's brows lifted and for a moment he seemed to hover between further rage and amusement. He seemed to choose amusement.

"I was here." He nodded to the giant ledger on its stand. "I wanted to look back over our records."

Thea noticed a pile of papers and an open notebook next to the reading stand. She wondered what it was that Gadsden had been looking for, but it didn't seem relevant, so she dragged her attention back to what was relevant to Master Paulin's death.

"And where were you?" she asked Gordie.

"There's an archive room in the basement," he answered, glancing down at his robes and wrinkling his nose. "I was there, gathering dust."

"And I was in my office, which is on the floor above, for most of the morning, until it was time to leave, then I came downstairs to meet Dalston. When he didn't show, I went back upstairs," Cedd told her, before she could ask.

"And what time were you due to meet?" she asked.

"Noon."

A trickle of ice worked its way across Thea's skin. Master Hannaford had been killed around noon, too. It seemed that the killer had a preferred time to strike. Just one more similarity between the deaths.

"Are you aware of any particular disagreements that Master Paulin was involved in?" she asked the three merchants.

They glanced at each other and then shook their heads. Gadsden was confident and if it had just been him in the room, she might have believed him. But the Trant brothers were far less assured, or perhaps she just knew them a little better. And all three of them had looked at each other first. They were lying. All of them. They did know something, and did not want to tell her.

She was tempted to bluntly ask why they were lying to her. She dismissed the idea as soon as it occurred to her. Not only would it be rude, more importantly it would not help. The merchants ran their own business, and their guild, answering to no one apart from the Ageless, and even then only grudgingly. So a direct question would not help. She would have to find another way to get the information she wanted.

"Perhaps a disagreement also involving Master Hannaford?" she prompted.

"We have disagreements all the time," Gadsden said, voice cold, staring at her with flat eyes. "It's part of our role. But there is nothing unusual about that."

"So, nothing that you can think of that would have put Master Paulin at risk?" Thea prompted, following her instincts. The merchants were hiding something. It may or may not be important, but the fact they were hiding information after two of their number were dead made her curious.

"Nothing that stands out, no," Gadsden answered, still staring at her, unblinking. "Now, we have answered your questions. What more do you need of us?"

"I need to speak to the staff," Thea reminded him. "I also want to go back to Master Paulin's office just now, and may want to visit another time."

"I'll instruct the clerks to show you in," Gadsden said, face pinching in displeasure. Not wanting her back in the building specifically, Thea wondered, or the Watch in general? "I expect a swift resolution to this matter."

"I will do my best," Thea promised. "May I suggest, sir, sirs, that you take care of your own safety as well?"

"What do you mean?" Gordie asked, brows lifting.

"Two Master Merchants have been killed within two days," Thea said. "And at the moment there seems no clear reason for it. Please be careful."

"Senior Sergeant Sutter would be pleased to give you some advice on personal safety," Ware said. He had been standing beside Thea, observing in silence.

"That's it? Speak to the Sergeant?" Gadsden asked, his icy displeasure turning to the burning anger he had shown earlier. "Unacceptable."

"There's a killer that seems able to get past a locked door and leave without a trace." Ware held the merchant's gaze. "I have no doubt that Investigator March will uncover the truth of the matter. Until then, you would be wise to be careful."

Before Gadsden could say anything else, Ware turned his shoulder on the merchant and looked at Thea and Niath. "Shall we go and see what Iason and Dina have found?"

Chapter Thirteen

Dina and Iason were still in the room, Master Paulin still settled behind his desk, when Thea, Ware and Niath reached the offices again.

Sutter took the news he was to brief the merchants on their personal safety with a wry twist to his mouth.

"Do any of them have magic around them?" Thea asked Niath, remembering the elaborate protections around the Summer House.

Niath lifted a brow, perhaps thinking she should have been able to sense that for herself. But he answered readily enough. "None that I could sense. Cedd and Gordie Trant both had traces of old magic on them. Cleaning spells, I think."

"Probably from Odilia," Ware suggested, before Thea could. "She often shares her spells."

"That makes sense." Niath frowned slightly, looking at Thea. "Is it strange that Master Hannaford had a fortified house and magic around him, and these merchants don't?"

"I'm not sure what to make of it," Thea said. "It's something to keep in mind, I think. I don't imagine that the protections which Master Hannaford had were cheap, or common." Which made her wonder, again, just what Bordan Hannaford had been so worried about that he had been willing to spend on his protection. Just for him, too. There had been no such consideration for his estranged wife.

"And yet, the killer managed to get through the defences there and leave no trace," Ware said, breaking through Thea's musing. "Whereas here, it seems a much easier thing to achieve. At least, it looked that way. Dina, Iason, what have you learned?"

The examiner and physician exchanged glances. They were standing on either side of the desk, Iason next to Master Paulin.

"Not much," Dina admitted, her frustration clear. "Whoever did this killing left no trace. Same as with Hannaford. I mean nothing. No footprint, no disturbance of the papers on the desk, nothing."

"And as we know, the key was in the lock on this side," Iason added. "So it looks as if the door was locked from the inside."

"Then how did the killer get out?" Thea asked, looking around the room as if a secret door might reveal itself.

"We don't know," Dina said, glaring at the wall nearest her. "A building like this could easily have a servant's passage or two, but we've not found anything."

"May we come in?" Thea asked. She, Ware, Niath and Sutter were all gathered just outside the door, looking past each other's shoulders.

"Yes," Dina said, waving a hand. "There's no evidence for you to destroy," she added, sounding more annoyed than ever.

"Was this the same killer, do you think?" Thea asked, moving to stand near Iason.

"Based on the angle of the wound and the depth of it, I would say yes," Iason said, and glanced up at her. "It looks like Master Paulin simply sat here and let his attacker stab him."

Thea nodded, taking in the details of the body. Paulin was settled into his chair, his shoulders against its back and his face pointing upward. She followed his gaze again, as she had earlier, and again saw nothing.

"It's odd that both men were in the same position," she said, mostly to herself.

"It is. Even with the same killer, you would expect the bodies to be settled differently," Iason agreed, frowning.

"Does that mean that they were staged? Posed after death?" Thea asked, attention sharpening.

"We've found nothing to suggest that," Dina said, "but that doesn't say much. A killer who can get through a locked door, or through the defences at Hannaford's house, can probably rearrange a body."

"And it was just one blow?" Thea asked Iason.

"Yes. The killer did know what he was doing," Iason added, confirming her suspicion.

Thea frowned at the dead man for a moment more. It really did look as if he had been stabbed facing his attacker, and had done nothing to defend himself.

She turned her attention to the papers on the desk. A neatly placed ledger, open at entries for the current month, an inkwell and pen ready for use, and some scattered parchment with what looked like hastily written notes. Summaries of cargoes, she saw, and prices. Doubtless to be added into the ledger. It all seemed quite ordinary, and to be expected of a merchant's desk.

Everything was in its place, everything as it should be, apart from the body.

And yet there was something trying to catch her attention. Something that wasn't right, except she could not see it. Apart from the body.

"What is it?" Ware asked.

"I don't know," she answered, hearing the irritation in her voice. "Something. I think I need to see Master Hannaford's desk again. Not the one here. The Summer House."

"If you're going back that way, I want you to take more people with you," Ware said at once.

"The warriors?" Thea asked. In her focus on the mystery in front of her, she had all but forgotten the attack and Mage Waters. "You think they'll try again?"

"I don't know. But I don't want to take any chances. I'll ask Commander Reardon to arrange an escort for you," Ware said, in a tone that didn't permit any debate or discussion.

All the same, Thea opened her mouth to argue. She didn't want to be beholden to Reardon.

"I'll make the arrangements," Ware said, before she could say anything more. "You'll want to go tomorrow?"

"Yes. First light," Thea said, giving in, and then looked at Niath, colour rising. "Sorry. I was just assuming I could borrow a horse, and that you'd want to come with me."

"I wouldn't miss it for the world," Niath said, eyes gleaming with mischief.

Chapter Fourteen

As Thea and Niath left the guild building, they almost ran into a familiar figure coming up the steps. Odilia Trant stopped in her tracks when she saw them.

"There you are," Odilia said.

"Who were you looking for?" Thea asked. "Me or Niath?"

"You, actually," Odilia said.

"I'll leave you to catch up and see you at first light, Thea," Niath said. "Good day to you, Mage Trant."

Odilia barely acknowledged Niath's departure, which sharpened Thea's focus on her friend. As well as being one of the friendliest people Thea had ever met, Odilia also had a fascination for the Citadel's most infamous mage.

"What's wrong?" Thea asked bluntly.

"First light? I'm sorry, I didn't realise you were so busy," Odilia said, shoulders slumping. "I hoped you'd have time for a meal and some drinks."

"I'm sorry," Thea said gently, "not tonight. Another time. But we can walk for a bit?" she suggested. Odilia lived a short distance away from Thea, in a very different part of the city.

"I suppose," Odilia said, and fell into step beside Thea.

Thea glanced down at her friend and could not help frowning. The mage's sleek black hair was straight and tidy, but there were unfamiliar signs of strain on her face. There were smudges under her eyes and a tightness around her mouth that had not been there the last time Thea had seen Odilia.

"Do you want to talk about it?" Thea asked, more gently than she had before.

Odilia blew out a breath and wrapped her arms around her middle, continuing to match Thea's strides. "Not really. My brothers are being idiots."

"Can you be more specific?" Thea asked, and drew a short, sharp laugh from the mage.

"They've been annoying you, too, I see," Odilia said, unfamiliar bitterness in her voice. "They seem to think the Watch is the enemy."

"Actually, they seemed the more reasonable ones of the group," Thea said, remembering the other three Master Merchants.

"Oh, my," Odilia said, eyes wide. "That's bad."

Thea turned her laugh into an unconvincing cough. "The merchants seemed very angry," she said.

"They are." Odilia fell silent. Thea waited, sensing her friend had more to say. She did not have long to wait. The mage drew a breath, then let out a torrent of words. "They seem to think they should be above the law. I spent all of last night's dinner listening to them go on and on about it. I tried to tell them that only applies to the Ageless. And then Cedd told me I was a silly girl and didn't know what I was talking about. So I threatened to turn him into a frog. He just laughed. And papa said that my magic wasn't good for anything apart from cleaning."

Thea paused, gently placing a hand on Odilia's shoulder, not sure if it would be welcome or not in Odilia's frame of mind. "I'm sorry."

Odilia stopped, facing Thea. She blinked, a pair of tears rolling down her face. "Thank you. You're lucky you don't have older brothers who think they know better," she said, bitterness still in her voice.

Thea said nothing, old and familiar grief stinging as she remembered Theo. Her twin would never have spoken down to her the way Odilia's brothers had to the mage. Knowing Odilia, and Mistress Trant, Thea found it hard to believe that the Trant brothers had got away with that kind of attitude growing up. She suspected that the arrogance of the other Master Merchants was having an effect, and could only hope that Cedd and Gordie did not follow their fellow merchants' examples too closely.

Odilia shook her head, as if trying to get rid of the bad feeling. "I told them they could do their own cleaning from now on," she said, a hint of mischief chasing some of the sadness away. "Wait until Gordie spills ink on his robes again. We'll find out just how useless my magic is."

Thea remembered Gordie frowning down at his robes, dusty from his visit to the guild archives, and thought that it would not be long before he was trying to cajole some cleaning spells from his sister. It didn't seem to be helpful to tell Odilia, so she tried to distract her instead.

"Or, you know, you could always make his robes glow again," Thea suggested. It was a trick that Odilia had pulled on her brothers many years before, when she had first been learning magic, and her brothers had apparently been particularly annoying.

"Now, that's an excellent idea," Odilia said, eyes bright. "Oh, or I could turn his robes green so he looks like a giant frog." Odilia skipped a stride or two ahead. "I'm so glad I found you. I knew you would cheer me up. Thank you." She turned back to Thea and flung her arms around her.

"Anytime," Thea said, returning the hug, careful not to squeeze too hard. Odilia was human, and fragile.

The mage went on her way with a lighter step, leaving Thea to finish her journey home, wondering what revenge Odilia would find to exact on her brothers.

Thea reached her mother's house and went through the gate at the side of the building, wanting nothing more than a hot bath and a long sleep. A light in the garden drew her attention. There was a lamp lit and placed on the ground near a chair and one glance around told her she would not be getting either her bath or her sleep for now.

Her mother was standing in the garden, a light shawl wrapped around her shoulders against the cooler air of evening. She was not alone. Reardon was there, too, dressed more casually than Thea had ever seen him, in a plain, pale shirt and dark trousers. He was in his human *aspect*, his wings tucked away, and if she had not known him, she might have assumed he was human.

It was startling to see them together. As far as Thea knew, the last time they had spoken, her mother had shut the door in Reardon's face, making it clear he was not welcome. She could not imagine what had happened to change her mother's mind.

"Mama, is everything alright?" Thea asked, concerned.

"I'm fine," her mother answered, not meeting Thea's eyes, glancing aside to Reardon. Her mother paused, drawing the shawl more closely around her shoulders, a restless movement that caught Thea's attention. "We've been talking," her mother said, still not looking at Thea. "There are some things you should know."

Apprehension slithered over Thea's skin, chilling her to her core. The last piece of new information her mother had disclosed was that she had known, had always known, who had killed Theo. Not for the first time, Thea wondered what other secrets her mother was keeping. "What do you mean?"

"Perhaps we should sit down?" Reardon suggested.

Thea had an impulse to tell him to leave, that he had no right to be here, not in her mother's house. She held the words back, though. Her mother did not look worried by Reardon's presence. And it was her mother's house. If she did not object to Reardon, then Thea would not.

So Thea moved with her parents to the small group of chairs in the middle of the garden, wondering if her mother had pointed out Theo's memory stone in the midst of the greenery. Her twin's body might be half a world away, but sitting here she could always remember him, with his tousled dark hair and ready smile.

"I want you to know that everything I have done, everything I have said. Everything. All of it. Has all been to keep you safe. Losing your brother was awful. I was not going to lose you, too," her mother said without warning. She was sitting in her chair, hands grasping the arms, knuckles white.

"I know, mama," Thea said softly. It had been one of the fundamental truths of her life ever since Theo had died.

"So when I didn't tell you about Aldric, that was why," her mother went on.

Thea's brows lifted and she could not help but look at Reardon, trying to judge his reaction. He was stony-faced, jaw tight. Someone had told him who had killed his son. Perhaps her mother.

"I know, mama," Thea said, the anger she had carried sliding away. She understood.

"That's not the only thing I didn't tell you, though," her mother went on, not looking at Reardon, staring at Thea with unblinking, unseeing eyes. "And it's time you knew that. More than time, truth be told," she added, a crack in her voice.

Thea's brows lifted, the apprehension returning. She opened her mouth, no sound emerging, and tried again. "What do you mean?" The words were thick and heavy in her mouth. She did not want to know more. And yet she did.

"I kept you hidden from the Ageless," her mother said, eyes bright now with unshed tears, "because I told you that they would Conscript you."

"Yes," Thea agreed. "And I've seen the Ageless and the Archon's soldiers Conscript Ageless-born in the city."

"The ones who can't claim an Ageless parent, yes," her mother said, face and voice stiff.

"I don't understand," Thea said, glad she was sitting down.

"You are my child," Reardon said, voice softer than she would have believed possible. "You and your mother could have claimed kinship with me. Named me. And you would not have been Conscripted. There would have been a place for you, for both of you, in any Citadel, and an apprenticeship if you had wanted."

Thea's vision was fading around the edges and she realised she had been holding her breath, trying to take in what was being said. And not said. She drew in some much-needed air and let it out, puzzling through the words. They didn't make any sense.

What Reardon was saying was that she or her mother could have walked into any Citadel across the lands, invoked his name and been accepted. There would have been places for them both, and no forced service.

The words tumbled over in her mind, fragmenting and pulling apart. Nothing made sense. What Reardon had said went against everything she had been taught. Everything that she knew.

Everything that her mother had told her.

The wood of the chair arms creaked as she tightened her grip. Her mother had lied. More than once.

"I don't want to work for the Ageless," she said. It sounded childish in her ears, even if it was true. The Ageless were selfish and cruel. They took what they wanted and discarded everything else. That was what her mother had taught her. And it was what she had seen with her own eyes, time and time again. It was not all lies. But it seemed there was something false in what her mother had taught her.

Thea wanted to be sick.

"After what happened to your brother, I can understand that," Reardon said. She could hear pain in his voice. He had only recently learned he'd lost a son before he even knew he had one. "You don't have to work for the Ageless. Not now, not ever," Reardon said, still in that soft voice, pain fading. She believed him. She couldn't explain why, but she believed him, and trusted him in that moment. He was no longer some faceless, unknown Ageless who had hurt her mother, but someone that she was slowly getting to know, and what little she knew told her that he did not give information or make promises easily.

Thea found she was holding her breath again, trying to make sense of what she was being told now, and what she had been told before.

"You told me that I would be Conscripted," she said to her mother, voice hard and flat. "You told me that. More than once. And you told me that if I was found, even now, that we would be taken to the Citadel. Both of us. Made to work for the Ageless."

"I did say that, yes," her mother said, voice not quite steady, a tear trailing down her face. "I was trying to keep you safe," she added, voice hoarse. "I grew up around the Ageless. They are many of them as cruel and selfish as I said."

"But not all of them," Thea said slowly, realisation crawling over her skin. She had never really questioned that before, despite memories of Trymian, who was not cruel or selfish. And although she did not know Reardon well, what she had seen of him suggested he wasn't cruel and selfish, either. Not entirely. Arrogant and secretive, yes. But she had yet to see actual cruelty from him.

"No, not all of them," her mother echoed. She was gripping her hands together in her lap now, still with those white knuckles.

"Why are you telling me this? Why now?" Thea asked. There were so many things that didn't make sense, so many questions flying around in her head. But that question she thought might be a simple one to answer.

Her mother's face tightened and she glanced across at Reardon.

"I came to ask Elise why our daughter fought better than most soldiers in the Archon's army," Reardon said, voice sharper than it had been. He glanced back at Thea's mother.

"And I told him that you had been trained to defend yourself as necessary," her mother said, glaring at Reardon. "Because he was not around to do it."

Reardon flinched as if he had been struck, colour rising in his face.

Thea drew a sharp breath through a tight throat. Her mind scrambled for a moment to work out when Reardon might have seen her fight, and then she remembered the warriors of Alayla. He and Trymian had been flying towards her and Niath. They would have been able to see most of the fight from their higher vantage point.

Her parents were silent and she realised they were glaring at each other, both of them with tight faces, anger pinching their mouths.

"I would have been here. If I had known," Reardon said. It sounded as if he had said it before. More than once.

"And how was I to know that?" her mother snapped back. "Not one communication in nearly thirty years. You left without a backward glance."

Reardon got to his feet and paced away. Not leaving, just putting some distance between himself and her mother. He circled around the small open area outside the storeroom.

Thea looked between her parents, wanting to speak, but knowing that it was not her business. She had lived with her mother's anger and grief for her entire life, her mother believing that Reardon had abandoned her, deliberately ignoring the messages she had sent. Except that was not the truth. They had sent each other messages, and none had been received. Thea wanted to know more about what had happened to those messages, but lately her mother had not been willing to talk about Reardon at all, having banned him from the house. And Thea had not felt bold enough to ask the Commander of one of the Archon's garrisons, an almost total stranger, what he thought might have happened to the letters he had sent to her mother.

He was far less intimidating and remote just now, out of his uniform, channelling his frustration into movement. This version of Reardon was far more approachable, but now was not the time to ask him why he thought his messages had disappeared.

And it seemed that it was going to take some more time before her mother's anger and grief faded.

Meantime, Thea had pain of her own radiating through her chest. Her mother had lied. Again and again and again. Not just about Theo's killer, but about the Ageless and what might happen to them if Thea was discovered to be Ageless-born.

"You made me afraid," Thea realised, the words out before she knew what she was going to say. "You made sure I was afraid of the Ageless. Afraid of Conscription. Made sure that I kept quiet and avoided people who might betray us."

It hurt. It felt as if her chest was being ripped open. The certainties of her life stripped away. Everything around her seemed insubstantial. Unreal.

"It's right that you are afraid," her mother said, voice rising in pitch. "The Ageless could have taken you. Could have Conscripted you."

"That's not what you said," Thea answered, her own voice rising. "You made it seem as if we would never see each other again if I was Conscripted. That I would most likely die in service." Her voice cracked, and tears ran down her face, fury and grief and betrayal choking her, stopping more words from coming out. She had spent so long being afraid, hiding in plain sight, watching what she said, how she moved, who she spoke to. Even turning twenty-five and being free of the threat of Conscription had not really lessened the fear, as her mother had assured her that the Ageless could still find ways to force them both into service.

And so Thea had been careful. Had tried not to be noticed. Had tried not to think too much about what the future might hold, because it could all be taken away from her in a moment. Or so she had believed.

It was not all lies, Thea knew. Conscription did happen. And the Ageless were known to simply take what they wanted, with no regard for others' feelings. If the Ageless decided that she was worth having, then she would have no say in the matter, even now when she was past the age of Conscription.

But her mother had exaggerated the danger. Kept Thea frightened of her own shadow.

She was on her feet, striding towards the gate.

"Wait, where are you going?" her mother said.

"I don't know. Away from here." Thea stumbled to a halt, pain sharpening as she realised that she had nowhere to go. This house, and her mother, were the only safe spaces she had ever had in this city. The only places she had not needed to be afraid. Where she could be herself.

There was a hard lump in her throat that resisted her attempts to speak around it, and there was a block of ice in her middle. She had accepted what her mother had told her because she loved her, because she knew her mother loved her and wanted what was best for her. And there had been lies. Lots of lies. Lies that she had not seen. She flinched, wondering what other falsehoods she might uncover.

"There is a place for you at the Citadel. If you want it," Reardon said unexpectedly. He had come to a halt near one of the storeroom doors, a careful distance away from both her and her mother. He was watching her with an expression she could not read. All she could tell was that he had meant what he said.

Her mother uttered an inarticulate protest.

"No," he said, voice flat, raising a hand to cut off whatever her mother might say. "Thea is old enough to make up her own mind."

"Thank you," Thea said, forcing the words out past the lump that was sliding down into her chest, hurt blooming out across her skin so that the light touch of fabric was almost unbearably painful. "But I do not belong in the Citadel," she said. She didn't know where she found the grace for that refusal, but saw Reardon's mouth turn up in an unexpected smile.

"You may not believe so, but from the fighting I saw, you are quite wrong," he told her.

She blinked. In the revelations of her mother's lies, she had missed the fact that he had paid her a sincere compliment. He had said to her mother that she fought better than most of the Archon's soldiers.

The last compliment he had paid her was that she seemed competent at her job.

This one was better. She had improved in his eyes. She wasn't sure how to feel about that.

But she was sure about one thing.

"I don't want to fight for the Archon," she told Reardon plainly. It was close to treason, in the eyes of most Ageless, but even with the certainties of her life shaken, she was still sure of that.

To her surprise, Reardon's mouth lifted in a smile. He looked younger, almost human.

"No, I don't suppose you do," he said. He hesitated. "The offer of a place to stay is yours, if you ever change your mind."

"Thank you," Thea said again, the words coming a little more easily now. She glanced aside to her mother, who was still sitting in her chair, fingers twisted together. "For now, this is my home." Her eyes were hot, burning with unshed tears. "If you'll excuse me, I have a long day tomorrow."

She turned to go into the house.

"Thea," her mother said, voice high.

Thea stopped, half-turned, looked over her shoulder. "I know you meant it for the best," she said, jagged fragments stabbing into her chest, aimed for her heart. "But I can't. Not just now."

"Alright," her mother said, tears on her face.

Thea left without another word, catching a glimpse of her parents through one of the windows as she went up the stairs to her room. Reardon was still standing, staring at her mother, who was looking at her hands. They both looked tense, on the verge of anger.

She had an impulse to go back, to stand between them and absorb some of the anger. The impulse died as soon as it had been born. Her mother was in no danger from Reardon, and doubtless the two of them had things to say that they didn't want an audience for.

Thea got ready for bed with mechanical efficiency, making sure her uniform was clean, ready for the next day, settling into her old, familiar bed, Gilbert finding his way to his normal resting spot, tucked under her chin. He started to purr, as if oblivious to the tension in Thea's body.

She lay for a while, staring into the night, and waited for the tears to come. They never did. Instead, the pain in her chest dimmed, little by little, with Gilbert's purring, enough so that she eventually fell asleep and did not dream.

Chapter Fifteen

Thea felt hollow all the way through when she left the house the next morning, sneaking out before first light and successfully avoiding her mother. The world around her was leached of colour, a perfect reflection of her mood as she made her way through the city, trying to focus on details around her rather than the revelations of the night before. There was a tavern sign that needed painting. Further down the street, a house with a brilliant display of flowers in a window box, several useful herbs mixed in amongst the flowers. A glimpse through a window showed her a quiet domestic scene; a couple settled at a table sharing a meal with a single candle between them. Ordinary, everyday things.

When she had first started venturing more freely around the city, Thea had wondered how the citizens of Accanter managed to continue their day-to-day lives with the oppressive presence of the Citadel overhead, the constant reminder of the Ageless and their unfettered power. She had wondered how ordinary people managed to get through their lives without the daily fear and worry that she carried. She had decided that most people simply didn't think about the Ageless, or the impact that their rulers had. Not unless they had to.

And now she had another explanation. She doubted that the other citizens of the city had mothers who had drilled that wariness into them every day of their lives in this city. They probably had not spent hours and hours tucked in a secret room, frightened to move or breathe too loudly in case the Ageless or the Archon's soldiers should find her and take her away into Conscription.

Her mother had said, more than once, that she had lost one child and did not want to lose another. And Thea had her own grief to carry as well. So she had not questioned her mother's restrictions. Not really. She had always understood why her mother was so careful.

And now it seemed it had not all been required. Not really.

It made her wonder what else she had got wrong. What else she had thought she knew that would turn out to be false?

And it made her more determined than ever to be ordinary. To not stand out. She had never wanted to be different. She had just wanted to blend in, to be accepted, to do her job, to find some justice for Theo. She had never wanted to be Ageless-born, not since she had understood that it made her different. And it was worse now, now that she knew she was Ageless, her wings tightly hidden away. She didn't want the wings. Didn't want to be known as Ageless. Didn't want to think about what that might mean, and how Reardon or her mother might react if they knew.

She shook her head, trying to shake off the things she had learned, and focus instead on the day ahead.

The tantalising smells from the Harrow bakery distracted her enough to realise that she had missed a meal the night before. It would not do for her to faint from hunger during the day.

There were a few other Watchmen and women at the bakery already, those finishing the night shift. She exchanged greetings with some of them, noticing that they seemed a little less wary of her than they had been since her former Sergeant's arrest and sentencing to a black ship.

The food, and the little bits of ordinary, everyday conversation, brought a bit of colour back into the day and took care of the hollow feeling in the pit of her stomach so that she felt almost whole when she arrived at Middlefield Watch Station brushing crumbs from her uniform just as daylight was breaking across the city rooftops.

She had time to get a new notebook and pencil from the Watchman on the front desk before movement outside and the brilliant white wings of an Ageless drew her attention.

She left the building in time to see an Ageless touch down on the ground, folding his wings away, returning to his human *aspect*. She didn't know him. He had sleek blond hair and a square-jawed face that many women would find attractive, his skin tanned from working outdoors. He was wearing the black uniform of the Archon, a stylised set of wings stitched in silver above his heart declaring that he was one of the Archon's winged warriors. In Accanter, that put him under Reardon's command.

"Investigator March?" he asked, surprising Thea with a courteous tone.

"Yes." She stopped where she was. The last time an unknown Ageless had been close to her, she had been snatched up from the city streets and carried to the Citadel.

"I am Lucan. Commander Reardon asked us to provide you with an escort today. Said there might be some warriors of Alayla around." Far from being disgusted by the assignment, Lucan seemed pleased, his eyes gleaming with what looked like keen anticipation.

"Us?" Thea repeated, latching on to the ordinary word. She looked up and saw a group of Ageless warriors hovering in the air above them, their wings blinding white. A half dozen in all. She blinked. Reardon had sent an entire wing of his garrison to escort her. "Ah. Yes. We encountered some warriors on our last journey back from the Summer House. I'm hoping not to see them again, to be honest."

"Well, we'll be here if they do turn up," Lucan said, sounding almost cheerful. "The commander sends his regrets. He'll try to join us later."

"Oh. I see," Thea said, sounding stupid in her own ears. She did not know how to feel. On the one hand, she was relieved not to see Reardon, the conversation of the night before too new and raw in her mind. And it made sense that a commander had far better things to do with his day than provide an escort for a Watch Investigator. And yet, a small part of her, that she had not known existed before now, felt disappointed that she wasn't important enough to warrant his personal attention. It was a new feeling, and one she didn't like. She would never question her mother's need to be elsewhere. She had always understood that her mother's work was essential to providing their home, food and clothing, and that her mother's work would take her elsewhere. She had also been blessed with time with her mother, like their lunches in the kitchen swapping the news of the day.

Reardon, on the other hand, had been a mystery most of her life and now seemed to drop in and out with no warning and Thea had to admit, in the quiet of her mind, she found it unsettling.

"We offered to provide transport," Lucan went on, not seeming to find anything odd about her reactions. "But the commander said you had horses organised."

"Yes," Thea said, not able to form more than that one word for a moment. She had experienced the Ageless' idea of providing transport once, at Reardon's command, and would be happy to never experience it again. Relief was followed by the strangest impulse to blurt out that, if she wanted to, she could fly herself to the Summer House. She kept her mouth shut. She was not ready to speak about that. Not yet. And probably not ever. And certainly not to a strange Ageless.

Before she could say anything more foolish, she heard hoof beats behind her and turned to find Niath and Sam riding towards her, spare horses trailing after Sam. She blinked but, no, she had not imagined it. There were four riderless horses, not the one she had been expecting.

"Good morning," Niath said, lifting a hand. "Lucan. Are you coming with us?"

"I am," the Ageless confirmed, and grinned, shocking Thea as she realised he was perhaps younger than she was. "The commander thinks it will be good for me," he added.

Niath laughed. "I'm sure. Thea, have you met Lucan?"

"Only just now," Thea said, glancing between the two of them, wondering what in the world a Citadel Mage and an Archon's soldier would have in common.

"He has a bit of a reputation for rule breaking," Niath confided, smiling, "but he's good at his job."

"I see," Thea said, feeling she had to say something, even though she didn't understand at all. "You know each other, then?"

"We've been friends since Niath arrived at the Citadel," Lucan said easily, laughing at a memory. "Some of our cadets tried to use him as target practice. A few of them are still waiting for their hair to grow back properly."

Thea looked between the two men as they laughed at their shared memories, and smiled in turn, imagining the army cadets getting an unpleasant shock when they tried to target Niath. The mage had more than a few tricks up his sleeves.

"We can talk more later," Niath suggested. "I imagine Thea is anxious to get started."

"Yes, I am," she agreed.

"We brought spare horses so we can make a faster pace," Niath explained as Sam led one of the spare horses forwards for Thea. Not the same horse, Hern, that she had ridden before, but a chestnut that could be the twin of Niath's horse. Thea paid attention as Sam gave her the horse's name and some tips on riding him, missing whatever further conversation there was between Niath and Lucan.

By the time she was in the saddle, ready to go, Lucan was back overhead with the rest of his wing, rising higher into the sky as she and Niath rode forward, Sam following with the spare horses.

By the time they reached the edge of the city and the road that led to the Summer House, Thea had settled onto her new horse and had plenty of time to think about the long road ahead and all the possible hiding places for the warriors of Alayla. She could only hope that the wing of Ageless above would be enough to deter the warriors.

In the end, their journey to the Summer House was perfectly routine. Thea didn't see any shadowy figures in the trees along the road, and no one tried to kill them. If it hadn't been for the fast pace that Niath set, meaning they had to pause to change horses on the way, it would have been an almost boring journey.

The Summer House was still bristling with magic when they arrived. Thea and Niath had no sooner got off their horses than Fionn appeared at the front door.

"What do you want?" Fionn asked as soon as they were in earshot.

Her tone and her manner were rude, in sharp contrast to their previous visit.

"Something wrong?" Thea asked.

"What do you want?" Fionn repeated, ignoring the question.

Thea exchanged glances with Niath. "We'd like to see Master Hannaford's study again. There was another death in the city yesterday, and I'd like to see if I missed anything the first time."

Fionn gave an audible sniff, eyeing Thea up and down with disfavour, her mouth tightening. "I suppose," the steward said, with reluctance, "although you might need to wait a bit."

"Wait?" Thea asked, startled. She had agreed with Fionn that the study would be left undisturbed, and did not think that the steward was someone to go back on her word.

"It's easiest if I show you," Fionn said, sounding more exasperated than anything else. "Come on, it's this way."

"We remember," Thea said, following Fionn as the Ageless-born steward started striding away into the building. The steward didn't pause, and Thea had to stretch her legs to keep up.

As they drew closer to the study, Thea could see that the door was open, daylight spilling out into the corridor. There were odd sounds coming from the room. As if things were being thrown about inside.

Before Thea could ask what was going on, Fionn took a step to the side and stopped abruptly.

"You're on your own from here," she said. "I've been ordered to stay out."

Now deeply curious, Thea moved past the steward until she reached the doorway of the study, then stopped.

The room, which had been beautifully ordered when she had last seen it, was in total chaos. The shelves had been emptied, with books and parchments strewn across the floor. The papers on the desk had been swept aside into a careless heap next to the empty chair. The furniture in the room looked as if it had been moved, too. One of the chairs was on its side, another out of place.

In the midst of the chaos was a slender woman, perhaps as tall as Thea's shoulder. The stranger had her back to Thea, a heavy ledger held carelessly in one hand, a low muttering carrying to Thea's ears.

"Not here not here not here. Where did he put it? Where? Where?" The distracted words reminded Thea of Mage Waters' mad utterances and sent a chill across her skin.

"Ma'am," Thea said firmly, taking a step into the room, then stopping in her tracks as the bitter ice of ancient Ageless power slid over her skin. The impact of it held Thea in place, caught the breath in her throat and dried her mouth. Power filled the air so that she was momentarily blind to anything else. The weight of centuries pressed against her shoulders, weakening her knees so she had to lock them to remain upright. There was only one Ageless old enough to carry that weight. Only one. Thea might never have met her in person before, but the Ageless in front of her was unmistakably Edris, the Archon. Ruler absolute of most of the known world, with ambitions to conquer the rest.

Thea wanted to turn and run. Far away, and as fast as her legs would take her. She did not want to attract Edris' attention. No one sane wanted Edris' attention. Thea could not move, though, no matter how much she wanted to. Her feet were locked to the ground, heart thudding in her neck. And with the next breath she realised that there was no point in running. Edris was faster, and stronger, than she was.

The Ageless whirled, white-blond, waist-length hair spiralling out around her, and stared at Thea. Edris was in her Ageless *aspect*, the bones of her face sharp and brittle, black eyes a stark contrast to her pale hair.

The force of Edris' presence, the air around her crackling with Ageless power and the scent of frost, held Thea still, her mind scattering, noticing random details as she tried to get her breathing under control.

The absolute ruler was clothed in a brocade jacket and matching split skirt of deep blue covered in pinpoints of light from the gems sewn across the fabric, her hair pinned back from her face with jewelled combs. There were rumours that Edris never wore the same outfit twice. Rumours which Thea had discounted as exaggerated gossip. But it was clear that Edris did like fine clothing. Even one of the combs in her hair would have kept a family in Accanter housed, clothed and fed for two years or more. Thea doubted that Edris would know, or care, about the yawning gap between her wealth and her citizens. Everything Thea knew about the Archon suggested Edris saw the people under her rule as things to be used.

"What?" Edris said, voice as sharp as the angular planes of her face, slicing through Thea's scattered, panicked thoughts. "How dare you disturb me."

"Eminence," Thea said, voice too high and thin, managing to gather herself enough to put her hand on her heart in a gesture of respect. She did not want to attract Edris' famous temper. "I did not know you were here."

"Well, of course not," Edris said. "What I do is of no concern to you. What are you doing here?"

"Eminence, I'm conducting an investigation into the deaths of Bordan Hannaford and Dalston Paulin." For the space of one heartbeat, Thea wondered if Edris had been involved in their deaths. She dismissed the idea as quickly as it had occurred. The men had been killed by someone adept at covering their tracks. The sheer force of Edris' presence in the world would have lingered in the rooms. And Edris would have had no reason to cover her tracks. She could have killed the men in the middle of a crowded marketplace and faced no consequences. She was the supreme ruler.

"Who are they?" Edris demanded, still with that hard edge to her voice.

"Bordan Hannaford was the human merchant who owned this house. Dalston Paulin was another human merchant," Thea said, trying to hide her surprise. Edris did not seem to know whose house she was in, which made Thea even more curious as to what the Archon was looking for. She half-opened her mouth to ask, then thought better of it. Edris might answer. Or she might decide Thea needed to be taught a lesson.

"Bordan. Yes. An irritating man. Dead, you say? Well, that's something," Edris said, seeming to realise she was still holding a ledger. She glanced down at it. "Useless." She flung the ledger aside, turning away, not caring where it went.

The ledger flew through the air towards Thea. She managed to catch it, needing both hands, and stood, holding it, heart thumping again. If she had not inherited the non-human quicker reflexes and greater strength from Reardon, the ledger would have hit her head and injured her. Perhaps worse. It was heavier than it looked, more than weighty enough to kill a person.

Edris had not seemed to notice, prowling back around the room, beginning to mutter to herself again. The Archon seemed to have completely forgotten about Thea.

With the ledger clutched to her chest, Thea slowly backed away towards the door, only then realising that Niath was beside her.

She didn't take her eyes off Edris until she was out in the corridor, glancing at Niath to find him on edge, his normally blue eyes shaded with a hiandar's darkness, the angles of his face slightly shifted to his other *aspect*.

"She's disturbing a crime scene," Niath said in a very quiet voice, when they were a few paces away from the open doorway.

"I'm not going to be the one to tell her that," Thea answered, in an equally soft voice. She was still clutching the ledger as if it was armour that could guard against Edris' temper. Not even Dina would expect her, or Niath, to order the Archon out of a crime scene. And Thea realised that she would far rather face Dina's wrath than Edris'.

Thea forced her attention away from the study for a moment, finding Fionn standing a short distance down the corridor, arms folded over her middle, as if she, too, wanted some armour.

Thea glanced down at the ledger, recognising it as some kind of merchant's records, then tucked it under one arm, the bulk of it awkward and heavy against her side, and went to stand a few paces from Fionn, careful to position herself so that she could see the study doorway as well as the steward.

"How long has the Archon been here?" Thea asked, keeping her voice low. Edris didn't seem to be paying them any attention, but that could quickly change.

"Since early morning," Fionn said, pressing her lips together. "She landed on the roof. Set all the alarms off," she added, still pale. "Insisted on seeing all the rooms the master occupied. She's taken apart his bedroom, dressing room and the sitting room." Fionn's face tightened. "She's thrown a few things, too. One of the maids is still unconscious."

Thea felt the weight of the ledger in her hand and realised again how lucky she had been to avoid serious injury. Edris had not cared.

"All the other rooms are like the study?" Thea asked, brows lifting. She could only imagine how Fionn, who seemed to run an orderly household, felt about the chaos Edris was leaving behind. And, worse than that, what Edris might do if she did not find whatever it was she was searching for.

"Yes."

"Do you know what she is looking for?" Thea asked. She could not help the question. The Archon had spent a great deal of effort searching, in multiple rooms.

"I offered to help her find whatever it was," Fionn said, "but she wouldn't tell me. Told me to get out of her sight, but then gets annoyed when I go too far."

"You, girl." Edris' voice cut through whatever else Fionn might have said, or Thea might have asked. The Archon came through the door of the study, still in her *aspect*, her wings flickering into being behind her, fluttering partly open as she strode the short distance down the corridor.

With a shock, Thea realised that Edris was barely taller than her mother, and just as delicately built. There was no other resemblance between the two, though. Thea's mother was warm and clever and human. The Archon was something other, at the moment seemingly made of nothing but power and temper, dragging with her the weight of centuries of life and the assurance of absolute rule over her empire.

Before Thea could react, Edris had reached out, lightning-fast, and grabbed one of Fionn's arms, dragging the steward forward. From the grimace on Fionn's face, Thea guessed that the Archon's grip was tight enough to bruise bone.

Edris went back along the corridor, Fionn scrambling to stay with her, and stopped at the open doorway.

"This is it? This is all he had left in the room?" the Archon demanded.

"Yes, ma'am. All his business records and ledgers are here."

"There's nowhere else in this building?" Edris asked, shaking Fionn's arm, twisting it as she did so.

"No, ma'am. Just here," Fionn said, tears starting down her face.

"You. What's that?" Edris asked, pointing to Thea and the ledger she held.

"One of Master Hannaford's merchant records, ma'am," Thea said, holding the ledger out. "You're welcome to have it."

"No. Useless. All of you. Useless." Edris dropped Fionn's arm, but only to backhand the steward across her face, sending the Ageless-born woman flying through the air until she hit the opposite wall of the corridor with a crunch that made the breath rush out of Thea, mouth dry, heart rate picking up. That had sounded like a fatal landing. "It's not here. Where else did he work?" the Archon asked, staring at Thea with pitch-black eyes that seemed to bore into her.

Pinned with the full force of Edris' rage and power, skin crawling at the murder she had just witnessed, Thea opened her mouth, no sound emerging. She was freezing from head to toe, trembling as if she was on a cliff-edge, preparing to dive over.

"Edris."

Reardon's voice had never been so welcome.

The Archon sniffed, a haughty little gesture that sat oddly on her angular face and against the weight of years she carried. She tossed her head, the white-blond hair spilling around her, and turned her glare to Reardon, somewhere behind Thea's shoulder.

"What are you doing here?" she demanded, in the same tone she had used with Fionn.

"Warriors of Alayla have been seen in the area," Reardon answered easily. "I'm checking in with my patrol."

"Warriors of Alayla? How quaint," Edris said, all her rage disappearing into apparent amusement. "What next? An escalus? Another forest giant? Or perhaps Alayla herself? The bitch is long dead, whatever her warriors think."

"Eminence, I don't know about the other things, but we captured one of the warriors a couple of days ago. He killed himself before we could get any information," Reardon said.

"Of course he did," Edris said, tossing her hair again and walking past Thea as if she did not exist.

Thea turned, following Edris' movement, not wanting the Archon at her back, in time to see Edris put a hand on Reardon's chest. From the tightening of his face, it was not a welcome gesture. The Archon did not seem to notice.

"Is your business here concluded?" Reardon asked. On the face of it, a perfectly polite, perfectly reasonable question. And yet there was an undercurrent in his voice. Not pleased at Edris' presence here, if Thea had to guess, although he was not openly hostile to his ruler. Of course not. Open hostility to Edris tended to result in a very short life expectancy.

Of course, even politeness could result in a short life expectancy, too, Thea realised, shivering as she glanced at Fionn, who was lying crumpled on the floor nearby.

"It is. I trust you will be at tonight's concert?" Edris asked, beginning to walk away down the corridor. The change in tone and subject made Thea blink, wondering if she had heard right. The Archon had changed her mood and her focus in a blink.

"If my duties permit, yes," Reardon said to the Archon's back.

"See that they do," Edris said over her shoulder, before reaching out in what looked like a careless gesture and punching a hole through the wall, daylight flooding in where there hadn't been any. The Archon stepped through the opening, her wings unfolding, and through the newly created gap, Thea could see her rising into the sky.

"I'll make sure she leaves," Reardon said, stalking along the corridor to the gap.

"Fionn," Thea said, flinching as she remembered the crunch of the steward hitting the wall. She ran to the woman's side, dropping the ledger as she moved.

The steward was lying too-still, one side of her face a mass of swelling and bruising. Thea knelt beside her and held a hand close to her mouth, reassured by the puff of breath against her skin. Fionn was still breathing, at least.

"Still alive. But she needs healing," Thea said, glancing up at Niath. "Do you think the house will have some spells?"

"I think we can do better. I sensed Mage Fisk earlier. Let me get him," Niath said, and strode away before Thea could ask him how he had sensed the other mage, or what good it would do getting the arrogant mage.

She was left alone in the corridor with the unconscious steward and stayed kneeling, not sure if her legs would support her, shaken to her core, trembling with the after-effect of Edris' presence.

Thanks to an early childhood in Kellto, Thea had met a good number of Ageless in her life, but none of them had carried the shock of the Archon's presence, or the weight of her years.

Even thinking about Edris made Thea look over her shoulder, as if the Archon was still there, with her sharply angled face and mad, black eyes. There was no one else in the corridor with her, but Thea's breathing picked up all the same. There had been rumours for years, bare whispers when Thea and her mother had first moved to the city, that the Archon was not quite right in her mind. And having met her, Thea could understand why people would think so. Edris had lived so long that the normal human lifespan was a mere blink to her. But she still had some anchor to the here and now. Her determination in searching the house was evidence of that.

Thea's mind sharpened. The Archon had been searching for something. Even if she could not imagine what on earth a Master Merchant might have had that would be of interest to the Archon, there was a solid object somewhere that Edris wanted. And that made Thea curious, bringing some warmth back to her body so that when Niath came back towards her a few minutes later, Mage Fisk behind him, Thea was staring into middle distance with a frown on her face, trying to think where a human merchant might have hidden something. Somewhere there was a lock that fitted the key she carried, and she wondered if whatever the Archon was looking for might be behind that lock.

Chapter Sixteen

To Mage Fisk's credit, he did not waste time with pleasantries or protests, simply knelt at Fionn's side and put a hand on her chest. The sensation of magic being used wound up Thea's arms, surprising her with its warmth. It was not anything like the compelling feel of Niath's magic, but it was pleasant, carrying none of the chill she associated with most human magic and at odds with the arrogance Fisk normally displayed.

She straightened and took a few steps away from Fionn, giving the mage room to work, and frowned at him. When she had met him before, he had seemed purely human. But now she wondered if she had been too quick to judge, seeing only the arrogance, and whether she had missed something. And if she had missed his true nature, what else she might have missed?

"Mage Fisk is a natural healer," Niath told her, his eyes on the mage working on Fionn. He glanced up and held Thea's gaze for a moment. "They are rare, but their healing gift is very strong."

"For all the good it does me," Fisk said, with his hand still on Fionn's chest. "She's got broken bones in her back and her skull is in pieces. I can heal her, but it's going to take a while. And I'll need some food."

"Here." Niath drew a pair of cloth packets out of his robes that Thea recognised. The packets would most likely contain oatcakes. She was tempted to ask for one herself, but Fionn's need for healing was far greater. "That should help to start with, and I'll ask the kitchen to send you some more."

"Should we try to move her?" Thea asked.

"Not unless you want to do more damage," Fisk answered, setting the food from Niath to one side and putting his other hand on Fionn's head. He glanced up. "Didn't you hear me? This is going to take a while."

"Alright," Thea said, and took a careful step back, away from the mage. Her foot bumped into the ledger on the ground and she bent to pick it up. "We'll leave you be for the time being."

"There's a bell in the study," Niath said, looking towards the door. "Assuming it's safe to go in?"

"I don't see how we can possibly do more damage," Thea said.

Niath's mouth lifted in an unexpected smile and he went into the study, heading for the fireplace. There was a small, old metal bell hanging above the fireplace and he rang it once. The small sound echoed through the house, carrying with it the faint trace of magic.

Fascinated, Thea went into the room to inspect the bell more closely.

"A lot of the larger houses have them," Niath explained. "They're connected to the servants' quarters downstairs. One of the household staff should be along in a moment."

"I don't remember seeing them at Brightfield House," Thea commented. It made a certain sort of sense to have a ready means of calling for servants in a house this big.

"No," Niath agreed, turning to the room around them. "What do you think Edris was looking for?"

"I don't know," Thea said, putting the ledger down on the desk. "But we need to see if we can find a lock for this key." She dug it out of her pocket and held the oddly shaped key up to the light. "I don't remember seeing anything that it might fit when we were here before." Looking around the room and the chaos Edris had left behind she shook her head. "And I'm not sure how we're going to find anything in this mess."

"We will," Niath said, with absolute confidence.

"How can you be so sure?"

"Well, Edris didn't find anything in the places she looked. So we'll look at the rest of the room." Niath grinned at her expression. "I have some experience of looking for things," he added.

Thea's brows lifted as she took in the room. Edris had searched through the bookshelves, the desk, and even ripped the stuffing out of one of the chairs. The floor was covered with ledgers, parchments, and torn pages. The Archon's search of this room might have been hasty, but it had been thorough, from what Thea could see.

Before she could challenge Niath's assumption, a servant appeared at the doorway, pale-faced as he glanced back along the corridor to where Mage Fisk was working on Fionn.

"You rang, mage?" he asked, tone perfectly polite.

"I did. Thank you. Mage Fisk is going to need some food to help him heal the steward," Niath explained, and went across to the door to confer with the servant.

Deciding that he was more than capable of dealing with that, Thea turned back to the room, puzzling over the idea of searching the places that Edris had not looked. She knew that some old houses had servants' passages in the walls. It was possible that there was a hidden door somewhere that Edris had missed.

There was a flat stretch of wall next to one of the bookcases that seemed a possible candidate to have a hidden door. As she made her way over to it, her attention snagged on the nearest bookcase. The back of them and the shelves were made of old, dark wood, but there was a misaligned joint against the wall at one point, one piece of wood standing slightly proud of the others. Curious, Thea put her hand on the wall, feeling along the length of wood. The house had been crafted by masters of their trade, and none of them would have left such a badly aligned piece of work, even at the back of a bookcase.

As she smoothed her hand along the wooden panel, she felt a corner under her palm and stopped, curling her fingers around the edges of the wood and pulling back.

Part of the back panel came away in her hand, lifting out so smoothly she knew it was intentional, and not an accident. There was an ancient-looking metal plate behind where the panel had been, with a small, dark opening that might fit a key.

She set the panel on the floor, leaning against the wall, and turned back to the metal plate. It looked as if there might have been some writing on it once, or some decoration, but it seemed to have worn away over the years. It was longer than her forearm and half as tall, taking up almost the entire back wall of the shelf. She put her hand onto the metal, feeling it cool to her touch, the old writing or decoration standing out under her fingers.

"Niath, come and look at this," she said.

"I see it," he answered from just behind her shoulder. "Does the key fit?" he asked.

She didn't need to turn around to know that his eyes would be gleaming with interest. He was naturally curious, and they had just found a mystery.

She put the key into the small opening and her brows lifted. It slid into place and then turned easily under the slightest pressure, a distinct clicking noise telling her that the locking mechanism had opened. Not seeing any obvious handle, she pulled back slightly on the key.

The metal plate swung out, hinged on one side, revealing a metal box as deep as the plate was long, the available light showing a stack of what looked like old books and loose papers.

Thea reached in and lifted the contents out into the daylight, going still as she read the first line of the topmost page.

Alayla, goddess of war, have mercy on our souls…

"This is about Alayla," Thea said, looking up at Niath.

"Really?" Niath was trying to read over her shoulder as Thea flicked through the first few pages. "Most of that looks old."

"Yes," Thea agreed, and stopped when she reached what looked like a letter in bold, crisp writing, the parchment free of any age spots. "But this isn't. Can you clear a space on the desk?" she asked, carrying the bundle over there.

Niath simply swept the tumbled papers and ledger onto the floor. Thea opened her mouth to protest, but then remembered that everything had already been disturbed by the Archon. So, instead of a useless protest, Thea moved across to the desk.

The clear surface of the desk triggered a memory of her mother at the kitchen table, her ledger open in front of her, turned at an angle that was comfortable to write on. She stopped, drawing in a breath.

"That's it. That's what was wrong," she said, mostly to herself.

"What?" Niath asked.

"I've realised what was wrong with the desk here and at Master Paulin's office. They were too neat. Everything was set out square, lined up with the edges," Thea said. Niath was frowning at her and she shook her head slightly. "When you are studying a text, or writing, do you have the paper square to the edge of the desk? Or do you have it at an angle to write or read better?" she asked.

"I see." Niath's confusion cleared. "So if everything was too neat, that suggests that someone did pose the bodies after they died."

"Yes," Thea agreed. "It makes more sense, and also explains why everything looked like it hadn't been touched." Pleased with that small bit of progress, she set the bundle she was carrying down and started spreading the papers and books out on the desk's surface.

"This is old magic," Niath said, picking up one of the books. It was barely bigger than his hand, a crudely made volume which opened at his touch revealing pages covered in cramped handwriting. "A mage's journal," Niath murmured.

"Is it dangerous?"

"The book itself, no," Niath answered, most of his attention on the writing. "But these are spells. Old ones. It looks like the mage was trying to refine them. The writing is difficult to read."

Thea turned her attention to the rest of the papers, picking up the more recent letter. It had been written with the careful, precise lines of a clerk or merchant's handwriting, each letter and word carefully spaced and easy to follow. Her brows lifted as she read.

"This is from Kendrick," she said, glancing at the signature. "And he's asking Bordan to come back to the city for a celebration of some kind." She frowned, glancing across at the metal safe. It seemed an odd letter to keep so securely. There was a strange marking at one corner of the page which fizzed against her skin when she touched it. "Niath, is there magic on this page?"

Niath looked up from the book and frowned at the page. "Yes, there is. Hold on." He put the book away in his robes, almost carelessly, and took the page from Thea, putting one thumb on the odd marking. A trace of his magic slid across Thea's skin and the words on the page shimmered, changing to something quite different. "Ah. It's an old mage's trick. Write a very boring letter over the information you want to send," Niath said. He turned, holding the page so that he and Thea could read it together.

Applying magic had revealed a quite different letter. The polite, formal covering words were gone and in their place were far more blunt sentences with an almost threatening tone. Thea's brows rose as she read it through. She was on her second read through when the words began blurring, returning to the false covering letter, but she had seen enough to realise that whatever assumptions she had made about Bordan Hannaford had been quite wrong. He had been no ordinary merchant.

The letter referenced a conspiracy involving Kendrick, among others, and referencing Alayla. Kendrick was trying to persuade Bordan Hannaford to join them, with a not-too-subtle reference to "unwanted consequences" if Bordan did not comply.

"No wonder Master Hannaford wanted to keep it," Niath said. "Do you need to see it again?" he asked.

"Yes," Thea said, pulling out her notebook. "How did it start? *'We're gathering at Roe's house in two days to perform the ceremony.'* Then what?"

Niath read the letter to her and she copied it down, barely able to believe it even as she was writing the words. Kendrick was describing a ceremony to bring forth the goddess Alayla.

She remembered the golden woman who had turned up in Middlefield Market, claiming to be the goddess herself. A woman who had possessed extraordinary power but who had, to Thea's senses, seemed artificial. As if someone had created her. And here, in this letter, was Thea's first written evidence of that. The letter referred to creating a vessel for the goddess' power.

"So, Kendrick was part of the Hand of the goddess," Thea murmured, reading over her notes. "I suppose we knew that already. Sort of. Along with at least Roe Gadsden, and possibly Bordan Hannaford as well."

"Although Kendrick seemed to be trying to drag Master Hannaford into it," Niath observed, staring at the letter. It was back to the innocuous, false cover, but Thea was sure that Niath could remember the words of the actual letter as well as she could.

"Are all these papers about Alayla?" Thea wondered, turning to the desk and beginning to look through the papers and books. Everything else looked far older than Kendrick's letter. There were other letters, addressed to names she did not know, none of them disguised in the same way as Kendrick's letter. The name Alayla featured prominently, as did the word goddess. She opened one of the books and wrinkled her nose. The handwriting in it was as cramped as the writing in the book Niath had picked up. It would take a long time to read through, assuming she could understand it at all. The first line she tried to read seemed to be in a very arcane form of the common language. The sort of flowery language that had not been spoken, or written, for hundreds of years.

"It looks like this is a library of sorts, for the goddess' followers," Niath said, staring at the document he was holding.

"Why in the world did Master Hannaford have these? How did Edris know they were here? Why was she looking for them?"

"You think this is what Edris was looking for?" Niath asked.

"What? Oh, sorry, I was talking to myself. Bad habit. Yes, I think this is what she was looking for. There's nothing else that interesting here. But why?"

Before Niath could answer, a bell started ringing somewhere in the house. Not just one bell, but many of them, all different tones, the force of sound vibrating through Thea until it was the only thing she could hear, the noise tasting bitter in her mouth.

"What is that?" she asked, putting her hands to ears. It didn't help. The sound was overwhelming.

"The perimeter alarms," Niath said, looking out the window and swallowing, hard. "I think the warriors of Alayla have found us," he said.

Thea followed his gaze and saw at least half a dozen shadows moving across the landscaped gardens outside. She spat out a curse and gathered the papers hastily together, clearing the desk, shoving everything back into the metal safe and locking it again, trying to ignore the fact that her hands were shaking. The Archon might have left the building, but the impressions of the Ageless' presence were still with Thea. Added to which, she had barely survived the last attack by the warriors. They were far more skilled than she was. Impossible to defeat. She knew she had to try. But she could not imagine how she would succeed.

She was putting the wooden panel back in place in front of the metal safe when the bells abruptly went quiet, the silence ringing through her ears as loudly as the alarm had done. She turned from the bookshelves in time to see Reardon appear in the doorway, face shifting to his Ageless *aspect*, eyes darkening.

"There are warriors outside," he told them. "Lucan and his wing are on their way to deal with them."

"We can help," Thea said, words out before she knew she was going to make the offer.

"The mage is still healing the steward," Reardon said, with a shake of his head. "We can't move her yet. You can help by looking after them."

"Do you think the warriors will get inside?" Thea asked, speaking to Reardon's back as he stalked away. She did not get an answer, which, she suspected, was answer enough.

"Do you want your sword?" Niath asked.

"Yes, please," she said, and patted her pockets, making sure the key and her notebook were sealed away. "And there's an armoury here, too, isn't there? We should make sure the household staff are armed."

"Good idea," Niath said, and led the way out into the corridor.

Mage Fisk was still kneeling beside Fionn. There was a tray beside him, covered with empty dishes. The mage was pale, frowning as he stared down at the steward. Fionn was looking almost normal, Thea saw, almost all the bruising across her face gone.

"She'll be fine in a little while," Fisk said, not looking up. "I could use some more food, though."

As she drew closer, Thea could see that Fisk was not just pale, but also looked hollow, great dark smudges under his eyes.

"Here, this should help," Niath said, handing over a couple more cloth packets. "We might not have time to get you much more just now," he added.

"I know," Fisk said, taking the cloth packets with one hand, his other hand staying on Fionn's chest. "I made the alarms, remember?" he added, a trace of his old arrogance appearing as he looked up. "That many going off at once means that there are attackers on their way."

"We were going to organise the staff," Thea said.

"Unlikely you'll need to," Fisk said, and turned back to Fionn, opening one of Niath's packets one-handed and shoving the oatcake into his mouth, barely chewing before he swallowed.

Thea was going to ask him what he meant when she saw movement out of the corner of her eye. Turning, she found a half-dozen members of the household staff running towards them, carrying weapons.

"Those who can fight are armed," one of the servants reported. She recognised him as the one who had answered Niath's earlier call, although she could not place his name for a moment. "The rest are going to the safe rooms."

"Safe rooms?" Niath asked, brows lifting, looking intrigued.

"A moment," Thea said, before the servant could answer. "Is there any food in the kitchen? Mage Fisk needs some more."

The servant's face tightened as he looked down at Fionn's still form and the mage. He nodded, once, and turned, giving instructions to the rearmost pair. They turned and ran back the way they had come.

"We have some spare weapons, if you need them," the servant said, turning back to them, "and Fionn's weapons, if she's able to use them." The armed pair of women behind him unloaded an impressive array of weapons onto the ground, stacking them up along the wall near Fionn.

"She really should rest," Fisk said, not looking up. "Otherwise I might as well not have bothered."

"What protections are built into the shields?" Thea asked, eyes drawn to the half-dozen spare shields the women had set down. The shields were half as tall as she was, and would provide a decent amount of protection. Assuming they could withstand the warriors' weapons.

"I added some standard magic to them," Fisk said, glancing up, mouth flat.

"They won't last long against the warriors," Niath said, "but they are better than nothing," he added, glancing back to the study, as if he could see through the walls. Doubtless wondering, as Thea was, where the warriors were and whether the Ageless had managed to hold them back.

"We'll protect Fionn with our lives," the servant said, lifting his chin.

"You may need to," Thea said, voice sharper than she had intended. "As soon as she's ready, you all need to get to the safe rooms. I'm assuming they have stronger protections around them?"

The servant nodded, but opened his mouth to argue, interrupted by the sound of something heavy thumping against the wall of the study, quickly followed by the sound of breaking glass.

"Impossible," Fisk said, looking up with a sour scowl. "I tempered that glass with the strongest wards I could."

"Thea," Niath said, and held out her sword. "Stay here," he told the others, before picking up a shield and stalking forward. Thea picked up a shield of her own, finding it awkward and heavy on her arm compared to the light, superbly balanced sword. Even if, as Niath had said, it was better than nothing, she doubted it would last long against the warriors.

Chapter Seventeen

Fresh air met her as she and Niath stepped through the doorway of the study. The wall opposite them, which had held wide windows, was gone. The remnants of the stone wall and fragments of glass were tumbled together inside where the wall had been, adding extra hazards to the already chaotic room.

She and Niath arrived just in time to see a pair of black-clad warriors leap through the opening, their swords already in hand. The warriors did not hesitate when they saw her and Niath, one of them lifting a hand and flinging a now-familiar blot of magic across the room at them.

Niath blocked the magical weapon with magic of his own, then raised his shield as the other warrior threw a knife in his direction. The knife lodged securely in the shield. Thea doubted that the warriors would try that again.

The warriors were moving forward, another blot of *fyr na dathan* flying through the air. Towards Thea this time. She raised the shield and ducked, not sure if it would do any good. The warriors were skilled and powerful. Fisk's magic was competent. And she was no match for the warriors. She had barely held her ground against one in their last encounter.

The force of the magical weapon sent her stumbling back, the shield bursting into flames, which consumed the entire thing in mere moments. She flung it aside before it could burn her.

Niath flung *fyr na dathan* of his own back to the warriors. They stepped aside, Niath's magic flying out the window and finding a target somewhere outside, from the cry of pain. Thea could only hope it was not one of their allies who had been hit.

Not deterred, Niath tried again. This time, he struck one of the warriors, the other one ducking past him and attacking Thea. She lifted her sword, remembering how difficult it had been to fight the warriors before. They were seasoned and skilled. She was one person, with little experience of actual combat. All the training in the world couldn't make up for that.

The shock of impact rang up her arm and she set her jaw, pressing back, determined to at least try to hold her ground. She might be able to buy the others some time to form a better defence.

"Thea!" Niath yelled.

"What? I'm a little busy," she said, warily circling the warrior. He might not have a face, but she felt he was laughing at her nonetheless. She could even imagine the taunts he might fling at her. *Weak little girl. Who are you to imagine you can defeat me?*

"What's wrong? Stop fighting like a human," Niath said, shocking her into lowering her sword and turning to stare at him.

There was no time to ask questions as the warrior took advantage of her distraction to come at her with a sweep of his blade. It would have sliced through her neck, if she hadn't managed to get her sword up in time, blocking the attack.

As she stared into the warrior's masked face, feeling the weight of his attack, struggling to hold her ground, she realised Niath was right. Her mind was still full of the revelations of the day before, tangled up with the shocking realisation of her true nature. She did not believe she could win against the warriors. She had been holding back, not using her full strength. Making that belief true.

A memory surfaced. She was in the secret training room at her mother's house, drenched in sweat, every limb aching, facing one of the trainers her mother had hired. Thea had hated that particular trainer. He had been rude, dismissive and brutal in his methods. That day she had carried bruises from head to toe. The bruises took weeks to fade.

On that particular day, she had been sent to the floor more times than she could count, and was close to giving up. Only her promise to her mother to try and learn something had kept her in the room this long.

The trainer stared at her, pitch-dark skin shadowed in the room, whites of his eyes startlingly bright. He was holding a heavy staff in front of him. Ready to attack her again. He swept the staff towards her and she jumped back, lifting her own weapon reluctantly. She did not want to take another beating, or end up on the floor again. The door was behind her. Only a few paces away. She was much closer than he was. She might be able to escape.

Then he stopped, surprising her.

"Get out of your head, girl," he snapped at her, voice low and hard.

She had not really understood what he meant, not then. But he had provoked her into attacking him, almost losing her temper, and she had landed her first strike against him. It drew the tiniest nod of approval from him. The only praise she had ever had from that particular trainer.

She remembered the words now, mixed with Niath's plea.

Get out of your head.

Stop fighting like a human.

Stop thinking. Fight.

That had been another saying from another trainer. One Thea had actually liked, and listened to. Her body knew what to do, that woman had said. She just needed to get out of its way.

Her focus snapped back into the here and now, the weight of the warrior's sword against hers, the pressure on her arms, the tension in her muscles, the feel of the hilt in her hands, the brush of air against her face. *Stop thinking. Fight.*

She turned, pivoting on the balls of her feet, bringing herself closer to the warrior, sliding her blade along his so that she could jab her elbow up towards his face, sending him stumbling back in surprise.

And then she got out of her head and stopped fighting like a human, not caring who might see or what they might think. The warriors were simply enemies trying to kill her. They were men underneath their masks. And men could be stopped. Thea had spent years and years learning how to fight and stop stronger and bigger opponents.

The warrior fell a few moments later, struck unconscious by the hilt of her sword. The other warrior was also down, although she had not seen what Niath had done. She glanced outside, through the gap where the window had been, seeing more warriors fighting the Ageless. The sword was light and ready in her hand. But it was not the best weapon here. She needed something with a bit more reach.

"Can you make me a staff?" she asked Niath.

"Yes," he said, not asking questions. He picked up a piece of wood, his magic filling the air, and then handed her a staff, weighted with iron at one end. She spun it, finding it perfectly balanced in her hand. She thanked him, handed him the sword and made her way out through the broken window, joining the fight with the Ageless.

Thea no sooner stepped outside the building than two warriors were on her and Niath. Niath sent one of them flying with a blast of magic. Thea met the other's sword with the iron tip of her staff and had the satisfaction of seeing the warrior take a step back. The length and extra weight of the staff added more power to her swing.

There was no time to think, barely any time to breathe, as she held her ground, putting herself between the house and the warriors. The last line of defence to prevent them from getting access.

The staff moved with her, smooth and almost effortless in the moment. A sweep, deflecting a sword strike. Turning, feet moving in old, familiar patterns. Staff up. Blocking another strike, the impact barely felt. Twisting her wrist, spinning the staff, the iron tip of it thumping against a warrior, sending him back. No time to celebrate as there was another warrior there, trying to move past her. She caught him with the weighted end of the staff and spun to meet him. And the next and the next.

She was vaguely aware of flashes of white. Ageless wings. Reardon and Lucan's wing harassing the warriors from the air and occasionally on the ground, but she and Niath were the ones on the ground outside, stopping more warriors from getting into the building.

Again and again Niath fired magic at the oncoming warriors, each of his blasts as strong as the last even though the mage himself was swaying on his feet beside her. The magic kept the warriors from attacking in a group, leaving Thea with only one or two to defend against.

A brief cry from one of the others, Thea was not sure who, was the only warning she had before the building behind her exploded, bricks and glass and wood and furniture spewing out into the open space where she and the others were fighting.

The force of the explosion lifted her off her feet, sending her through the air. She twisted in mid-air, hours of training and practice coming to her aid, and landed on her feet, dropping to a crouch, the staff still in her hand, looking around for the next warrior to fight.

But there were no more enemies to fight. There was a pair of dark-clad bodies on the ground, but the others had vanished.

She was breathing hard, hot under her clothes, the staff a great weight in her hands as she turned, slowly, making sure there were no more attackers.

There were none.

Just an audience of Ageless, and Niath, all staring at her.

Heat rose up her neck. "What?" she asked, her voice faint in her ears, wondering if she had something on her face or, worse, if her wings had somehow appeared again. She was tempted to turn and check, but she could not see any white feathers at the corner of her eye.

"As fine a display as I've ever seen," Lucan said, sounding as if he was a great distance away. He put a hand on his heart, and bowed a little. "Lady, you are welcome on our training grounds at any time. It would be a pleasure to spar with you."

Thea wasn't sure what to say to that. It seemed rude to tell Lucan that the last place she ever wanted to be was the Citadel. She pushed herself to her feet, wincing at sore muscles, and stared at a piece of glass sticking out of her leg. It wasn't a huge piece, perhaps the length of her thumb, but she hadn't noticed it striking her. She pulled it out and tossed it onto more glass nearby. She would heal quickly, thanks to her other nature.

The grass around her was littered with more glass, and bits of stone, splintered wood, the remains of an armchair, and a sea of scattered papers.

She turned back to the building and stopped, blinking. There was a great hole in the side of the building, where the study and the rooms above it had been.

Across the ruins, inside the house, Fionn and Fisk were standing, leaning on each other, staring at the devastation.

"What happened?" Thea asked. Her head was ringing. She put a hand to her ears, fingers coming away sticky with blood.

"The warriors inside must have blown themselves up," Niath said, coming to stand next to her. He held out a familiar-looking packet. "Here. You look like you need this."

His voice was very faint and the edges of her vision were blurring. She nodded, tucking the staff under one arm and taking the food. He had some for himself, and she saw the Ageless getting supplies out of their own pockets.

This was the bit that tall tales and stories missed, she thought, sitting down on a bare patch of grass before her legs gave out. The aftermath of battle wasn't the feasting and singing and drinking. No, it was this shaky, sick-and-hungry feeling where her body wasn't quite sure the fight was over and she couldn't quite hear or see or think straight.

Niath settled on the grass beside her. He looked as worn out as she felt, as if all his resources had been stretched thin.

"Well done," Reardon said. He had moved to stand in front of them and now crouched down so he was closer to eye level, back in his human *aspect*. "I think you may be even more proficient with a staff than with a sword," he added, a slight smile tugging his mouth. She had thought her capacity for surprise had been exhausted by the day so far, but here was the Commander of one of the Archon's garrisons settled at eye level, looking at her as if she was his equal, and not something beneath his notice. Something had changed. Perhaps the revelations of the night before, the memory of which still sent searing pain through her. Perhaps something else.

Proficient.

She had the sense that Reardon rarely gave out compliments. And that word was a vast improvement from the first word he had used to describe her, which was competent. She chewed the oatcake and stared back at him, not sure what to say or what she thought or felt about it. He seemed pleased by her expertise. But he had had no part in it and she had a spike of irritation that he seemed proud of her. He had not practised with her for hours in secret, or scraped to save enough money for illegal weapons or highly paid weapons trainers. Her mother had done that, knowing all the time the risks she had been taking.

"I've always liked working with a staff," she said eventually. That seemed a neutral-enough thing to say. "Thank you," she added, turning to Niath. "It's a magnificent weapon."

He smiled, seemingly pleased, showing straight white teeth, blue eyes bright. "Keep it," he said, when she moved.

"I can't. It's not exactly easy to hide," she said, fingers tightening around the polished wood, not wanting to let go even as she knew she had to give it back.

"Give me a moment," Niath said, and put his hand on the staff. She felt the warmth of his magic under her fingers, coursing through the length of the weapon. "Now, it will disguise itself. Try it. Say 'hide'."

"Hide," Thea said, her hand still on the staff. The wood shimmered under her hand, reducing to become an innocent-looking cudgel, like the sort carried by the Watch from time to time. It would fit perfectly into the slot at her uniform belt. Her eyes widened. "That's impressive," she said.

"If you want it to go back to being a staff, say 'come out'," Niath said, rummaging in his robes for something and sighing when he didn't find it.

"Hungry, mage?" Reardon asked. He was still crouching in front of them.

"Yes. I gave most of my supplies to Mage Fisk," Niath said, turning towards the house. "Oh, Fionn is on her feet. That's good."

"Here," Reardon said. He was holding out a cloth-wrapped packet to each of them. "Stay there for a moment while we make sure they're really gone," he said, tone making it an order, getting to his feet. "And then we can talk about what the warriors were looking for," he added, his tone that of a superior officer wanting answers. He stared down at Thea for a moment before turning and striding away to join the other Ageless.

She ignored the food in her hands, frowning after him. First Edris and now the warriors of Alayla had approached the house. It seemed likely that both the Archon and the warriors had been looking for the same thing. And she found she did not want to tell Reardon about what she and Niath had found. He was Ageless. And whilst she suspected he did not completely agree with the Archon on all things, Edris was still his ruler and his superior officer. He owed her loyalty.

He was giving orders to the Ageless soldiers just now, all of them listening to him with clear deference and respect. Whatever he said had a pair of Lucan's wing taking off a moment later, rising into the air overhead, and a third Ageless taking to the air, heading in the direction of the city. At least, Thea believed it was towards the city. Her brain was not quite fully functioning. The other Ageless warriors started walking along the walls of the house. Carrying out some kind of patrol, Thea guessed, as Reardon went inside the house.

"Are we going to tell him?" Niath asked, voice very soft.

She did not look at the mage, keeping her eyes on the Ageless she could see, picking a bit of food out of the packet Reardon had given her. It was some kind of game pie, and the scent teased her senses as she hesitated, wondering how to answer Niath. After a moment, she shook her head.

"Good," Niath said, still in that soft voice. There was a rustle as he opened his own packet of food. "I think the information could be dangerous. We need to know more before we share it."

Chapter Eighteen

When she and Niath had finished the food, they got up from the grass by mutual, silent agreement, and made their way through the debris from the house. Thea's new staff fit perfectly into the loop at her belt, the slightest bit of additional weight that she adjusted to after a few strides.

Amid the broken glass and shattered wood were bits and pieces of the black substance Thea remembered from Iason's mortuary. They had been lucky that the black shards had missed them.

"Is that what caused the explosion?" Thea asked, crouching beside a small pile of the fragments, ignoring the protest of her muscles.

"Probably," Niath said, crouching beside her. "I wonder if we should collect a sample for Dina?"

"Only if you can put it in the same spell that Reardon and Trymian used," Thea said, her eyes still on the fragments. "I don't want to ride back to the city with any bit of that able to work free."

"That's a good point. I wonder if Reardon would share the spell," Niath said.

"I can, or you can ask Trymian when he gets here," Reardon said from behind them.

Thea started, almost losing her balance, then got to her feet, glaring at the Ageless warrior. She opened her mouth and then thought better of whatever it was that she might have said.

"Trymian is on his way here?" Niath asked, getting to his feet with far more grace than Thea had managed. She had to resist the urge to roll her eyes. Of course the mage would want a chance to meet Trymian again, and doubtless was already preparing a list of questions for the Ageless scholar. Niath had said Trymian was the greatest scholar since Gaderian. Even Thea had heard of the legendary Ageless mage who had been responsible for most of the magic used by the Ageless and human mages alike. Thea could only imagine how much Niath wanted to ask Trymian.

"I sent for him. And the physician and examiner," Reardon added. "I thought they might be helpful." He lifted a brow at Thea, as if daring her to disagree. She kept her mouth shut, jaw clamped tight. His mouth quirked, as if hiding a smile, and it took all of her self-control to stay silent. After the difficult revelations of the night before, then the encounters with Edris and the warriors of Alayla, her temper was frayed. She could almost feel the bits of it drifting inside her, flame-hot and ready to spark at a moment's notice.

"I am sure Dina will want a sample of these," Niath said, pointing to the fragments littered around. "We're lucky that none of them struck us."

"I managed to raise a shield of sorts around us," Reardon said. It was not a boast, just a simple statement of fact, but it made the food in Thea's stomach churn and the torn bits of her temper quiet down. It was all too easy to forget, when faced with their sharp, angular faces and the spread of brilliant white wings, but the Ageless were also born with the ability to work magic. They were generally more powerful and at least as capable of complex spell-working as human mages. And better, if the Ageless chose to study.

Niath had said she could learn magic, too. When her wings had appeared, revealing her to be Ageless, and not Ageless-born as she had always believed. She had refused. She had not wanted any part of being Ageless. Wanted to deny it completely, and returned to her wingless state. So far, she had succeeded. In the quietest, most private part of her mind she did wonder, from time to time, just how long she could deny her nature. How long she could hide. And the conversation with Reardon and her mother the night before had just stirred everything up again.

"Thea, are you alright? You've not been yourself all day," Niath said, cutting across her spiralling thoughts.

"I'm alright. Just some, er, family business," she answered, managing a smile for the mage, conscious of Reardon listening. "We should see if anything in the study survived," she added, and started walking towards the building, confident that Niath would understand that she was only interested in one particular thing.

When they reached the house, they found that Fionn had already organised some of the household staff to clear a path through the debris. They were carefully sweeping the black fragments aside. The fragments clinked together like glass as they were piled up, but they did not otherwise move.

The steward was standing in the doorway. Or, rather, leaning against the doorpost. She looked pale, but the awful bruising had gone. Past her shoulder, Thea could see Mage Fisk settled on the floor on the other side of the corridor, what looked like a tray of food next to him.

Satisfied that they were fine, Thea turned her attention to the study itself. The power of the explosion had completed the destruction started by Edris. The floor had buckled with the force of the explosion, and the ceiling overhead was shattered, daylight gleaming through holes to the upper floor.

By something of a miracle, the panelled wall of the room where the metal safe was hidden was intact. It was badly scarred, probably from the black fragments, but otherwise undamaged. Thea dragged her eyes away from the spot before Reardon could notice her attention, and turned to Fionn instead.

"It's good to see you on your feet," she said.

"Indeed." Fionn glanced back over her shoulder to where Mage Fisk was sitting, her expression tight. "Hard to believe I owe my life to him."

"It was my pleasure," Fisk said, in a sharp-edged, bitter voice, searching through the tray beside him as if looking for more food. He sighed when he didn't find what he was looking for and pushed himself to his feet.

He was in better shape than Fionn, Thea realised. The extra food had helped him recover, while Fionn still looked as if a strong wind would blow her over.

The steward was ignoring the mage, staring at the devastation in front of her, face set, eyes over-bright.

"It's going to take years to repair," she said, voice low and harsh.

"If it can be repaired," Thea said, and earned a sharp look from the steward. "I'm sorry. I know you care about this place, but the damage is extensive. This part of the building will need rebuilding, at least."

"This is our home," Fionn said, her voice tight and too high. "We have nowhere else to go."

"Did this belong to Master Hannaford?" Thea asked.

Fionn nodded once, as if not trusting her voice.

"Then it will go to his wife. You should talk to her," Thea said.

"Wife?" Fionn asked, brows shooting up. "The master had a wife?"

"You didn't know?" Thea asked. That explained why the steward had not mentioned it, at least. But it was odd in the extreme that she had not known.

Fionn shook her head, face tight again, eyes still bright with unshed tears. "He said he had no family," she said.

"Well, he and his wife have not been on the best of terms. But they were still married. I think you'd like her," Thea said, not sure what prompted that last, personal comment. "She lives within the Citadel perimeter, and makes a living baking fancy cakes for fancy parties."

The steward stared at Thea, her nose wrinkling in clear distaste. "You think I will like her? She sounds frivolous."

"Well, why don't you visit and see?" Thea suggested, biting the inside of her lip to hide a smile. She didn't know why, but she was absolutely certain that Megan Hannaford and Fionn would find a great deal in common with each other. She remembered Fionn's care for her staff, and the collection of people that Megan had around her. People that might not find a home elsewhere.

"Do you think she might need a mage?" Fisk asked. He sounded bitter, as if not expecting a positive response, arms folded around himself. He met Thea's eyes for a brief moment. "What? Don't judge me. One of my most prominent clients was killed within my protection. And now the house has blown up. I'll be lucky to be able to sell a simple ward after this."

"Or you could use some of your other talents," Thea suggested, the words out before she thought better of it. "There's an infirmary in the city that is always short-staffed. They would be glad of a healer."

Fisk opened his mouth as if to dismiss the idea out of hand, spots of colour high on his cheeks. He closed his mouth with a snap and glared at Thea instead.

"I know it's not as well-paid. But it's highly unlikely anyone will try to kill you," Thea told him.

"They might even thank you," Niath added, grinning.

"And Mistress Hannaford might want a mage, but most likely for healing or household matters," Thea said.

"We'll go tomorrow," Fisk announced, glancing at Fionn. "You can be my reference of good work."

Fionn glared at the mage, clearly wanting to argue, but stayed silent. She turned her shoulder on the mage and back to Thea. "Is there anything else you need just now?"

"Commander Reardon sent for Physician Pallas and Examiner Soter. They should be here soon."

"I'll have someone bring them here. I take it you want the room undisturbed?" Fionn asked. She was perfectly serious, but Thea had an impulse to laugh, glancing around her at the utter destruction. It would be almost impossible to tell if anyone did come into the room. Apart from the narrow, clear path that the staff had swept, everything was chaos.

"It might be wise for you and the staff to stay in the safe rooms," Thea said. "The warriors might be back when we're not here."

"They did seem quite determined," Niath agreed.

Fionn glared at them both, bristling with temper. Perhaps not happy about being told what to do in her own domain. But she cared about the staff, and Thea was confident that they would all be in the safe rooms overnight, letting the warriors have the run of the place if they returned.

The warriors had not got what they wanted this time, Thea knew, a tight knot forming in her stomach. Somehow. But they had seemed to know not only that something valuable was in the house, but also where to look.

Which made her wonder just how they had known. Both what was here, and where to look for it.

And made her wonder the same thing about Edris.

She could not imagine that the Archon had much in common, if anything, with the warriors of a long-dead and almost forgotten goddess. And even though Edris had not said what it was she was looking for, Thea had a cold certainty that it had been that metal safe with its varied contents. A library of materials devoted to Alayla.

Edris had not got what she wanted, either. But unlike the warriors, the Archon had searched the rooms in the house. It was unlikely she would be back. Or so Thea hoped, for the sake of the household staff. Then Thea had to shake her head, and admit to herself that her concern wasn't just for the household staff. Edris had been terrifying, and Thea didn't want to see her again.

Dina's expression when she saw the destruction of the study was one Thea would remember for a very long time to come. For once, the examiner was speechless.

Iason, a man of few words at the best of times, was also silent as he stood next to Dina in the doorway, staring around the room. He then looked back at the hallway, at the other, much smaller, hole and lifted a brow at Thea.

"The only thing the Ageless would say is that we were needed," he said. "Perhaps you can tell us more, Thea?"

"I didn't think you had it in you," Dina added, still staring around.

Thea blushed, aware of Trymian, Reardon and Niath nearby.

"When we got here this morning, the Archon was here," Thea said, adopting Niath's favourite posture, hands behind her back.

"Edris?" Dina's brows shot up again. "What did the old witch want here?"

Thea choked on an inappropriate laugh, and out of the corner of her eye saw Reardon's expression tighten. That sobered her at once. Disparaging the Archon was punishable, according to Accanter laws.

They were not in Accanter, though. And although Reardon was not pleased, he kept quiet.

"She didn't say. She was definitely searching for something. Apparently she's been through Master Hannaford's personal rooms, and this was the last one she was in," Thea said, not looking at the panelled walls. "She made the hole in the wall out there when she left," she added, nodding in the direction Iason had been looking.

"Well, that explains some of it," Dina said, "but are you telling me that Edris also blew up this room?"

"No. The warriors of Alayla did that."

"You have had a very busy day so far, it seems," Iason said. "I take it that the warriors caused the destruction in here?"

"Yes," Thea confirmed, and glanced at Niath. "You'll notice the black fragments. We think that they somehow blew themselves up."

"It fits," Dina said, taking a careful step forward, on the clear path that the household staff had made, and crouching so she could get a better look at the fragments. "Trymian and I have been studying the piece that I have. It's fascinating. And very dangerous. If Trymian and Commander Reardon hadn't managed to stop the warriors blowing up in the mortuary, we'd all be dead." The prospect seemed to fascinate rather than dismay Dina, which did not surprise Thea. Even the idea of her own death was a matter of scientific enquiry for Dina.

"What have you learned so far?" Niath asked. The question was directed at Dina, but the mage was looking between Dina and Trymian.

"The examiner has a formidable scientific mind," Trymian said. "We've learned more in the last day than I believe the Ageless have in all the time we've encountered the warriors."

Dina simply nodded, acknowledging the Ageless' praise. She knew her worth, Thea realised, and didn't need anyone else to tell her.

"The fragments are like glass," Dina said, pointing at one nearby, but not moving to pick it up. "Except they are not. They are extraordinarily strong, very sharp, and not quite solid."

Thea's brows lifted. She was sure that Dina had meant something significant by that description, but it had only confused Thea. And, from the expressions on Niath and Reardon's faces, she was not the only one.

"Glass is made by super-heating sand," Trymian said. It was a well-known fact, but Thea sensed there was more to come. "What seems to have happened with the warriors is that they super-heated their own bodies, turning them into these fragments."

"But glass is solid and still when you look at it under a lens," Dina continued, straightening from her crouch. "This stuff isn't. It is in a constant state of movement."

"And extremely dangerous," Trymian added. "If left alone, it will stay still, but if approached, it will react."

Thea looked across the room, at the clear path the house's staff had created. "Does it only react to living things? The staff here used brushes to make the path."

"We think so," Dina said, nodding.

"I see you also have a sharp mind, Investigator March," Trymian said.

Thea's face heated up and she ducked her eyes away, uncomfortable with the praise. "Did you learn anything more from the fragment or the ash?" she asked Dina.

"Not much," Dina said, nose wrinkling. "The ash is more like normal human remains. Nothing particularly special about it."

"The fragments contain some magical properties," Trymian added, "but that seems to be destroyed when they are reduced to ash."

"Fascinating," Niath said, eyes bright. "Commander Reardon suggested that you might teach me the holding spell to contain the fragments?"

"I think that would be wise," Trymian said, perfectly serious. "It seems the warriors are making their presence felt again, and it would be useful to have someone else with the skill to deal with them. Come, I think I saw some more fragments outside. It will be safer if we practice there."

Thea watched, more than a little amused, as Niath followed Trymian outside, almost tripping on the Ageless scholar's heels in his haste to keep up with him.

"The warriors might come back?" Dina asked, brows lifting, turning to Thea.

"It seems likely," Thea said. "We think they were looking for something in this room. And didn't find it. They don't seem the type to just give up."

"Very true," Dina said, looking around the room with more interest. "I wonder what it was they were after?"

Thea held herself still, not looking at Reardon. Or the book case.

"We don't know," Reardon said, surprising her. "Or what the Archon was looking for earlier, either."

"Looking for the same thing?" Dina asked.

"Possibly," Reardon said, face tight.

He knew something, Thea realised. Whether it was something about what the Archon had been looking for, or something else, she couldn't tell. But he had not told them everything. Then again, neither she nor Niath had told him everything, either.

She had an impulse to tell Reardon what she and Niath had found. It died quickly. If she told him, he would doubtless feel obligated to bring the papers to the Citadel, and then she would never see the information again.

If the papers were a library for Alayla's followers, they may have used that information to create the goddess herself. The warriors of Alayla clearly had access to potent and dangerous magic, including *fyr na dathan* which was one of the few things that could harm one of the Ageless. There might be other, equally powerful, spells in the papers and Thea did not trust what the Archon and the Ageless would do with that information. If the Ageless thought that the warriors were a threat, and if they believed that people in the city were helping them, or giving shelter to them, then the Ageless would not care who they hurt or killed pursuing the warriors.

Edris had hurt Fionn with a casual violence that still chilled Thea, giving her a close-up reminder of just how powerful the Ageless were. If Fisk had not been in the building, Fionn would most likely have died. Edris would not have cared. Thea could all-too-easily imagine Edris taking that anger out on the city's population. The Archon had punched through a wall with a casual blow. Truly angry, she could level the entire city.

Chapter Nineteen

Thea lost track of Niath, Reardon and Trymian during the rest of the daylight hours. She caught glimpses of them outside now and then and from time to time a ripple of Niath's magic would wash over her, distracting her from Iason and Dina's work.

With no bodies to inspect, and the fragments posing a real danger to everyone, there wasn't much that the examiner and physician could do, but they took the opportunity of making a study of the scene, trying to trace the origin of the explosions and gauge the force that had been generated.

They were used to working together, firing questions and theories at each other in scientific shorthand that Thea barely understood. Still, it was fascinating. And she did not have anywhere else to be just now. With the threat of the warriors, she was not willing to travel back to the city on her own, and suspected the others would not want to do so, either. So she was there until the others were ready to leave.

Her mind kept wanting to turn back to the conversation at her mother's house, to the realisation that a lot of the things she had believed to be true might now need to be questioned. She did not need to be as afraid of the Ageless as she had been. They were not necessarily the heartless, cold monsters her mother had taught her.

And she did not want to think about that. Her mother's instinct had been to protect her surviving child. Thea understood that, but it still hurt. She and her mother had only had each other for a long, long time.

She dragged her thoughts away and back to the investigation. Going over what she knew and didn't know about the two deaths and the possibility of a magic-wielding assassin was useful, at least.

Two Master Merchants, killed in places where they should have been safe, both of them behind doors locked from the inside. Both of them stabbed from the front, with no signs that they had resisted their attacker or tried to defend themselves.

Thea found it hard to believe that there were two such assassins operating in Accanter. So it was likely the same killer. And likely that there was a common motive, even if she did not understand it yet.

It might be the trickster that she and Niath had met when they had last worked together. It had appeared as a weak old man, close to death, but it could take on any form it wanted. Thea shook her head slightly. She wasn't ready to dismiss the idea, not yet, even if she didn't believe it fit with what little she knew of tricksters. They liked to stay in the shadows and manipulate people. Directly confronting and killing someone did not seem like something a trickster would do.

With the papers that Thea and Niath had uncovered, and the arrival of the warriors, it looked as if there was a connection of some sorts to the Hand of the goddess, and the warriors of Alayla. Warriors who possessed magic. It was more than possible that the warriors knew spells that would allow them to sneak past perimeter defences and kill a man without being seen or heard.

"What's wrong?"

Dina's voice broke through Thea's tangled thoughts. She started, realising that both Iason and Dina were staring at her, and the room was darkening as daylight faded.

"I'm sorry. I was just thinking about the investigation," Thea said.

"That explains the frown," Dina said, and tipped her head towards the door. "Fionn has had a meal prepared, and rooms if we want to stay overnight."

"We can talk about the case over a meal," Iason suggested. "And I can update you on Master Paulin's examination."

With a shock, Thea realised that Master Paulin's death had only occurred the day before. A lot had happened since then. And she had not even thought to ask Iason whether he had found time to examine the dead.

"Oh? You found something interesting?" Thea asked.

"Food first," Dina said firmly, waving her hands to usher both of them out of the room.

The house's dining room was mercifully free of shattered windows and walls. The long table had been set with perhaps a dozen places, the heavy sideboard laden with dishes that gave off tantalising scents as Thea, Dina and Iason came into the room.

Fionn was there, giving the room a quick look-over, nodding her satisfaction at the closed curtains, the fire burning low in the grate and candles set along the length of the table.

"I've told the Ageless that there's food here for them, and the mages, too," she said, taking a step towards the door. She hesitated. "We'd welcome some company overnight," she said, not meeting Thea's eyes.

"I think it's too late to travel back anyway," Thea said. "And we've plenty we can do here." Not just waiting to see if the warriors of Alayla returned, to keep searching.

Fionn relaxed a bit, tension easing from her shoulders. "Most of the staff are in the safe rooms. But we're keeping an eye on the bells, so ring if you need anything else."

The steward left the room, the door closing quietly behind her. Dina was already piling a plate high with food, pausing at Iason's sideways glance.

"What? I'm starving. I've been in the workroom most of the last two days," the examiner said, and took a place at the table.

Thea picked up a plate of her own, following Iason down the length of the sideboard and discovering that she, too, was truly hungry.

When the three of them were settled, she lifted a brow at Iason. "You found something on Master Paulin?" she asked.

"I did." Iason reached into a pocket and held out a familiar-looking key on a chain. "He was wearing this under his clothes."

"Another key?" Thea took the object and turned it over in her hand. It was a similar design to the one that Master Hannaford had carried. "I wonder what this one opens," she said, tucking it into a pocket. Whoever had designed the Watch's uniforms had somehow known that plenty of pockets would be useful. It had taken Thea some time as a new recruit to find them all.

"Sounds like you found something," Dina said, eyes sharp as she stared at Thea across the table.

"Niath and I did, yes," Thea said, hesitating.

"And you haven't told the others," Dina concluded, mischief sparking across her face. "Well done. Let us know if we can help."

"I will. Thank you," Thea said, meaning it. Dina and Iason would not tell a soul, she was quite sure.

Before they could have any more conversation, the door opened and Niath, Trymian, Reardon and Lucan came in, all looking a little weary.

"We've summoned another wing to watch the skies overnight," Reardon said as he sat down at the table, plate piled with food. "Lucan's wing will patrol the grounds."

Thea was glad she was not required to say anything at that point, not sure how she felt about being surrounded by Ageless both in the air and on the ground. It also made her wonder how she was going to get back into the study and retrieve the contents of the metal safe. With the building compromised, she didn't want to leave such potentially dangerous materials here.

If she was quiet, it was not noticed. Niath might be tired, but he was also delighted to have Trymian sitting near him, the two of them keeping the conversation going and never seeming to run out of things to talk about.

Drinking her tea at the end of the meal, Thea's chest constricted, the lively discussion between mage and Ageless reminding her of the discussions that had taken place in her home, so many years before, on Trymian's rare visits.

It was something of a relief when the group parted ways a little later on, Lucan and Reardon heading outside on patrol, Trymian saying he would check on the household staff. Dina and Iason were going to the rooms that had been made up for them.

Thea hesitated as the others left, Niath staying with her.

"Are you sure you're alright?" Niath asked, surprising her. "It's none of my business, but you don't seem yourself."

Thea was about to lie, to say she was fine, but the words wouldn't come. He had seen her at her worst not once but twice, first when they had taken the enclosed platform to reach the Citadel and then when her wings had appeared. He had not shied away from her, and did not seem to think less of her for the weakness she had shown. She did not want to lie to him. Not Niath. She shook her head, throat tight. "You asked me once why I hate the Ageless so much."

"I remember," he said.

"It's because my mother taught me to fear them, to keep me safe. Or so I've always believed. And now it seems she didn't tell me the truth. Not entirely," Thea said, voice too high and brittle. "I'm sorry. I know it must seem silly."

"No," Niath said, and shook his head. His mouth lifted in the hint of a smile, although there was no humour in it. "It's hard, learning that the people you trust and love the most haven't been truthful."

There was a story behind that, Thea sensed. But now was not the time or the place to ask. "So, I am fine, really. It's just been a shock. And I haven't had any time to think it through," she said. No time to think about what her life might be like with the lies stripped out. If she didn't have to be so afraid of the Ageless. If she didn't have to be afraid, then she could make her own decisions about her future.

"I realise that we have not known each other long," Niath said, "but I hope you will count me as a friend, if you need one."

Thea nodded, not trusting her voice. Friends were rare, and treasured, things in her life.

"I think we all need some rest. But before then, if you will trust me with the key, I can get the papers," Niath offered.

"Trust you? Of course," Thea said, blinking. She pulled out Master Hannaford's key. "But how-" she broke off her words, shaking her head. Niath was hiandar. He could make himself invisible if he needed to.

"I can take you with me, but it will be a bit of a strain," Niath said, mouth twisting. "I haven't used this much magic in a single day for a long time."

"No, it's alright. I could really do with some rest," Thea said, and hesitated again. "How will you ..." She closed her mouth before she could finish the words, not sure if she had been about to insult Niath's resourcefulness. The papers were too bulky to be hidden in even the mage's robes, but he doubtless had other means of concealment.

"I'll give the papers to Sam. He'll make sure they're safe on the spare horses tomorrow," Niath said. It was a sensible and practical arrangement. No magic involved.

"And what then? We need somewhere to examine them," Thea said, the answer coming to her even as she spoke. She was far more worn out than she had realised, if her mind was this sluggish. "Mort. I'm sure he has somewhere we could keep the papers."

Niath's eyes gleamed with mischief. "I'm sure he does. And his shop is well defended, too."

Thea was going to say something, but a huge yawn took over her entire being. "Sorry," she said, face hot.

"It's been a long day. I'll see you in the morning."

"Good night, Niath. Good luck."

"Luck?" Niath repeated, mischief across his face before he faded from sight in front of her eyes. "Good night, Thea," he said, his voice coming from somewhere near the door.

Chapter Twenty

There had been no disturbance during the night, and the morning brought no further surprises. The additional wing of Ageless, who had kept watch overnight, seemed disappointed that they had not had a chance to try their skills against the warriors of Alayla.

Reardon would make arrangements for Ageless to keep watch over the house, he told Fionn, but he thought it was unlikely that the warriors would be back.

From the tight expression on Fionn's face and the shadows under her eyes, Thea suspected it would be a long time before the steward felt safe in the house again.

But they could not stay forever and left in the early morning, the horses fresh from their rest. The Ageless took to the skies, leaving the rest of the party on the ground.

Even with a larger group, the journey seemed far quicker than the previous ones. Dina and Iason were each in talkative moods, sharing old tales and legends of the land they were riding through, making Thea very glad they were travelling in daylight.

They parted ways when they reached Middlefield. Niath and Sam were going to take the horses back to his house. Dina and Iason were headed back to their offices. And Thea needed to make a report to Ware and Sutter.

Niath nodded to Thea when she met his eyes. They had not managed any private conversation, but she was sure he had managed to retrieve the papers, and somehow that nod told Thea that he would take the papers to Mort as soon as he could.

Which left her back on duty, with obligations to fulfil.

She didn't have far to walk to the station, but was glad of the little bit of exercise to ease stiff muscles.

The station was bustling with activity when Thea arrived, weary from a disturbed night and journey back to the city.

The main room was full of grim-faced Watchmen and women, with Sutter in the midst of it, handing out orders. No one had any attention to spare for her as she paused in the entrance.

"What's wrong?" she asked Watchman Hobbs at the front desk. If anyone would know, it was Algar Hobbs. There were several of the Hobbs family across the Watch, all of them honest and hardworking. And if Watchman Hobbs' normal genial manner had cooled a bit around Thea, after she had turned her former Sergeant in for his corruption, she did not blame him. He still did his job, and treated her with perfect politeness.

"Kendrick's loose." Watchman Hobbs wasn't looking at her, but at the gathered Watchmen and women listening to Sutter. He looked as if he wanted to join them, except Thea could not remember Hobbs ever leaving his post at the front desk.

Thea silently repeated his words, shock running through her. That should be impossible. Except that Algar Hobbs was as down-to-earth a person as she had ever met, and not inclined to make things up. "Escaped?" Thea asked, voice faint.

"Ay. Managed to get off the black ship somehow. It wasn't docked here, but he might be headed back here."

"I've never heard of such a thing," she said, still in that faint voice.

"Ay," Hobbs said again, shaking his head. "No one has. The Ageless are all aflutter trying to work out how he did it."

"I can imagine," Thea said. All too easily. The black ships belonged to the Archon and were used for Ageless business, and nothing else. They were the ultimate punishment, reserved for the worst and most hardened criminals, and supposed to be escape-proof. She had been close to one of the ships only once before, her skin still crawling at the memory. The overseers of the ships were harsh in their treatment of the prisoners, using brute force and magic. One of the prisoners she had met had chosen death rather than return to the black ship.

When the Ageless had taken Kendrick to the black ships, he had been deliberately separated from anyone he might have known. At the time, it had seemed overly cautious to Thea because, apart from death, no one escaped a black ship.

It seemed, though, that the Ageless had not been careful enough and they had all underestimated Kendrick's abilities. Somehow, the former Master Merchant, who had kept his own personal army within the city limits, had managed to escape his captivity.

Thea's skin prickled. He would be coming here. She was quite certain. Accanter was where he had been born, where he had enjoyed power and influence. Even disgraced, he would still have access to wealth and allies within the city.

Like the merchants' guild. Who had petitioned Ware for his release already.

She looked into the main room, where members of the Watch were grouping into fours and leaving under Sutter's orders. There was a map of the district pinned to the wall, sectioned off with different coloured ribbon. A search, Thea guessed, to see if Kendrick had reached the city already.

Sutter came out of the main room, heading for the stairs, frowning, and checked in his stride as he saw her.

"Thea. I'm sorry, I didn't see you there. Were you looking for me or Ware?"

"Both, if possible," she answered.

"Come on up," Sutter said, and headed up the stairs.

The Watch Captain's door was closed, which was a rare sight, but Sutter knocked once, then opened the door a fraction.

"Thea's here," he said into the room.

"Good." Ware's voice answered, although he sounded exhausted.

"Come on," Sutter said, and went into the room.

Thea followed and discovered that Ware was alone in the room. She had half-expected to find angry merchants berating him.

He looked as worn out as he had sounded, deep lines etched around his mouth, shadows under his eyes. He was sitting behind a desk piled high with papers, a plate with a few crumbs resting on one of the higher piles.

"Did you hear about Kendrick?" Ware asked, sitting back in his chair as she and Sutter took seats opposite his desk, with a view between the piles of paper.

"Watchman Hobbs told me he'd escaped the black ship," Thea said, and shook her head. "If it hadn't been him telling me, I'm not sure I would have believed it."

"I know what you mean," Ware said, rubbing his false eye. "I've had merchants and lawyers and bankers and Ageless and Ageless knows who else in here since the news broke, all demanding that I find Kendrick, and a few of them wondering why we didn't kill him when we had the chance."

Ware's voice was rough. Lack of sleep, and something else. Frustration. Anger. Or so she thought.

"We don't kill people," Thea said. "Or, at least, we try not to," she amended, remembering the several dead bodies she had left in her wake.

"So I've reminded them. And also told the merchants that a few days ago they were demanding that he be released." Ware blew out a breath and focused on Thea. "But I don't imagine you came here to talk about Kendrick."

"No, sir, that's true. I didn't know about him until I came into the building." Thea hesitated, wondering where to begin. There was a lot she needed to tell them both.

"You went back to Hannaford's place yesterday, didn't you? The Summer House. Learn anything?" Ware asked.

"Quite a few things, actually," Thea said, and glanced across to make sure the door was closed. Assured of that, she gave Ware and Sutter what she had intended to be a brief report of the day before, from discovering Edris in the study to discovering the papers hidden behind the wall, to the warriors' attack.

Sutter and Ware interrupted with dozens of questions, Ware almost losing his voice until Sutter went to the door and yelled for one of the junior Watchmen to get them some lunch.

Thea had never heard Sutter raise his voice before, and would wager that most of the people in the station hadn't, either.

Lunch turned up within moments. Hearty pies from the Harrow bakery and huge mugs of tea, steam curling into the air.

Thea wasn't quite ready for lunch, but she sensed that Ware wouldn't eat if she refused, so she relented. Besides, she wasn't sure when she'd get to eat next.

Between mouthfuls of the bakery's fabulous pies, she answered Ware and Sutter's continued questions.

"So, where are the papers now?" Ware wanted to know, finishing the last of his tea.

Thea hesitated, glancing at Sutter, not sure if he was aware of Ware's involvement in the other group.

"Sutter knows about Mort and the others," Ware said, lips twitching. "It is very difficult to keep anything secret from him for long, you'll find."

"Thank you, sir," Sutter said modestly. "So, you've got the group involved?" he asked Thea.

"Yes. Niath has taken the papers to Mort. There's a lot of information there, and we need some help deciphering them," Thea said. "Odilia is a good mage, but I think this may be beyond her knowledge. I'm going to meet Niath at sundown, when the shop closes."

"Good. Keep us informed," Ware said.

"Do you think the Archon was looking for those papers?" Sutter asked.

"I've been wondering that myself," Thea answered. "Honestly, I don't know. I thought so for a while, but I can't work out how the Archon would have known the papers were there, or why she would be so interested in papers about Alayla. She thinks that the goddess is dead, and didn't seem worried about her." Thea frowned, remembering the Archon's mutterings and her apparent confusion about whose house she was in even as she tore apart the study in her search.

Thea realised that some of her inner doubts must have shown on her face as Ware and Sutter were both looking at her with raised brows.

"I don't know how-" she began, then blew out a breath. "Sorry. It's just that the Archon didn't seem quite herself," she said. There. That was fairly neutral. Even if Thea had no idea what the Archon was normally like.

Ware and Sutter exchanged glances.

"We've never had the pleasure of meeting her," Ware said, speaking slowly, as if he was choosing his words with care, "but there has been some talk about her not quite being herself lately."

Thea was glad she was sitting down. Speaking ill of the Archon was considered a crime in the eyes of the Ageless. And even in the privacy and safety of this office, that was the most that Ware was prepared to say.

She could not help remembering the comments made by members of the Hand of the goddess about Edris being half-crazed. At the time, she had just dismissed the things they had said. The Hand had no love for the Ageless. But now she wondered.

"Who else knows about the papers?" Ware asked, turning the subject.

Thea tried to hide her relief. The papers might relate to a long-dead goddess, but they were a safer subject than the Archon's health.

"Dina and Iason know that we found something, but not what we found. Apart from that, Niath's groom, Sam, probably guessed we were carrying something back with us, but not what it was. And we didn't tell anyone else," Thea answered.

"Good. Let's keep it that way. The Archon might not think that these warriors of Alayla are dangerous, but I think she's wrong," Ware said, expression grim.

"Sir," Thea acknowledged. "I'm not sure how long we'll be able to keep the papers hidden. The Ageless who were there knew that the warriors were looking for something. And the Archon was there, too. But I just thought - still think - that we need to keep them contained as long as possible. Until we understand what's there." Commander Reardon would not be happy, she knew. And if the Archon had been looking for the papers about Alayla, Edris would be furious that they had been within her grasp. Problems for another day, Thea told herself. Once they knew what the papers contained and just how dangerous they were.

"Agreed," Ware said, without hesitation.

"What's next on your list?" Sutter asked.

"Well, I want to go back to Master Paulin's office and see if there's anything there that will fit the key. If that doesn't work, I'll need to try his home," Thea said. "And we haven't questioned the staff at the guild yet. I'll try to get to that tomorrow," she said, shaking her head slightly. "But I'm not expecting much. None of the staff at the Summer House had heard or seen anything unusual before Master Hannaford's death." She hesitated, and then went on, "And I want to speak to Master Merchant Gadsden again, once Mort and Niath have had time to look over the papers we found. It looks like Master Gadsden is involved with the Hand as well. He might be a target. Or he might know something that will help us find the killer."

"We made it clear that the other merchants should be careful," Sutter told her.

"They weren't happy," Ware added, with a certain sour satisfaction. "They wanted protection from the Watch. I told them we don't do that. I think Cedd and Gordie might have asked Odilia for some help. No idea what Master Gadsden has arranged."

Thea nodded, wondering how Odilia felt about having her brothers come and ask her for help and protection after they had been so rude to her only a handful of days before.

"Do we think that the killer is finished?" Sutter asked.

"I don't know," Thea answered, hands curling into fists for a moment. "I can't figure out what the motive is. Not yet. I mean, we think that both Paulin and Hannaford were somehow involved with the Hand. But I'm not sure how that would lead to their deaths."

Ware rubbed his false eye again. "Damned meddlers. Why in the world the merchants are involved with the Hand, I can't figure out."

"What do you mean, sir?" Thea asked, intrigued. It wasn't something she had considered before.

"They pretty much have their own way," Ware said, sitting back in his chair and turning to glare out the window. "Yes, they pay taxes, but they would do that anywhere."

Thea's brows lifted as she puzzled that through. "You mean that the merchants aren't really that affected by the Ageless, so there's not really a strong reason for them to be involved with the Hand. Because the Hand seems to be about opposing the Ageless. Huh." She sat back in her chair in turn, and stared at nothing while she turned that over in her mind. "I had not thought of that before."

"That's because you don't need to get involved in politics," Ware told her, sour smile pulling his mouth, "while my whole day is sometimes taken up with them."

"I'm sorry," Thea said automatically. It was an instinctive response. But she meant it.

Ware's face lifted into a smile that chased some of the tiredness away. "It's part of the job."

Before he could say anything more, the door opened, with no knock preceding it, and Reardon stepped into the room.

"I hear Kendrick has escaped from a black ship. The Citadel is concerned," the Ageless Commander announced. "I'm here to help you find him."

Chapter Twenty-One

Thea left Ware and Sutter to deal with Reardon's offer of assistance. Kendrick might be a former Master Merchant, and once have had access to power, but he had been stripped of his borrowed magic along with his position as Master Merchant, and he was now simply a cunning, determined human and being hunted by the Ageless. She couldn't do anything about the disgraced merchant. Even though she itched to join in the search, to make sure Kendrick was caught as soon as possible. Half the city was looking for him. And there were other things needing her attention. Away from the Ageless.

She made her way towards the merchants' guild, not far from Middlefield Watch Station.

The afternoon passed in a blur and she came into focus standing outside Mort's shop in the middle of Brightfield. She blinked. It felt like no time at all since she had been in Ware's office, and yet the sun was setting overhead.

"Thea. Are you alright?"

Niath's voice came from somewhere behind her. She started. She had not realised anyone was nearby. That was bad.

Even worse, when she turned around, she found that Niath had company. Trymian was standing next to him, both of them frowning at her.

"Good evening," she said, gathering her wits and her manners.

"Are you alright, Investigator March?" Trymian asked.

The echo of Niath's question made her shiver.

"I don't know," she said honestly. "Just tired, I think." She frowned, looking around. "I am not sure how I got here, though."

"May I?" Niath asked, and held out his hand. She put hers into it without hesitation, remembering another time when she had done this.

"You think I met the trickster?" she asked Niath. A creature who had pretended to be one of Kendrick's captives, giving Thea some useful information before vanishing. She hadn't been able to learn much about the creatures, but they were not known for their kindness.

"No," he said, his magic curling over her. "There's no trace of him, and you are definitely yourself. But ... have you encountered any herbalists today? Has anyone given you something to drink?"

"I don't think so," she said, blinking. "I mean, it's possible," she added, trying to remember who she had seen and spoken to that afternoon. Her last clear memory was leaving Ware's office. After that, she was not sure.

"I think you've been given a potion of some kind," Niath said. "It's not harmful, but you're not quite yourself."

"I feel fine now," Thea protested, even though it was not quite true. She felt heavy and uncoordinated, weary to her bones. "And we should go inside before we draw too much attention," she added, moving away from the pair.

The door opened as she approached and Mort appeared, face breaking into a wide, welcoming smile. She had a moment of displacement, seeing Trymian's features on the younger man. The two looked so similar, even though she knew they were quite different people.

"Investigator March, it's so good to see you again. Do come in." He stepped aside for Thea to pass, nodding greetings to Niath and Trymian.

When they were all inside, Mort closed and locked the door behind them, turning the shop sign to "closed". He waved a hand towards the back of the building. "I have the papers in the back room."

"Are they protected?" Trymian asked, a hint of disapproval in his voice.

Mort rolled his eyes and winked at Thea. "If you did not already know that Trymian is my esteemed father, you surely must have guessed now. Only parents can be so critical and get away with it," he said. He was smiling, though, as he turned back to Trymian. "Yes, the papers are protected. Niath put spells around them earlier, and you yourself taught me how to ward buildings."

"Very well," Trymian said, a hint of a smile on his own face. Not offended by his son's prickly reply. Instead, it sounded like an exchange they had had many times before over many years. Well-worn and familiar to them both.

"My father was one of the founders of this group," Mort confided to Thea as he led them through the shop. "His knowledge is a valuable resource."

"I'm so glad to be useful," Trymian said in a dry tone, belied by the humour dancing in his eyes.

"It's a good reason to keep you around," Mort answered back, provoking a laugh out of Thea, which she tried to turn into an unconvincing cough. She had often thought that Trymian would be a wonderful father, and it seemed that she was right.

Mort had set up a screen to shield the back room from view of anyone in the shop. The shelves of writing materials that Thea had seen before had been joined by a series of writing stands, with papers laid on each, along with fresh parchment and pens. Her fingers itched to touch the parchment. It looked far finer than anything she had used in her life before. Far too good for simple note-taking. But she still wanted to touch it all the same.

"Did you hear that Kendrick has escaped?" she asked Niath, in an effort to drag her attention away from the parchment.

"Yes," Niath said, face as grim as she had ever seen it. "Half the Citadel is looking for him. The Ageless are trying to keep it quiet, but it's only a matter of time before word spreads."

"This is the merchant that escaped from a black ship?" Trymian asked, brows lifting. "I did not know such a thing was possible."

"No," Thea agreed.

"I'll keep an eye out as well," Mort said, shaking his head, his normal cheerful manner subdued. "It was a truly awful business, what he did. The sooner he is back in chains, the better."

Thea agreed, and from the expressions on Niath and Trymian's faces, they were of the same mind.

"What have you learned so far?" Thea asked, not wanting to think about the escaped convict anymore, looking around the room and then turning back to the others.

"Not much," Niath said, with a grimace.

Not much still took a while to tell. Niath and Mort had made an initial review of the documents and books and made an inventory of them. But they had not made a detailed study, waiting for Trymian, who had far greater knowledge of language and spells than the other two.

What they had learned, though, was confirmation of what Thea had suspected. The papers were, in effect, a library of knowledge for the followers of Alayla. Incantations for the goddess. Spells in her name. Old, long-forgotten magic. A lot of the spells and magic were vicious things, Niath said. She was the goddess of war and destruction, after all.

And then there were the other spells, contained in the old book that Niath had picked up. Spells which might explain how the false goddess had been created.

Spells which required blood to power them. Thea could not help remembering the scar on Bordan Hannaford's arm and the cuts on Mage Waters. Blood magic. Just the thought of it made her skin crawl. But it backed up what Waters had said, in his mad state. The spells would have needed someone skilled in magic to perform them, Niath said. It was not possible to just read the spells and carry them out. He and Trymian offered to give her an explanation as to why. She declined.

By the time Niath and Mort had finished their summary, Thea's head was spinning. Suspecting was one thing, but the confirmation was something else. Something far more dangerous.

And she could not help wondering why a Master Merchant, the Citadel's most prominent mage and his apprentice had worked together to bring forth a copy of a long-dead goddess. Waters had been at the pinnacle of what any human mage could achieve. His apprentice only one step removed from that exalted position. And Master Merchants were powerful in their own right, answering to no one but the Ageless.

Then there was also the question of whether the warriors of Alayla were affiliated with the Hand, or how the warriors might feel about their goddess supposedly being brought back to life. With the powerful magic that the warriors commanded, it seemed to Thea that they could have recreated their goddess at any time. And had chosen not to, perhaps out of respect for her memory.

"The warriors have been in the city before now," she said, into a small break in conversation. "If they are looking for the papers, they will not hesitate to come here."

"They won't find them," Niath said, with absolute confidence.

Thea looked between him, Mort, and Trymian, and trusted their assurance. If anyone could hide items from the warriors, it was them. It left her free to investigate the seemingly impossible murders, which she felt no closer to solving now than when she had first seen Bordan Hannaford's body.

Chapter Twenty-Two

She left Mort's shop not long after she had arrived. With no knowledge of magic or languages to contribute, there was little for her to do. Niath and Trymian would most likely work through the night, the pair of them barely able to contain their excitement at the mysteries waiting for them in the papers.

Thea refused an escort, not wanting to pull them away from their work. As she left the shop and began making her way home, she found she could barely keep her eyes open, her body heavy and uncooperative. It was an almost impossible effort to get home, and she stumbled more than once, heat rising in her face. She must have looked as if she was drunk, rather than so tired she wanted nothing more than to just lie down and sleep.

Somehow she made it home and up to her own bed, asleep before her head hit the pillow, only to pass a restless night with vague, menacing dreams of shadowy figures approaching her and an all-too familiar disgraced merchant sneering at her from too short a distance away. She had no idea why Kendrick had invaded her dreams, but he was not welcome.

Waking in the morning took what seemed like forever, even with Gilbert pawing at her face and shoulder, demanding to be petted before she let him out of her bedroom window. She stayed by the window for a while, the cool morning air waking her up a little more. Enough to get dressed, at least.

Settled at the kitchen table, she made her way through several mugs of tea and twice as much food as she would normally eat, only then beginning to feel more like herself.

As she woke up, she realised that she had not yet visited the merchants' guild. She had meant to go the day before, but could not remember going. When she tried to remember what she had done the afternoon before, a headache bloomed behind her eyes. Checking her notebook revealed no further notes or information, and made the headache bad enough that she took some of her mother's foul-tasting painkiller, trying not to think about the afternoon before or the fact that there were several hours of her day that she just could not remember. That had never happened to her before.

Still feeling tired, and also worried, with the headache finally fading, she set off for the guild again.

"Good morning, Investigator March."

She jumped, clamping her jaw shut against an undignified squeal. She was annoyed with herself for being taken by surprise for the second time in less than a day.

Turning, she found Matthew Shand standing in the shadows between two buildings, with someone standing a little distance behind him.

"Master Shand. Good morning to you. Is there anything wrong?" she asked. She could not think why he was seeking her out, let alone so early in the day.

Matthew was the head of the largest night kind clan in the city, and his success as a leader could be measured by the fact that very few humans knew that there was a night kind clan in the city, and by the size of his clan. They occupied a self-contained part of Brightfield, growing their own produce and generally keeping to themselves.

"We fear that there is something badly wrong, yes," Matthew said. "This is Iva. She is newly arrived in the city." He stepped aside to let the person behind him step forward, closer to the light.

A woman, a little shorter than Matthew, with close-cropped fiercely red hair and dark, penetrating eyes in an angular face. She was leanly built, wearing close-fitting clothing and looked like a warrior, although she was not openly carrying any weapons. Not in this city, where bladed weapons were banned.

And she was night kind, Thea realised. It was very subtle, but something in the way that she moved, and stared back at Thea, betrayed her nature.

"I know about Kendrick's escape," Thea said, assuming that was what Matthew had referred to.

"Yes. Word is spreading," Matthew said, face tight, "but that's not why we are here."

"No?" Thea prompted.

"You do not have your shadow with you this morning," Matthew commented.

"Not today, no," Thea said. Matthew had been one of the first people to call Niath her shadow. She still wasn't entirely sure what it meant. Niath had given her an explanation, and yet she was sure he had been holding some information back. Still, she was not about to ask Matthew about something better asked of Niath.

"We will come with you," Iva said. She had a deep voice, with an accent that Thea could not place. Not from here, anyway.

"But you don't know where I'm going," Thea said, blinking.

"You're going to the merchants' guild, because you believe you forgot to go there yesterday," Matthew said.

"What?" Thea stared at him, trails of ice running across her skin, wondering how he knew and just what had happened in those missing hours. She had meant to go to the guild. But she could not remember being there, or asking any of the questions she had, or examining Master Paulin's office to find the home for the key in her pocket.

"I told you," Iva said to Matthew, no satisfaction in her voice.

"May we come with you?" Matthew asked Thea.

She hesitated. Although Matthew Shand had been helpful before, he was not a member of the Watch. And she wasn't sure how the merchants would feel about him in their building. They had seemed protective of their space.

"I promise, we will not impede your investigation," Matthew said, "but we have business at the guild, too."

"I should be glad of the company," Thea said, realising it was true. She might have grown up with very few people to talk to, but she had become used to having more company these days, and she was missing Niath's presence. Besides, she had learned that Matthew Shand did and said nothing without a purpose. She wanted to know what Matthew and Iva believed was wrong, and had a feeling she would soon find out.

The streets around the merchants' guild were busier than normal for the time of day, and hearing the odd snippet of conversation, Thea quickly understood why. News of Kendrick's escape had spread. She heard a few rumours, her sharper hearing picking up words from the crowd. Kendrick had been seen at the docks. In a tavern nearby. On the road to the Citadel. In a marketplace.

All the bits of information were exchanged in hushed voices, the people with their heads together, seemingly partly horrified and partly thrilled by the gossip. Kendrick had not been popular with the common folk in the city, it seemed, and they were not happy to have him back.

She exchanged glances with Matthew, knowing that his hearing was at least as good as hers. He nodded, expression unreadable. He had heard. She wondered which, if any, of the rumours were true, and how much time and energy the Watch were having to spend chasing down phantom sightings of the disgraced merchant.

Past the crowds of people, the merchants' guild was exactly as she remembered it from her first visit with Niath. She had an odd moment of displacement, setting her foot on the first step up to the front door, as if a memory was trying to surface. A vague impression of being here alone, climbing these steps, with the afternoon sun at her back. The headache she had endured earlier resurfaced and the brief memory faded, the pain disappearing along with it.

Matthew and Iva had not answered her questions on the way here, so she still did not know what they were here for, or what was wrong. But she trusted Matthew enough that he meant her, and the city, no harm. He had earned that much.

The clerk behind the desk in the reception hall looked up from his papers, face tightening into an expression of clear distaste. Thea's brows rose. Dislike of non-humans was common among the human population, even if most humans couldn't tell the other races apart. But both Iva and Matthew did an excellent job of holding their human *aspects*. That first, brief glance should not have been enough to tell an ordinary human what they were.

Then Thea realised that the distaste had been directed at her, not the night kind, and her brows rose again. She did not remember doing anything to offend the clerk. Or perhaps the clerk had picked up the Master Merchants' disdain for the Watch.

"Good morning," Thea said, keeping her voice pleasant. There was no point in being rude. "I'd like to see Master Paulin's office, please."

"Haven't you asked enough questions?" the clerk asked, voice sharp.

"Unfortunately not," Thea answered. "I can show myself up," she added, taking a step past the desk.

"Not with them," the clerk added, as Matthew and Iva moved with her.

"They are assisting me," Thea said. It was close enough to the truth that it didn't feel like a lie on her tongue. "I am sure that the guild wants the deaths of Master Hannaford and Master Paulin solved as quickly as possible."

The clerk's face pinched again. He looked like he was trying to find a good argument, and failing. Thea kept moving, wondering how long it would take the clerk to alert the rest of the guild that they had unwanted visitors.

She didn't see anyone else until they reached the floor where Master Paulin's office was. Turning away from the stairs, she saw a newly familiar figure walking along the corridor towards them. The other clerk, the one who had been there on her first visit to the building. Thea had only the barest impression of her as neatly presented and efficient.

Thea opened her mouth, about to say good morning.

"That's her," Iva said from just behind her shoulder.

The clerk ahead of them froze, staring past Thea to the two night kind, and her face shifted, losing some of its human *aspect*. Another night kind, Thea realised, startled. She had not taken the woman for anything other than human.

Before she could react or say anything, Iva shoved past her, pushing Thea hard enough that she stumbled against the wall, Matthew following his companion.

The clerk dropped the papers she was carrying and drew a blade out of her robes. She stabbed forward, trying to attack Iva.

Iva jumped, twisting in the air so that her feet landed on the wall, pushing off and barrelling into the clerk. The clerk's blade clattered to the ground, Iva wrestling with her, Matthew trying to grab the clerk's feet.

"Thea, your rope. Now," Matthew said over his shoulder. His voice was deeper, carrying more than a hint of his other nature.

Shocked out of her stillness, Thea reached for the Watch rope at her waist. As she did so, the clerk somehow wriggled out from under the two night kind, and rushed forward along the corridor, grabbing up her blade as she did so, heading for Thea. Her face had completely shifted to her other *aspect*. Not just night kind, but the same as Matthew Shand. Fiandar. Who were supposedly nearly harmless.

There was nothing harmless or friendly about the woman running towards Thea, naked steel in her hand.

Faced with a threat, Thea's training kicked in, pulse speeding up, everything around her coming into sharp focus. She took a half-step sideways and drew the staff from her belt and said, "Come out." The length shivered, the staff springing into existence in her hands just in time for her to block the vicious swipe of the sword.

The clerk didn't stop, though, kicking out under the length of the staff, hitting Thea's knee at just the right angle to make it crumple, sending Thea sideways into the wall, her head thumping against the wooden panelling.

Thea brought the staff up in instinctive defence, but there was no need. The clerk had gone.

She stumbled to her feet, wincing at the pain in her knee, and limped towards the stairs, overtaken by Iva and Matthew, both of them in their night kind *aspects*. They ran down the stairs, quickly out of sight. Thea followed far more slowly, using the staff as a walking stick, her knee beginning to truly hurt. She tried to distract herself from the pain by puzzling out what had just happened, and why. She only remembered meeting the clerk on her first visit, and trying to picture the clerk's face made her head hurt again.

When she reached the basement level, she found Matthew and Iva at the open back door of the building, back in their human *aspects*, both of them grim-faced.

"She's gone?" Thea asked, knowing the answer.

"She must have mapped out several escape routes," Iva said, frustration clear. "It will take us an age to find her again."

"You've been looking for her?" Thea asked.

Before Iva could answer, a trace of familiar magic washed over Thea. Niath was close by.

She turned her head just before he came around the corner of the building, running, out of breath, robes flapping around him.

"Thea. Are you alright?" he asked, stumbling to a halt in front of her.

"You've not been doing your job, shadow," Matthew told him, voice tight. "If your lady wasn't such a good fighter, she'd be bleeding right now."

To Thea's surprise, Niath looked ashamed rather than angry. He inclined his head to Matthew, a gesture that looked almost like contrition, and then turned to Thea.

"You are hurt," he said, dismay clear.

"Twisted my knee. Banged my head," Thea said. "It will heal soon enough. You were going to tell me about the woman you are hunting," she said, turning back to Iva and Matthew.

The pair exchanged glances.

"Not here," Matthew said.

"I need to look at Paulin's office," Thea said. "We can talk there."

It was only as she turned back to the building, using the staff as a walking stick, that she realised that meant climbing up all the stairs again, with her knee stinging in protest every time she moved.

"Here," Niath said, pulling something out of his robes. "I asked Mage Fisk to provide some healing spells. I thought they might be useful," he explained, holding out a small glass vial.

"Good idea," Thea said. The potion tasted utterly vile, as medicines often did, but it soothed her knee so that by the time they reached the upper floor where the office was, she barely felt it, and the lingering ache in her head was completely gone, too. She put the staff away. "That's a powerful spell."

"That's what a natural healer can do," Niath corrected, then put a hand out, asking for her to stop. He was looking ahead at the office doors. "Were we expecting someone else to join us?" he asked.

"No," Thea said, regretting putting the staff away. She glanced across at Matthew and Iva, who both shook their heads.

"We'll go first," Iva said, brushing past Thea, Matthew following. The night kind pair took up posts on either side of the door, listening for a moment before opening it and flowing inside in a move that looked rehearsed. They had worked together before, Thea realised.

A cry of outrage sounded followed by a scuffle, Thea reaching the open door in time to see Matthew and Iva pinning Master Merchant Gadsden against the wall, the merchant's face flushed with rage.

"Unhand me at once. Don't you know who I am?" Gadsden spluttered.

"No. No idea," Iva said, sounding almost cheerful. "Investigator March, do you know this fellow?"

"Yes. That's Master Merchant Gadsden. One of the leaders of the merchants' guild," Thea said. "I think you can let him go. Perhaps you will tell me, sir, what you were looking for?" she asked Roe as he was released from the night kind's hold.

The merchant twitched his robes back into order with tight, sharp movements, face pinched with displeasure.

"It's guild business," he said, and glanced at the night kind. "They are not authorised to be here."

"They are assisting me," Thea said. The urge to apologise or explain died as soon as it was born. Her mother would be appalled by her lack of manners. But her mother was not here. And Master Gadsden had not answered her question. Not really.

"Did you know your clerk is night kind?" Matthew asked, his voice a calm, reasonable tone. He was still in his human *aspect*, but Thea could sense his other nature close to the surface.

"Does it matter?" Gadsden asked, brows lifting. Thea's opinion of him rose slightly.

"Yes," Matthew said bluntly. "She drew a sword on us just now."

"Really?" Gadsden seemed genuinely shocked. "That doesn't sound like her."

"We'll need her address, and any other personal information you have," Thea said.

"Yes. Of course," Gadsden said, smoothing his robes again.

"And we need to search Master Paulin's office again," Thea said, glancing around the room. It looked unchanged since her last visit, but she wasn't familiar enough with merchants' papers to be certain.

Gadsden looked as if he would argue, his face tightening, fists clenching by his sides.

"Did you hear that Kendrick escaped?" Thea asked, hoping to provoke a reaction.

She was disappointed. The Master Merchant merely nodded. "I'd heard," he said, turning away. "I'll get the clerk's information for you," he said over his shoulder as he left the room.

"Charming man," Iva said, in a voice full of false cheer. "What are we looking for?" she asked Thea.

Thea hesitated.

"Perhaps we'll wait outside," Matthew suggested, mischief on his face. "I'm sure we can find the answers out later," he added, going to the door with Iva. He closed the door behind them before Thea could come up with a response.

"Curious couple," Niath commented, looking around the room. "I don't remember seeing her before."

"Iva. I think she may be new to the city," Thea said. She shook her head. Another question for another time. She pulled Master Paulin's key from her pocket. "I wonder if there's a space behind one of the bookcases?"

"Or perhaps in the desk," Niath suggested.

"Really? What makes you think that?"

"It's a lot bigger than it needs to be," Niath said, making a slow circuit of the heavy piece of furniture. "I'm sure I've seen desks like this with concealed compartments."

Chapter Twenty-Three

With both of them working, it did not take long to find the false panel at the side of the desk that clicked away to reveal a large space containing a metal box about the right size to hold one or two merchants' ledgers.

After the discovery in the Summer House, Thea was disappointed to find that the metal safe in Paulin's office contained nothing more than business records going back a few years and a few letters, the parchment folded and re-folded so many times that the joins were wearing thin. The letters were written in a language that neither Thea nor Niath could read, and signed with an indecipherable scrawl.

There was no magic on any of it, Niath reported.

Satisfied that nothing in the box related to the Hand, Thea returned the contents to the box and the box to its hiding place. If she had more time, she would have liked to study the records in more detail. But she expected Master Merchant Gadsden to be back at any time, and she also had to see about finding the clerk.

She and Niath left Master Paulin's office as they had found it. She stuck her head out of the office to find Matthew and Iva standing on opposite walls of the corridor, their shoulders against the walls, in deliberately casual poses.

"Thank you for waiting," she said, and beckoned them inside. She still had questions for them, and a corridor was not the place to talk. A merchant's office seemed suitably private. The pair exchanged glances but came into the room, Iva shutting the door behind her. Thea had a moment of panic, shut into a closed space with three other people. But the room was big enough that she could breathe. For now.

"Master Merchant Gadsden came by. Left this for you," Matthew said, holding up a piece of parchment. "It's the clerk's name and address."

"It's not her real name," Iva said at once.

"You seem to know a lot about her," Thea commented, taking the parchment from Matthew. Her brows lifted as she read the address. It was a large house somewhere in Fallowfield. Not somewhere she would expect a merchant's clerk to be able to afford to live.

"She won't be there," Iva said. "It's probably a false address."

"You didn't answer my question," Thea said, looking up at the night kind warrior.

Iva stared back at her, face tight.

"Tell me, Investigator March, have you felt oddly tired over the past few days?" Matthew asked.

Thea blinked. "Yesterday," she said slowly, another chill running over her skin. She bit her lip, not wanting to go on and admit weakness. "I seem to have lost a few hours," she said, heat rising in her face. By the glances that Matthew and Iva exchanged, she realised that they had been expecting her to say that. Her mouth was dry as she forced a question out, "How did you know?"

"Her name is Kady. No last name," Matthew said. "She's well known among certain of my people."

"Oh?" Thea prompted.

"You know what we are," Iva said, eyes narrow, shoulders square as she stared at Thea.

"Fiandar. Yes. I don't pretend to understand it fully," Thea added.

"Among our strongest rules are that we avoid drawing too much attention, and we do not harm anyone. That means we only take what we need. Never enough to be noticed," Matthew said, jaw set. He meant energy, Thea knew. The fiandar, supposedly the gentlest of the night kind, drew energy from other living beings. Not blood, as some of the darker folk stories told.

"I assume that Kady does not follow these rules?" Thea said, mouth dry, understanding now what Matthew was telling her. She had been utterly exhausted the night before, barely able to get to her own bed, and sluggish when she woke up this morning, eating more than usual for breakfast.

"That is so," Iva confirmed.

"You will come to no lasting harm," Matthew said, meeting Thea's eyes, his own shading to the dark of his other nature. "She was not trying to take from you, only to obscure your memory."

"I'm sorry, what?" Thea asked, sure she had misheard.

"How do you think we avoid detection?" Iva asked, mouth lifting in a sour smile. "The strongest of us can cloud memories. It leaves our hosts to get on with their lives."

Thea's mouth opened, then closed. She swallowed. "Are you-" Her voice cracked. She swallowed again. Tried to speak again. "Are you telling me that she did something to my memories yesterday afternoon?"

"Can you remember what happened?" Matthew asked, eyes keen.

"Not really, no," Thea said, mouth dry. "I had planned to come here. I do remember that."

"You almost certainly did," Matthew said, his eyes still shaded to the dark of a fiandar. He glanced at Niath. "And you were alone, so she was able to steer you away."

"I don't understand why," Thea said bluntly.

"Nor do we. Not yet," Matthew said, looking grim. She believed him. Even as she thought that, a flicker of memory rose in her mind. The vaguest impression. An outline of a figure seen across the entrance way of the guild building.

A stab of pain shot through her skull and she hissed, putting a hand to her temple.

"Don't try to remember the hours you lost," Matthew warned. "They may come back to you in time, but if you try to force it, it will hurt."

"That explains a lot," Thea said, rubbing her forehead, remembering her earlier headache when she had tried to remember the afternoon before. The pain was fading, and she forced herself to think about something other than her missing hours. Fortunately, there were plenty of other things to discuss. "Why does my being alone matter?" Thea asked, frowning. "Is Niath immune?"

"I have protections in place," Niath said before Matthew could answer, "but even the strongest fiandar can only manage one person at a time."

"And having been caught by her once, you will be more vulnerable," Iva said, voice flat. "I suggest you don't go anywhere alone until we have found her."

"I understand that she has broken your laws," Thea said slowly, puzzling the matter through, "but you seem very determined to find her. Has she interfered with other people's memories? What else has she done?"

"I don't want to say more, not until we've had a chance to speak to her," Matthew said, before Iva could speak. "She can't harm us," he added, as if anticipating Thea's next question.

"And we're wasting time here," Iva said, taking a step towards the door. "She has a clear start on us."

"I'll make sure Thea is safe," Niath promised.

"See that you do," Matthew said over his shoulder as he followed Iva out of the room.

Thea turned to Niath when the door closed behind the pair and lifted her brows. "You'll make sure I'm safe?" she repeated, not sure how to feel about that. The doubts of a few days ago crept back in, unsettling and unwelcome. At the same time, having someone else keeping an eye out for danger was a new and interesting concept. And not unwelcome.

Niath wasn't looking at her. He had taken a ribbon out of one of his pockets and was scowling at it, a curl of his magic rising in the air around him. He spoke a few words, a spell cast on the ribbon, and then handed it to her, not quite meeting her eyes.

"Here. This will keep you safe if she tries to use her gifts on you again."

Thea took the ribbon and did not feel any different. There was a trace of Niath's magic in the fabric, warm against her skin, but otherwise it was just a bit of ribbon. She opened her mouth to ask questions, and stopped when Niath flinched. It was a tiny, almost imperceptible movement, but it was a definite move away from her and whatever she might have asked. He did not want to answer her. Not now. She could ask anyway. But something about the way he was standing, and the way he had spoken to Matthew, told her that there were things she did not understand. And perhaps did not want to understand. Not just now. She had enough to worry about. So she closed her mouth with a snap and tucked the ribbon away.

"Thank you," she said instead.

He nodded, a little bit of tension leaving his shoulders.

"Did you learn anything more from the papers at Mort's?" she asked him. That seemed a much safer topic.

"Oh, yes," he said, head lifting, eyes brightening with enthusiasm. "It's a remarkable find. There are spells and ways of using magic in there that I had not imagined were possible."

Thea could not help smiling back at his delight. "Anything useful for the case?"

"Sadly, no. But I do think we should be asking Master Gadsden about his involvement with the Hand," Niath said. "There are no invisibility spells in the papers, but it's possible that the Hand and the warriors know ways of slipping past locked doors."

"And killing unsuspecting merchants?" Thea suggested. "And perhaps Master Gadsden will know why the Hand of the goddess would want Bordan Hannaford and Dalston Paulin dead. Let's go find him and ask."

After the earlier drama of Kady's attack and escape, it was something of a shock to find the rest of the building felt as calm and still as it had on Thea's previous visits. This might be a place where merchants conducted business, but they seemed to do so quietly.

None of the offices had been occupied, so they were forced to look elsewhere for Master Gadsden, and had not found him by the time they reached the reception hallway. The doors of the building were open, letting in the early afternoon sunshine.

There was no clerk at the desk, or anyone in earshot, and Thea was getting annoyed. Master Gadsden had not wanted to answer her questions before, and she could not help thinking he was deliberately avoiding her.

Before she could begin a more comprehensive search of the building, running footsteps outside drew her attention.

A Watch messenger ran up the steps of the building, wide-eyed and a little out of breath.

"Ma'am, you're needed," he said to Thea, then had to stop to catch his breath. "Sorry, ma'am. Sutter said to run."

"Senior Sergeant Sutter sent you? Where does he want me to go?" Thea asked.

"Middlefield market, ma'am. There's been another death," the messenger said. "He said to tell you that the physician and examiner are on their way."

"Good. Thank you," Thea said, and handed over a coin into the messenger's waiting hand. She glanced at Niath. "It seems that we'll need to wait a bit longer to get answers from Master Gadsden."

Chapter Twenty-Four

The market was crowded with people and eerily still and silent when Thea and Niath arrived. The people were all looking in the same direction, towards the centre, so she excused herself through the crowd and made her way through the throng of people to find a ring of Watchmen and women facing outward, grim-faced.

In the gaps between the Watchmen and women, she caught a glimpse of a figure on the ground, what looked like a large knife sticking up out of its chest. Ware and Sutter were standing near the body.

"Thea, good," Ware said. "Jenkins, let her and the mage pass."

"Sir." The nearest Watchwoman stood aside. Thea recognised her from a previous case. Handy with a rope, and kept a cool head, she remembered.

Thea made her way past the ring of Watch, and then stopped, shocked.

The body lying on the ground was Kendrick. He had lost weight since she had last seen him - hardly surprising as the hard life on a black ship would be a far cry from his previous existence - but his sharp face was unmistakable even in death.

"We can tell the Ageless to stop looking for Kendrick, it seems," Sutter said as Ware was called away by one of the Watchwomen. He sounded more annoyed than pleased. "Our invisible killer got here first."

The scene was quite different from the previous deaths, but Thea could see at once what he meant. The knife was similar to the ones used before, and planted straight into the former merchant's chest.

"Do we have any witnesses?" she asked, glancing around. Beyond the ring of Watchmen and women, there was a decent-sized crowd. Upwards of forty people, she estimated. It seemed impossible that someone had walked up to Kendrick, killed him, and walked away without being noticed.

"No," Sutter said, now sounding both annoyed and disgusted. "There was a juggler performing over there." He pointed to one corner of the market square. "Most people seemed to be looking at him. No one seems to have noticed anything wrong until he had fallen over and didn't get up."

"So our killer took advantage of the distraction," Thea said. Jugglers and other street entertainers were relatively rare outside festival times, so it was no wonder the performer had drawn attention. "Do we have the juggler?" she asked.

Sutter's mouth lifted into a small smile. "Yes." He tilted his head back towards the corner again, and Thea saw a Watch Officer questioning a skinny man in bright clothing. "I don't think he was involved, but we thought we should ask," Sutter added.

"There's no magic here," Niath said abruptly. "However the killer disguised themselves, it's not a spell." He sounded as frustrated as Thea felt.

"So how are they doing this?" Ware asked. He was glaring down at Kendrick's body. "I thought he was annoying enough in life. It looks like he's going to be equally annoying in death. The commander is on his way," he added, with barely a pause, making Thea blink before she realised he was referring to Reardon. "Apparently, they had found no trace of him anywhere in his usual places. The commander was not happy when I spoke to him earlier."

Thea could imagine. As one of the Ageless, Reardon would be used to things going his way. That the Ageless could not find one human must have been frustrating in the extreme.

"The same killer again," Ware added. "Any ideas?"

Thea did not answer at once, tilting her head. "Maybe," she said, and glanced across at Niath. She lowered her voice so that it would not carry beyond their group. "I learned that there is a rogue fiandar in the city. One who can obscure memories."

Ware's brows lifted. "So you think that a night kind has been walking up to people, confusing them, then stabbing them?"

Thea's face heated. It did not sound very plausible, put like that.

"Yes," Niath said, startling them all. He rarely intervened in investigations. "It fits, doesn't it?" he asked Thea.

"Where is this night kind now?" Ware demanded.

"Matthew Shand and another fiandar, Iva, are trying to find her," Thea said.

"Iva?" Ware's brows shot up. "As in Matthew's Iva?"

"I don't know. We weren't fully introduced," Thea said, curiosity spiking. "But it might be easier to find them than the rogue."

"Very easy," Ware said, voice dry, looking past Thea's shoulder, "as they are coming this way."

"Sir, I'm concerned with this crowd being here," Thea said. "Can the Watch take names and let them go?"

"This is even better entertainment than the juggler," Ware told her. "But, yes, we should try. Sutter?"

"I'll see to it," Sutter promised, and moved away to the nearest Watchwoman. Jenkins again, Thea saw.

She had no more attention to spare as Matthew and Iva arrived within the circle at the same time as Dina and Iason.

Dina took one look around and both brows shot up.

"Just who has been trampling all over my crime scene?" she demanded, in a voice loud enough to carry across the whole, quiet space.

The crowd began drifting away almost at once, with no prompting from the Watch. In fact, the Watch had to follow the people to get their details.

"Well, this is a mess and no mistake," Dina said, turning back to the body. "Is that Kendrick? What in the name of the Ageless is he doing dead and out in the open?"

"We don't have answers yet," Thea said, when no one else volunteered a response to Dina's question.

"Thea tells us that there's a rogue fiandar in the city," Ware said, staring at Matthew and Iva. "Tell us more." His voice made it a command.

"We haven't found her yet," Matthew admitted, looking at Kendrick. "No witnesses?" he asked Thea.

"No. There was a juggler in the corner, apparently."

"And he's not involved, I take it?" Matthew asked.

Thea bit her lip, amused that the fiandar's clan leader was turning the tables on her and the other Watch members, making himself the questioner.

"No, he's not," Sutter said, as he came back to them. "The killer must just have used the distraction."

"It fits," Iva said to Matthew.

"And you haven't told us anything we didn't already know," Ware said in a silky soft voice that made Thea want to take a step back from him. "This man was wanted by the Ageless. They are not going to be happy that he's dead by someone else's hand."

"I can imagine," Matthew said, shaking his head a fraction. "You think Kady did this?" he asked.

For a moment, Thea wondered if he was asking her and could not work out why he thought she might know. But he was looking at Iva.

The other fiandar was scowling. "Could be. I haven't found any bodies in her wake before. But she has the strength to do this."

"This is the third body we've found," Thea said. "All killed like this. All of them Master Merchants."

"That doesn't fit," Iva said, shaking her head. "She might be a rogue, but she's always been careful with her victim choice. She was breaking our laws but didn't want to draw too much attention."

"Until now," Matthew said, looking at Iva. "She used her skill on Investigator March yesterday and attacked openly today."

"It's not like her," Iva said, turning to Thea, still frowning.

Thea realised that Iva was worried. The fiandar did not seem like someone who got worried easily, and Thea could feel her own concern rising.

"Well, why don't we find her and ask her?" Thea suggested. "Before another Master Merchant dies."

"We'll get the last Master Merchants into Middlefield Watch Station," Sutter said. "Keep an eye on them."

"Make sure that no one is left alone," Thea said, remembering what she had learned earlier. "Not even the Watchman at the door."

Sutter's brows lifted, but he just nodded and left the market, gathering a handful of Watchmen and women as he went.

"I know we're assuming it's the same killer," Thea said, "but I would still like to hear what the physician and examiner have to say."

"I thought you'd never ask," Dina said, grinning. Her humour faded as she exchanged glances with Iason. "From what we can see, yes, it's the same killer."

"Physician, would you mind checking to see if Kendrick also has a key?" Thea asked.

Iason's brows lifted, but he went back to the body to check, shaking his head.

"How would Kendrick have kept such a thing on a black ship?" Niath asked. There was no challenge in his voice, just simple curiosity.

"I don't know. But then, I don't know how he escaped the black ship, either," Thea said, hearing the edge of frustration in her voice.

She moved closer to Kendrick and crouched near his head, tracing the changes since she had last seen him. He looked older. When she had first met him, he had been arrogant, rude and clad in elaborate robes that befitted a Master Merchant. Now he was dressed in plain, dark clothing, his hair as close-cropped as before, showing hints of grey here and there, lines etched into his skin. Thea had never been on a black ship, but she had met some of the crew and the overseers before, and the prospect of the ships made her skin crawl.

A fragment of memory stirred and pain bloomed behind her eyes. She pinched the bridge of her nose, breathing out slowly, hoping the pain would pass. It died, replaced with the barest fragment. Her standing in a large internal space, two figures ahead of her. One dressed plainly, one dressed in elaborate merchants' robes. And a dark-clothed clerk moving towards her.

"Ouch," she said involuntarily as agony twisted through her mind.

"You're remembering, aren't you?" Matthew said, coming to crouch opposite her. The fiandar ignored the dead man, staring at her. "What do you remember?"

"Not much. I was in the merchants' guild, I think. There were two men there. I think one of them was Kendrick," she said, the realisation coming clear as she spoke. "I can't remember who the other one was. And then Kady appeared in front of me."

"That must be why she altered your memory," Niath said. He was standing not far away, looking unhappy. "You saw Kendrick in the merchants' guild."

"You're sure?" Ware asked. Matthew moved back to stand beside Iva, all of them looking at Thea.

"No, not sure. I can't remember clearly," Thea said, shaking her head. "I'm sorry," she said, anticipating Ware's disappointment.

"You didn't help him escape," Ware pointed out. "But it gives us more reason to question the merchants again. It's one thing for them to petition for his release. Quite another for them to welcome him back."

From the glint in Ware's eye, he was looking forward to putting some hard questions to the merchants. Thea ducked her head to hide a smile and looked back at the body in front of her. The snippet of memory faded, along with the headache, leaving her with just the here and now.

She frowned as she looked over the body again. Kendrick seemed to have survived his ordeal. More than that, he had managed to escape, which was something she had never heard of before.

"His clothes are clean," she noticed.

"Is that significant?" Niath asked, crouching on the other side of the body, his own robes a dark shadow around him.

"Well, it makes me wonder where he has been staying," Thea said. "He's an escaped convict. If he'd been living on the streets, he wouldn't look like this."

"That's a good point," Ware said. He sounded distracted. "I'll get Sutter to track down Kendrick's known associates. The ones who aren't on a black ship, that is. If you'll excuse me, that's the Commander arriving."

Thea looked up in time to see blinding white feathers spread out overhead. Not just Reardon, but a wing of Ageless with him.

Reardon landed lightly on the ground not far away, his wings folding behind him as he shed his Ageless *aspect*. His human face was only marginally less forbidding as he scowled in the direction of the dead man then looked up, his eyes travelling across the gathered group.

"Thea, will you take Matthew, Iva and Niath and begin your enquiries," Ware said, glancing over his shoulder before he moved to meet Reardon.

Thea's brows lifted, and she looked up to find Matthew and Iva staring at Reardon with set faces. There was no good feeling between the night kind and the Ageless. It made her curious, but it seemed that Ware had anticipated the tension, and had given her orders that would allow her to leave gracefully.

"Good idea," Thea said, straightening to her feet. "Let's go," she said to the others.

"That's right, just leave us, why don't you," Dina muttered as Thea passed her. But the examiner gave her a wink. Doubtless Dina had understood, far more quickly than Thea had, that Ware was trying to keep the night kind away from the Ageless' attention.

With the others gathered around her, Thea headed for the nearest exit from the market square, turning over possibilities in her mind as she went. There was an alleyway between two tall buildings not far from the marketplace and she turned in there, waiting for the others to follow her. She stopped halfway along the alley, glancing up to make sure the windows above them were closed. There was no one else in earshot.

"Mistress Iva, you said that Kady would not want to draw attention to herself. But these killings are high-profile," Thea said.

"That's right," Iva confirmed, leaning her shoulders against the nearest wall.

"What would make her kill like this?" Thea asked, looking across to make sure Niath was there, and listening. He was.

"I don't know," Iva said. Thea believed her.

"The killings have mostly been around noon. Is that significant?" Thea asked.

"Could be," Iva said, mouth pursing. "Most likely showing off."

"What do you mean?" Thea asked, holding on to her patience. Iva did not like sharing information, it seemed.

"You don't get many assassins in this city," Iva said, surprising Thea with a full answer, "but in the places where they are more common, it's considered a mark of some skill to be able to kill your targets at noon and get away without being detected."

Thea turned that over in her mind. It made a certain sort of sense. Noon was the height of the day, and there were almost always people about. It seemed risky, still, but perhaps, as Iva had said, Kady was showing off.

"What are you thinking?" Matthew asked.

"I'm thinking that I have been assuming that the Hand is behind these killings. I'm thinking that I don't know why the Hand, or Kady, would want to kill Master

Merchants. I'm thinking that I need to look for another motive, and perhaps if I find that, I'll understand what's going on," Thea said.

"The merchants couldn't think of a motive?" Matthew asked, brows lifting.

"Not any that they told us," Thea said, eyes narrowing. The merchants. "But we've never really had a chance to properly question them." She glanced at Niath. "Perhaps we should do that."

"Senior Sergeant Sutter is gathering them all at the station," Niath said, eyes gleaming. "It would seem rude not to pay them a visit."

"And we can try and pick up Kady's trail while you interrogate - ahem - speak to the merchants," Matthew said.

Thea's mouth twitched. She would wager that Sutter was not putting the merchants into Ware's office and making them comfortable. They would be out of their normal environment, and doubtless shaken by the new murder. A perfect time to get some answers.

Chapter Twenty-Five

Middlefield Watch Station was calm when Thea and Niath came through the front door. Watchman Hobbs had a junior Watchman sitting near him, with a stack of papers in front of him. Through the doorway, Thea could see that there were a pair of Watchmen in the main room. That was all.

"Good day, ma'am," Hobbs said, and nodded to Niath. He was perfectly polite, with a little more warmth than Thea had received from him for some time. It seemed she was slowly being forgiven for betraying her fellow Watch members, in Hobbs' eyes at least. The canny old Watchman knew it had been necessary, like all honest Watch members, but it did not sit well with him and it was taking him a while to trust her again. Thea did not blame him. It did not sit well with her, either, no matter how necessary it had been.

"Good day. I think the Senior Sergeant was bringing the Master Merchants here. Do you know where they are?" Thea asked.

"The brothers Trant are upstairs, along with Mage Trant," Hobbs answered. "Senior Sergeant Sutter left to go and find the other Master Merchant. You just missed him, ma'am. Said that he wasn't at the guild and they were going to try his house."

"Thank you." Thea glanced up the stairs. Gordie and Cedd might be more talkative without Gadsden there. And perhaps Odilia could help convince them to talk. "I'm going to talk to the brothers, just in case anyone is looking for me," she told Hobbs, and moved towards the stairs.

"Is it true, ma'am. Is Kendrick really dead?" the junior Watchman asked. He was sitting forward in his chair, eyes wide, waiting for her answer, when she turned to him.

"Yes, he is."

"Good riddance," the unnamed Watchman said.

"That's enough out of you," Hobbs said, scowling.

"But it is," the Watchman protested.

"Someone being killed is never a good thing," Thea said, frowning. "And his death doesn't help anyone as far as I can tell," she added as she started climbing the stairs.

By the time she reached the top of the stairs she was still frowning, turning her own words over in her mind. The lack of any obvious motive for the killings was nagging her, like an itch that would not go away.

Her frown vanished as she saw Odilia standing in the middle of the upstairs corridor. The mage had her arms wrapped around herself and looked as if she was on the verge of exploding into fury.

"Thea. Thank goodness. Will you talk some sense into my idiot brothers?" the mage asked.

"I will do my best," Thea said. "What's wrong?"

"They think they're in no danger," Odilia said. The rage was tempered with worry, Thea realised. "They don't think they should have to be here."

"Any particular reason why they aren't worried?" Thea asked.

"You'll need to ask them," Odilia said, words bitten off. "Come on, they are through here." She turned and led the way to a room that was very familiar to Thea. She had questioned suspects in there before. And they usually ended up dead. It was not a good start.

"Why don't we go to my office?" Thea suggested instead.

"Won't that be a bit crowded?" Odilia said, looking along the corridor to Thea's office door.

"Yes, but at least no one has died in there. That I know of, anyway," Thea said, going past Odilia to open the door to the room.

The Trant brothers were sitting side by side on a bench on the opposite wall, and turned near-identical frowns on her when she opened the door.

"Come on, we'll talk in my office," she said, and moved away, hoping that they would follow.

Somewhat to her surprise, they did follow her.

There were not enough chairs in her office so everyone stood, the Trant brothers with their backs to the wall, Niath near Thea and Odilia hovering in the doorway, still seeming to be torn between anger and worry.

"You'll have heard that Kendrick is dead," Thea started.

The brothers nodded, lips tight, staring back at her.

"What of it?" Cedd asked.

"He was killed in the same manner as Master Hannaford and Master Paulin," Thea said, "and I do not understand why anyone would want to kill all three of them. You need to start talking," she said bluntly, staring at the two of them. "You might well be next."

"That's ridiculous. No one would want to hurt us," Cedd said, waving a hand in dismissal.

"Are you sure? You didn't seem to think anyone had a motive to kill Master Hannaford or Master Paulin," Thea said, holding Cedd's eyes with her own. "Unless there's something you're not telling me?"

Cedd's brows lifted. "I assure you-" he began.

"Stop it," Odilia said. "Just stop it, both of you. You're hiding something. I know you better than Thea does. Tell us. Now."

"Or what?" Cedd asked, lip curling. "You won't hurt us."

"No, but I might," Niath said, in a mild voice that Thea had never heard from him before. He looked the brothers up and down, as if contemplating what he might do to them.

"What does it matter to you?" Cedd demanded, chin thrust out.

"At least one of your colleagues has been involved with some dangerous magic that could hurt a lot of people," Niath said. "So we need to know what you know. If you won't speak to Thea, then you'll be taken to the Citadel."

Thea drew a short, shocked breath in. That had been no idle threat from Niath. As a Citadel Mage, he could have the Archon's soldiers take the Trant brothers into the Citadel. And no one would be able to stop it. Not even her.

She had forgotten, in their working together, just how much power and authority he carried. Despite being the most powerful mage she had ever come across, he presented himself as mild-mannered, able to almost disappear into the background. But he had far more power in this city than she did.

"You-" Cedd began, and was interrupted again, this time by his younger brother putting a hand on his arm.

"We don't know much," Gordie said, turning from Niath to Thea. "I promise you. We just know that there were quite a lot of discussions behind closed doors, which is unusual. And Roe, Bordan and Dalston were arguing."

"Was that common?" Thea asked.

"There were disagreements from time to time," Gordie said, folding his hands in his sleeves in front of him. "We all think we know best when it comes to our business," he added, a rueful smile twisting his mouth, "even when we're proved wrong."

"You don't know for certain what they were arguing about," Thea said slowly, "but you must know something. What?"

"We don't know," Cedd answered. "No, really. We don't. They never spoke about it in front of us."

"There were meetings outside the guild," Gordie said. "And when Kendrick was ... well, when he left, they asked us to help get him back."

"They wouldn't tell us much. Just that they didn't think the Watch should have jurisdiction over us," Cedd added, face tight. "That we should answer only to the Ageless."

"You're idiots. Both of you," Odilia said, arms wrapped around her middle again. Her face was tight, eyes over-bright. "You know what Kendrick did. Kidnapped people. Enslaved them. And you were going to support him?" She paused, bit her lip, then said "Idiots," again. By the expression on her face, it was a far milder comment than she had wanted to make.

"What he did was wrong, no doubt," Cedd said, in a tone that suggested he was trying to be reasonable, "but he was a Master Merchant."

"Be that as it may," Thea said, before Odilia could vent any of the pent-up fury she was clearly struggling to contain, "he was not Ageless, and he lived and worked outside the Citadel's perimeter. All that put him within the jurisdiction of the Watch. It's also interesting, don't you think, that the Master Merchants don't want the Watch to interfere with Kendrick's activities, but are very quick to call us if you suspect theft from your warehouses?"

She had the mild satisfaction of seeing Cedd and Gordie flinch, doubtless reminded of the many times that they had called on the Watch's services over the years. Every merchant suffered their share of actual and attempted thefts, and every merchant demanded help from the Watch when that happened. In her few years with the Watch, Thea had lost count of the number of times merchants had turned up at Watch stations, full of fury, demanding action.

"Did you ever hear the other Master Merchants talking about the Hand?" she asked.

"A hand?" Gordie frowned. "Why would they talk about hands?"

"Not a hand, stupid. The Hand," Odilia said through gritted teeth.

"I'm sure I did," Cedd answered, ignoring his sister and speaking directly to Thea. "But I don't really remember when, or what the context was."

"What about Alayla?" Thea asked.

"Kendrick's mistress?" Gordie asked, brows lifting. "What about her?"

Thea blinked, taken aback, remembering the golden-skinned creation that she had met who had called herself Alayla, and Kendrick's clear contempt for the members of the Hand. She could not imagine Kendrick having any close association with the supposed goddess. "What do you know about her?"

"Not much. I just overhead Roe teasing Kendrick once, saying he was in thrall to his mistress. I'm sure her name was Alayla," Gordie said, turning to Cedd. "Don't you remember?"

"Something like that, yes," Cedd agreed, reluctance plain. "She was some simple country girl he'd set up in one of his houses," he added. "At least, that's what I gathered. I never met her."

"Mistresses?" Odilia hissed. "Do tell me, is that common practice for merchants now? I'm sure our parents would be so proud of the way you have turned out. And your wives, too."

Her brothers both flinched, colour rising in their cheeks.

"It's not common," Gordie said, not meeting his sister's eyes.

Odilia snorted, disbelief clear.

"Do you know where she lived? Where she is now?" Thea asked, before a full-on family argument could erupt. Kendrick had been staying somewhere after his escape from the black ship, and the Ageless would have searched all the properties they had known about. Perhaps his supposed mistress would have an idea where he had been staying, if Thea could find her.

"Lived? She's still there, as far as we know." Cedd gave Thea the address. A property in Lowcroft, only a few streets from her mother's house.

"This wasn't on the list of Kendrick's properties," she said, when she had taken a note of the address.

"No, it wouldn't be. He had a few secret places around the city," Cedd said.

"Do you know the addresses of those?" she asked.

Cedd pressed his lips together, glaring at her for a moment. "I hardly think that is of concern to the Watch," he said.

"It will be of concern to the Citadel, though," Niath said, in the same mild voice he had used before. "They like their taxes paid."

Cedd was glaring at Niath now, doubtless remembering, as Thea was, just how forcefully the Citadel would pursue unpaid taxes. The Archon's soldiers had burned entire houses to the ground before now, making the residents homeless, setting an example for others.

"Ask the clerk at the guild for details," Cedd suggested. "She was thick as thieves with Kendrick before he left."

"She? Do you mean Kady?" Thea asked, narrowing her eyes.

"Is that her name?" Cedd asked, as if astonished that the clerk had a name at all. Neither he nor Gordie had seemed to know how many staff worked in the guild building, Thea remembered. But Roe Gadsden had. And she would wager that Kendrick had, too. They had both been successful and wealthy merchants, and had paid attention to the detail of things around them.

Which made it all the more strange that someone had managed to walk up to Kendrick in a crowded, public place and stab him in the chest.

But it didn't fit. Kendrick had had his own clerk, who had turned over a damning ledger of evidence to Thea. He would not have needed to share information with the guild's clerk. Unless there was a good reason, which Thea could not guess at just now.

"We're looking for the clerk," she told Cedd and Gordie. "Did you know she is night kind?"

By the blank expressions on their faces, they had not known. But they had also not cared, and her opinion of them rose a little. Judging by the expression on Odilia's face, she was mentally rehearsing a few more choice terms for her brothers.

"You need to stay here," Thea told them. She watched their expressions change. They wanted to disagree.

"Or you can take your chances with an invisible killer who seems to like stabbing Master Merchants," Niath said, in his most falsely cheerful voice. "I'm sure Investigator March will take special care in investigating your deaths."

"As I do in all my investigations, yes," Thea confirmed. "But I am sure your families would prefer that you live, and it would certainly save me a great deal of paperwork if you were not the next victims."

"I'll stay with them," Odilia volunteered, "and make sure they don't leave until you let us know it is safe."

"That could be weeks," Gordie protested.

"Highly unlikely," Odilia snapped at him. "Thea is on the case. She's very good at what she does. Luckily for you. I'm sure she has suspects lined up already."

"We don't want to keep you here longer than we have to," Thea said, "but it would be much safer if you would stay here."

"What about Roe? Why aren't you looking after him, too?" Gordie asked.

"He refused to come in, and we're looking for him now," Thea said. "He's more vulnerable if he stays out on his own."

"You'd better find him before something happens." Cedd had drawn himself up to his full height, still shorter than Thea, and was staring at her with what he probably thought was authority and command. To Thea, he just looked sulky.

"So, now you expect Thea to work for you?" Odilia said, and rolled her eyes. "Go, Thea, I'm sure you have far more important things to do than to talk sense into my block-headed brothers. I'll keep them here."

"You can use the other room as long as you are here," Thea said, not wanting to leave them in her office. She watched, amused, as Odilia turned a glare on her brothers that had them moving out of the room and back along the corridor without a sound between them.

"Do you really think that the goddess Alayla was Kendrick's mistress?" Niath asked.

"No. Not even for a moment. But I do wonder who he has been keeping in that house."

It wasn't far from the station to the address in Lowcroft, and Thea suggested that they walk. She was sure that Sam would be somewhere close by with the horses, but she wanted to move under her own power and give herself a little time to think.

"Would you really have turned the Trant brothers over to the Citadel?" she asked, curious. It wasn't quite the thing she wanted to say, but it was getting there.

"Probably not," Niath said, sounding as if he was only now thinking it through. "I don't think it would help anyone," he said after a pause. Which made Thea wonder just what he would have done if he thought it would help.

"All the investigations, all the questions. You know, it never occurred to me that you had the power to compel people to answer," she said. It was said more bluntly than she had intended, but it got to the heart of what she really wanted to say.

Niath was silent long enough for her to look across, worried she had offended him. He was pacing beside her with an abstracted expression on his face, lost in thought.

"You know, it never really occurred to me, either," he said at length. "You are the investigator, not me. I find our work interesting. Far more so than what I was doing at the Citadel. And I'm not sure that constantly threatening people to drag them off to the Citadel would be effective for long."

Thea choked on an unexpected laugh. "No, you're right about that."

"And you know that you could do the same," Niath said, in a gentle voice she had not heard often from him. He was not looking at her.

"I don't want to talk about it," she said. He meant her wings. And she didn't want to think about them, let alone talk about them. Her mother might have exaggerated the danger from the Ageless, but Thea still wanted no part of them. "Can I ask you something?"

"Of course. Anything." He meant it, too.

"Matthew Shand called you my shadow, and he seemed to think you'd not been doing your job. You told me a little bit about it, but I don't understand. Is there something else I should know?" she asked, careful how she phrased the question. She was all too aware of having secrets she didn't want to talk about.

"Well, in centuries past, hiandar were used as bodyguards for royalty," Niath said, surprising her both with his answer and with his light tone.

"Really? Can you tell me more?"

"Well, the details are lost to time. The Archon has done an excellent job of wiping out most of the royal families when she took over their kingdoms. But the basic idea was that a hiandar was assigned to a particular member of the family and became their shadow. There was a bonding ceremony of sorts."

"So if you'd been born a couple of hundred years ago, you could have been a royal bodyguard?" Thea asked, fascinated. "Living in a palace. Following around some spoiled princess."

"I'm sure there were some nice princesses," Niath said cheerfully. "Or perhaps I would have been assigned to a royal who liked magic, and we could have studied together." He was serious by the end, and a little sad, as if longing for that imagined alternative life.

"But that makes me curious now as to what you do at the Citadel in our times," Thea said. She knew that Niath had spent time in the Citadel's library studying, but suspected that he had actual duties as well, even if she could not imagine what they were. "Can you tell me?"

"I don't see why not," he said, expression lightening, "though it is very dull."

For the rest of the short walk he told her about renewing spells around the Citadel's many buildings and finding lost items for the Ageless. He made it entertaining enough that Thea laughed more than once, even though she suspected he was not telling her everything. It seemed highly unlikely that the Ageless would keep a stable full of mages just to renew their housekeeping spells, or to find things. Then again, they were the Ageless.

The address that Cedd had given Thea proved to be a modest little cottage, one of the types with only a main room and a bedroom, surrounded by a lush, green garden. Thea remembered walking past it from time to time, always impressed by the skill of the gardener.

The door of the cottage was opened by a young woman, barely into adulthood, with long, dark hair and angular features that looked oddly familiar.

"You're not Kendrick's mistress, are you?" Thea said, blurting the words out without thinking. "Are you his daughter?"

The girl stared back at them, mouth set in a flat, determined line before she nodded once. Time enough for Thea to realise that the girl might not know her father was dead.

"I'm Investigator Thea March and this is Mage Niath. May we come in?" she asked, her voice softer.

The girl stared back at her for a moment, then silently stepped aside, waving them towards one side of the building.

Inside, the cottage was sparsely decorated with just enough furniture to keep one person comfortable. In the living area that they were standing in, there was a single, upright chair tucked under a small table, and a large, comfortable armchair that had seen better days. There were a few possessions on the shelves, and everything was impeccably clean and orderly. Through the door to the other side of the building, Thea could see a neatly made bed.

"Will you tell us your name?" Thea asked.

"Neda," the girl said, lifting her chin and staring back at her. "How did you find me?" Then she flinched, before Thea could answer. "You said mistress. Is that what he tells people?"

"Neda. I'm pleased to meet you," Thea said, and exchanged brief glances with Niath. "Yes, it seems that Kendrick has told people he has a mistress here."

Neda wrapped her arms around her middle, as if trying to make herself as small as possible. "What do you want?"

"I am sorry to have to tell you this, but Kendrick was killed earlier today."

Neda stared back at her, face blank of expression, for such a long time that Thea wondered if she needed to repeat the words. Then the girl blew out a breath, as if releasing years of built-up tension.

"Really? He's dead? Really dead?"

"Yes. I'm sorry."

Neda took a step back and sank into the chair as if her knees would not hold her any longer. She gripped the arms of the chair with white-knuckled hands, and stared at the floor, another long, deep breath easing out of her before she looked up, eyes bright, the beginnings of a smile around her mouth, making her look far younger than Thea had suspected.

"Finally. Finally," Neda said, and leapt out of the chair, skipping across the room, twirling as she went. "At last at last at last."

"You don't seem upset," Thea commented.

"Upset? Why would I be upset? He was an awful man," Neda said, coming to a stop, her face flushed, the stiff girl who had greeted them at the door completely transformed into a warm, vibrant young woman. "He kept me here. Wouldn't let me go out on my own. Had people watching me. If it hadn't been for Aunt Megan, I would never have left the house."

"Aunt Megan?" Thea's brows lifted. "You mean Mistress Hannaford?"

"Yes, yes. Kendrick's sister. She would come to visit me, and take me places," Neda said, face still flushed with warmth. "But I can go and see her now, can't I? If he's really dead, he can't stop me now."

"That's true," Thea said cautiously. "But before you do that, can I ask you a few questions?"

"I'm not going to sign the papers," Neda said, some of her earlier stiffness returning.

"Papers? What papers?"

"The ones Roe wanted me to sign," Neda said, wrapping her arms around her middle again. "Giving up any claim on Kendrick's possessions. I won't sign them," she said, jaw set. "I don't want all of it. Just enough to live on."

Thea drew a sharp breath in, an idea of motive finally falling into place. At least for Kendrick's death. With Kendrick alive and on a black ship, there was always the possibility, however slim, that he might come back to the city one day and claim his business and his properties again. Assuming he could get them out of the grasp of whoever had them now. But a dead Kendrick would have no claim on anything. And it was clear, from the existence of this house and this daughter, that Kendrick had more property and more secrets than the Watch had uncovered to date. Alive, he could have claimed the properties and, with the ruthless intelligence that he had built up his business in the first place, re-establish himself in the city. Dead, he could not. And all his assets that had not been seized already would fall to his next of kin. This daughter, who was bluntly refusing to give up her inheritance.

"And was it just Roe Gadsden who was asking you to sign the papers?" Thea asked.

"Yes." Neda stared at Thea for a moment. "You didn't know about that, did you?"

"No."

"So, why are you here?" the girl asked.

"There have been three similar deaths in the past few days," Thea told her. "Kendrick's was the last. Earlier today. I've not been able to find a reason for the deaths so far, so I wanted to speak to you to find out if you knew anything that might help."

"Oh. Well. Apart from the papers, the only thing I can tell you is that Kendrick has been staying here. He turned up a few days ago. Insisted I let him in," Neda said, voice sharp and bitter. "Said it would only be a little while and then he would be back in his own house."

Thea rubbed her forehead, feeling that she was in the middle of a maze and might get out if she could only work out the key to it all.

"So, Kendrick has been staying here. Did anyone come and see him when he was here?"

"No. I don't think anyone knew. He went out from time to time," Neda said, mouth in a flat line. "Came back in a foul mood every time."

"And when did Roe ask you to sign the papers?" Thea asked. There. That was it. That was the key. Or so she hoped.

"Oh, this was before. When Kendrick went away. Wait a minute. March. Thea March. You're the woman who caught him, aren't you?" Neda asked, face brightening again.

"Not just me," Thea said. "But, yes, I caught Kendrick."

"Thank you," Neda said, and flung her arms around Thea, giving her a hard hug before the girl stepped back, full of happiness again. "These last months have been wonderful, with him gone. I've been careful, just in case he had people watching, but it's been so nice not having him around."

"Well, he's not coming back again," Thea said, feeling she should say something. She hesitated, then added. "The Watch did not know about you when we arrested Kendrick. At the moment, all his property is being held by the Citadel. But as his daughter, you should be entitled to at least some of it." It was difficult to imagine the Ageless giving up everything that had been taken from Kendrick. The Ageless loved their wealth. But they had also made laws that the family would normally inherit. And, for one reason or another, the Ageless generally followed that law. So Neda should get at least something. Enough that she did not starve. It was not her fault that her father had been so awful.

"Thank you," Neda said, face flushed again, a smile hovering on her lips. "It would be nice not to have to worry about fixing the roof, or making sure I can get new shoes for winter."

"If Kendrick was staying here, did he leave anything behind?" Thea asked.

"No. He burned the clothes he had on when he got here, when I'd got him the other ones. But he didn't have anything else with him," Neda said.

"Do you know of any other properties he had where he might have gone?" Niath asked.

Neda jumped, startled, as if she had forgotten that the mage was there. She frowned, considering the question, then shook her head. "Nothing I know of. But I am sure he had other places. He once boasted that he owned half the city."

"Yes," Thea said, "I can imagine him saying that. One more thing. Have you heard of the Hand or Alayla?"

"The Hand?" Neda said slowly, frowning. "Wait. There was a gang at the market, wasn't there? I sometimes sell herbs from the garden to make some money," she added, perhaps reading Thea's surprise. "I'm sure that one of the older women there said that there were bullies calling themselves the Hand. But I never met them. And Alayla. Isn't that the name of an old goddess? From before the Ageless?"

"That's right," Thea said. "You've been very helpful. Thank you."

"No, thank you," Neda said, and gave a little skip across the room again, making Thea tense, wondering if she was going to be hugged again. "You've brought me such good news. I can't wait to tell Aunt Megan. Oh. I can go now, can't I? I don't need to wait until it's dark. Oh, what a good day," Neda said, and skipped through the room to her bedroom, coming back a moment later with a dull brown cloak which she settled over her shoulders. "If there's nothing else?"

"No," Thea said, trying to hide a smile. "Good day to you, Mistress Neda."

Thea and Niath stood outside the cottage and watched Neda walk away, skipping every few strides, her steps light and bouncy.

"And the best thing is that if Kendrick had known how happy she would be at his death, he would have been furious," Niath said, a smile pulling his mouth.

Chapter Twenty-Six

Leaving Neda's house, Thea turned without thinking, heading towards Middlefield.

"We're going back to the station?" Niath asked.

"Yes," Thea said.

"Why? I mean, it's getting late. What else is there to do today?" Niath asked. Thea wondered if he ever ran out of questions. And then realised that she never did, and he was far more curious than she was.

"I want to see if they've managed to find Master Gadsden. And there's something else," Thea said, and lapsed into silence, trying to puzzle it over in her mind. Something that Neda had said had made her wonder.

"Something else?" Niath prompted, when they were close to the station.

"Yes. I assumed that a merchant's property would go to their next of kin when they died. Including their business interests. But now I wonder."

"Interesting," Niath said, drawing the word out, as they reached the steps of the station building. "So, if their business interests don't go to their families, then who do they go to?"

"That is the question, isn't it?" Thea said, and ran up the steps.

Watchman Hobbs was still on duty, with the young Watchman beside him looking far less confident than he had earlier.

"Ma'am," Hobbs said. "The Senior Sergeant's not long back. Asked you to join him in the Captain's office if you came back before he left again."

"Thank you. Do you know if the Trants are still here?" Thea asked.

"Oh, ay," Hobbs said, a grin transforming his face. "They've been having some lively discussions. Last I heard, Miss Odilia was threatening to turn her brothers into frogs. Things have been a bit quieter since then."

"Thank you," Thea said, trying not to laugh.

"Does Mage Trant know a transformation spell that could turn a person into a frog?" Niath asked, sounding intrigued by the prospect.

"You should ask her," Thea said, laughing, as they reached the door. She knocked and then opened the door.

The air in the room was crackling with tension, the brothers sitting at opposite ends of the bench on the far wall, Odilia sitting at a bench against another wall. None of the siblings were looking at each other.

"Can we go now?" Cedd demanded, getting to his feet.

"Not yet," Thea said, putting on her best cheerful face. "There's still a killer at large. I wanted to ask you something else, though."

"What?" Gordie asked. He was still sitting, arms folded across his chest. He glanced up at Thea, then away.

"When a Master Merchant dies, what happens to their business?" she asked.

Cedd's brows lifted. "What do you mean?" he asked. But he had hesitated, and was also not meeting her eyes.

"It's a simple question," she said, looking between him and Gordie. "And I'd like an answer. It could be important."

"We have agreements in place," Gordie said, resting his shoulders against the wall.

"Gordie, shut up," Cedd hissed.

"No. Two of our fellows are dead, as well as Kendrick," Gordie said. "I don't want to be next. I want to see my children grow up." He turned to Thea. "There are certain trade routes which are split between the merchants. We have agreements as to who has what route and sometimes about the goods, too. Outside those routes, we can do our own business. But if one of us retires, those routes are open for assignment to other merchants. They don't pass to the families."

Thea turned that over in her mind, nodding. "That makes a certain sense. The families might not want to trade the routes, after all."

"It's normal for the new trader on the route to pay a gratuity to the family, where a merchant has died," Cedd added. "Death doesn't happen that often. More often, merchants retire."

"And am I right that a Master Merchant will hold at least one of these certain trade routes?" Thea asked, looking between the Trant brothers. Her guess was confirmed when they each nodded, clearly reluctant. "Thank you. That's helped a lot."

"You can't think that one of us had anything to do with this," Gordie protested, getting to his feet. "The trade routes pay well, but they're not worth the price of killing someone."

"Gordie, don't be so silly," Cedd said, lip curling in disgust. "Half of the merchants in this city would kill for just one of the trade routes the Master Merchants hold." Then he stopped and drew in a shocked breath. "That's what you think, isn't it?" he said, turning to Thea. "You think one of the merchants killed the others?"

"It's the first motive that I have identified which makes any sense," Thea said.

"I can't believe it." Cedd looked shaken.

"Why not?" Odilia asked, in a sharp, angry voice. "All you talk about is the price of things."

To Thea's surprise, Cedd didn't respond with an angry retort but looked down at his feet. Gordie shuffled uncomfortably. Odilia glared at them both, eyes over-bright, worry and anger still battling on her face.

Thea left the Trant family to their silence, closing the door behind her and staring into space for a moment.

"I've been assuming all along that the Hand were involved," she said to Niath. "I mean, we've got all this evidence. But what if they aren't?"

"I don't think the Trant brothers are involved. Not in the killings or the Hand," Niath said.

"I agree," Thea said. "But there's another Master Merchant we haven't spoken to today," she said, and turned towards Ware's office.

Sutter and Ware were poring over a map of the city pinned to the wall.

"No luck finding Master Gadsden, I take it?" Thea said, seeing their frowns.

"Not out in the open, no. We think he's in his house, which is here," Ware said, indicating a spot on the map. "We're just working out the best patrols round his house."

"You were just going to leave him there?" Thea asked.

"He doesn't want our help," Sutter said, turning from the map. He stopped, expression changing. "But it seems you may have more news. Do share."

Thea told them about Kendrick's daughter, the papers Roe Gadsden had asked her to sign, and the conversation she and Niath had just had with the Trant brothers. She saw Sutter and Ware's expressions change as they came to the same conclusion she did.

"That changes things," Ware said, glancing at Sutter. "We need to speak to Master Gadsden, and I'm not taking any more excuses from him."

"I'll gather some of the Watch," Sutter said, heading towards the door.

"Wait," Thea said. "Sorry, sir, but if Gadsden is involved with the Hand, there might be some magical traps laid in his house."

"Good point," Sutter said.

Everyone looked at Niath. He lifted a brow, lips curling into a smile. "You want me to go into a house where there might be traps laid and find the missing merchant for you? When do we start?"

"Right now," Thea said.

"I'll arrange some back-up for you," Sutter said, lips twitching. "Not that you need it, but a few more uniforms might help."

"Sir," Thea acknowledged, and headed out into the gathering night with Niath, the mage's strides light and eager beside her. He was looking forward to whatever they might find at Gadsden's house.

Master Merchant Roe Gadsden, despite his lofty title and wealth, had chosen to live in a perfectly ordinary-looking house. It was built of the local grey stone, two stories high, detached from its neighbours, its grounds marked off from the street by a head-height stone wall broken by metal gates. Through the gates, Thea could see that one side of the grounds was given over to outbuildings, a swathe of garden grounds around the other sides. Rather than the ornamental garden of a grand house, these gardens were practical, filled with edible plants, with some decorative shrubs and flowers mixed in. It was not at all what Thea had expected.

Despite the plainness of the outside, and the ordinary garden around it, the feel of the place set her teeth on edge. There was no welcome in any of the dark, blank windows facing the street or the plain, dark-painted wooden door.

"Is anyone home?" Thea asked Niath.

"There are people in the house, yes," he said in a distant voice, most of his concentration elsewhere.

"What's wrong?" she asked.

"There are protections around the house, which makes it hard to see inside. I don't recognise the magic." He sounded more irritated than alarmed.

"Well, let's go ask Gadsden," Thea said, and put her hand on the low metal gate in front of her. It warmed rapidly under her skin, and she pushed it open quickly, the metal continuing to heat as she took her hand away until it was glowing red hot. "Not very friendly," she remarked, going through the gate.

"No," Niath agreed, frowning at the gate as he walked through. "But it's not that dangerous."

"No?" Thea asked, looking at the gate, which was now white-hot. "It could have burned my hand off."

"Yes. But you had plenty of time to move away," Niath said. "It's more of a party trick than anything else."

Thea absorbed that in silence as they made their way to the front door. Gadsden didn't have magic of his own, and Thea knew enough about spells to know that they needed renewing from time to time. So the Master Merchant had paid a mage to set the spell on his gate, and to come back and keep the spell working. Perhaps Gadsden hoped that a self-heating gate would deter visitors, but it still seemed an odd thing to do.

As they reached the front door, the gate behind them exploded into a shower of white-hot splatters of molten metal.

They turned together, Niath flinging up a hand, the sensation of his magic washing over Thea as he spoke a spell which held the deadly shower away from them.

"Alright. I take it back. That is dangerous," he said, and spoke another spell which had the metal falling to the ground, rapidly losing heat so that the bits and pieces clinked as they landed.

"That is more what I expected," Thea said, her voice too high and too fast. Niath had reacted almost before she had realised that anything was wrong, but her heart hadn't worked out that the immediate danger was over. Or perhaps her body was more sensible than her mind. If Gadsden's house was entered by an exploding gate, she had to wonder what waited for them inside.

"Do you want the sword?" Niath asked as they turned back to the front door.

"Thank you, no. I'll stick with this for now," she said, taking the staff from her belt. She spoke the command and it shimmered into being, perfectly weighted for her hand. "You make excellent weapons," she told him before she used the staff to knock on the door.

"Knocking on the door? We're being polite?" Niath asked.

"I thought we'd try that first before violence," Thea said, conscious of the scattered bits of metal on the ground behind them.

"Do you think it will work?"

"No. But I can put it into my report," she said, trying not to smile.

"That is important," Niath agreed. She wasn't looking at him, but she could hear the smile in his voice.

No one answered the door. So Thea put her hand, carefully, on the doorknob and turned it. The metal stayed cool under her hand and the door yielded inward, revealing a deeply shadowed interior. There did not seem to be a single lantern lit anywhere in the house.

She glanced at Niath and saw his eyes gleaming with the dark of a hiandar. He nodded, signalling he was ready. She adjusted her grip on the staff, ready as she would ever be, and they went through the door together.

She was not surprised when the door closed behind them with a thump. The sound was oddly muffled, as if the air inside the house was too thick to carry the noise very far.

As well as the heavy air, there was almost no light at all. Somehow the house's windows were not letting in any of the star and moon light from outside.

"The people are somewhere to our left," Niath said. "Downstairs, I think, but there are distraction spells in this house that makes it difficult to tell."

In the dark, Thea wasn't sure if Niath could read her expression of surprise. He was a Citadel Mage, and a powerful one. From what Thea had observed, it would take a lot to distract or confuse him. Gadsden had access to powerful magic. Possibly from the Hand, or the warriors of Alayla. Possibly from somewhere else. Wherever he had got it, it was not good news for them.

And even with a few moments inside, her eyes had not adjusted to the lack of light.

"It's too dark for me," Thea said, her heart picking up pace again. "Can you provide some lights?" she asked.

She had no sooner asked than Niath's magic bloomed around her, motes of warm light rising into the air, expanding around them so that she could see.

Having come in the front door, they were in what should have been the entrance hall to the house. Except that Thea could not see any walls, just endless dark beyond the reach of Niath's lights. She looked up and there was no ceiling overhead, only more darkness. It felt almost like being underground, smothered by earth. It made her skin crawl.

"It's a disguise spell of some kind," Niath said. "I can lead us through it," he offered, and held out his hand. She put hers into it without hesitation, feeling his skin warm and real around her fingers. She held the staff upright, ready to use, next to her side, and let Niath lead her forward through the dark.

They had barely moved ten paces when something moved just out of range of Niath's lights. She stopped, tugging his hand.

"I see it," he said, more magic gathering around him. "Get ready." He said another spell, the words hard and loud in the dark, and the lights around them blazed, rising higher, as the darkness peeled away, revealing shapes all around them.

They were in a large room with plain wooden floors, painted walls and a low wooden ceiling. And they were surrounded by half a dozen armed men, all of them with weapons drawn and pointed towards Thea and Niath.

"Well, this is hardly a warm welcome for the Watch," Thea said. She had let go of Niath's hand and had the staff balanced in front of her, ready to defend herself.

"You came to my house uninvited." A voice she knew, belonging to the person she had come to find.

Gadsden was standing outside the circle of armed men. He was dressed in dark, close-fitting clothing quite different to the merchant's robes she had seen him wearing before, his pale skin and red hair gleaming in the light.

"Your gate almost melted my hand," Thea told him. "And we did knock at the door. No one answered."

"You're out of your depth, little girl. Best be going." That was a lighter voice, one that felt familiar, carrying with it a trace of power that set Thea's teeth on edge. In her pocket, the ribbon spell that Niath had given her earlier warmed, letting her know that it was working.

She turned her head slightly and saw another figure just outside the ring of armed men. The clerk from the merchants' guild. Kady. The clerk's face had shifted to her other nature, eyes dark.

Thea had a moment of displacement, remembering seeing that clerk's other *aspect* before. The night kind hidden under the disguise of a perfect, discreet clerk.

"No," Thea said.

"No?" Kady repeated, blinking in surprise. Then her eyes narrowed, and she looked at Niath. "You. You did something to her. She's not obeying me like she should."

"You changed my memories," Thea said, voice hard, staring at the woman. "Just to keep me from seeing Kendrick at the merchants' guild? That's all?"

Kady's eyes widened, and some of her assurance faltered. "You shouldn't be remembering any of that," she said, then her eyes narrowed again. "What did the mage do to you?" she hissed.

Thea ignored the question. Kady had all but admitted to hiding Kendrick's presence at the guild. And Thea could not understand why. The woman had killed the disgraced merchant shortly after that.

"So you're working for Gadsden," Thea said, keeping her voice calm, and trying to keep all of the armed men, Kady and Gadsden in view at the same time. It was impossible to keep track of all of them, but she did her best.

"Temporarily," Kady said, a sneer in her voice. "He pays well."

"You posed the bodies," Thea realised. As a night kind, Kady would have the strength to do that without causing a disturbance. The satisfied look on the woman's face confirmed Thea's guess. "Do tell me, though, how did you get out of the rooms when you'd done the killing?" Thea asked, voice light. "The doors were locked from the inside."

"Were they really?" Kady said, a smirk on her face. "Or were the doors locked, with the key on the inside?"

It was Thea's turn to blink. "Isn't that the same thing?"

"How are you still alive? You're so stupid. No, it's not the same thing. But I'm not going to give you all my secrets," Kady said. She turned to Gadsden. "You still owe me payment for earlier."

Earlier. Presumably when Kady had stabbed Kendrick in Middlefield Market. A sour taste bloomed in Thea's mouth. The woman was a killer for hire. Thea wondered what Matthew and Iva would think of one of their kind becoming a mercenary.

"And I told you, you get paid when I do," Gadsden said, a snap in his voice. "And don't try your tricks on me."

"Why not?" Kady asked, voice changing to become silky soft, almost seductive. "What are you going to do to me?"

"Have my men kill you," Gadsden said, the words dragged out of him. He shook his head, taking a step back as if trying to break free from Kady's influence. "I said don't try your tricks."

"As interesting as this is," Thea said, "I want you both to come with me to Middlefield Watch Station. I have questions for you both, as does the Watch Captain."

"No," Gadsden said, without looking at her. He flicked a hand at the armed men. "Kill them all," he said, and turned, leaving the room.

The armed men swarmed forward, aiming for Kady, Niath and Thea.

Kady yelled in fury, then moved with all the speed of the night kind and ducked out the same door Gadsden had used. Thea swore, seeing one of her quarries escape, but had no more time to do or think anything as she was surrounded by armed men, all trying to obey Gadsden's order to kill her.

A blast of magic sent a pair of the mercenaries off their feet, slamming back into the wall. Thea managed to disarm another with a sweep of her staff, turning her attention to the remaining three as Niath fired another blast of magic.

The mercenaries were wiser this time, and only one of them stumbled back.

Thea met the other pair with her staff, slamming into the swords they tried to attack her with, having the satisfaction of seeing them falter and hearing the grunt of surprise as she held against them. She disengaged her staff and turned it, spinning it towards their feet, catching them off guard and spilling the pair onto the ground.

That left the one who had stumbled back. He was standing, sword in front of him, near the door that Gadsden and Kady had disappeared through.

"I'm not getting paid enough for this," he said, in a heavy accent that Thea could not place, before he turned and left through the same door.

"We need to find Gadsden," Niath said, striding forward.

"Wait, let's tie these men up first. Otherwise they might come after us again," Thea said, pulling lengths of Watch rope from her belt. She had added an extra piece to her usual equipment, so had plenty to tie the five mercenaries up with. She secured one end of the rope around the door handle and left the men bound together, their weapons kicked to the other side of the room.

Then she and Niath went after Gadsden, into the dark of the rest of the house.

Chapter Twenty-Seven

"Are there any other people in the house?" she asked Niath, frustrated, when they had searched the fourth room without success. The house beyond the first room had been a series of rooms, all of them empty of furniture or people.

"Yes. I can sense at least one. Very close, but we can't seem to reach him."

"More magic?" she asked.

"If it's Gadsden, he doesn't possess any such magic," Niath said.

"You saw the gate, and the darkness spell. He's clearly hired someone to do the work. Mage Fisk?"

"No. This isn't Fisk's work. It's pretty blunt. Using some interesting spells, but with no finesse."

"Can you find Gadsden?" Thea asked, waving aside his interest in the other mage's technique. She just wanted to find her quarry and get out of the house. Even though the worst of the darkness had been lifted, she had a constant itch between her shoulder blades, as if someone was watching her from just behind her. Except every time she turned, there was nothing there.

"I do have a reveal spell," Niath said, clearly reluctant, "but it's pretty brutal. And it sometimes works in odd ways."

"Well, I'm willing to try brutal," Thea said. "This place is creepy."

"I agree," Niath said. He drew a breath, "Alright. Stand behind me."

Thea moved to where he had pointed and held her staff to her side.

The air grew heavier still, crackling against her skin, with the build-up of Niath's magic, heady and potent. She wanted to lean against him, absorb more of the warmth. She had never met anyone whose magic drew her as his did.

The magic released in a wave that scoured her skin, rolled across the floor, shaking the ground under them and making the walls tremble. The dark around them peeled back, revealing a plain room with a low, bare plaster ceiling and painted walls, and Master Merchant Gadsden sitting in a huge, ornate chair, a low table in front of him, watching them with a smirk on his face.

The smirk disappeared as Niath and Thea focused on him, then changed to astonishment as he stared at Thea.

"What?" she demanded, and took a step towards him, almost losing her balance.

Blinding white stretched to either side of her. Her wings. The wings she had folded away and managed to almost never think about. Revealed by Niath's magic.

She spat out a curse, glowering at the length of wing she could see.

"I told you it works in unpredictable ways," Niath said, unrepentant.

"You-" Gadsden said, then swallowed. "You're not human."

"No," Thea agreed, trying to step forward again and again hampered by her wings, which brushed against the ceiling. This was not a room designed for Ageless. She forced herself to stop, stand still, and take a breath. Gadsden did not seem as if he was going anywhere just now. And she needed to deal with the wings. She had managed to put away her wings before, and they had stayed hidden until Niath's magic had pulled them out. She could get rid of them again, she was sure, and go back to pretending that they didn't exist.

After a moment which seemed to stretch for an eternity, the wings flickered along their length and vanished and she was back to her own body again, light-headed with relief.

"Where were we?" she asked. "Oh, yes. Roe Gadsden, you are under arrest."

"I don't think so," he said, leaning forward. Too late, Thea saw the series of pots on the table in front of him, and the small burner, like one her mother used for brewing potions. He picked up one of the pots and tossed it over the burner, sending heavy, acrid smoke into the room that blinded Thea, stuffing up her nose and her senses so she was blind and deaf.

Until searing, blinding light broke through the dark and she found herself back in the same room, Gadsden trying to make his way past her. She reached out and grabbed his arm.

"No," she said. "You don't get to run away. Not this time."

He turned to her. Rather than the anger she had been expecting, he smiled. He put his hand over hers, his skin hot and dry. Dimly she heard Niath call her name, but then she was spiralling down into dark, the only thing she could see Gadsden's face and the only thing she could hear his voice.

"You are out of your depth," he said. "You have no idea what you are interfering with."

"Do tell me," she invited. "You had Kady kill Hannaford and Paulin and Kendrick. For what? So you could get their trade routes?"

"Stupid creature. You have no idea what those routes are worth. It makes me as rich as the Archon."

"I doubt that," Thea said, lip curling. "I've seen inside her Treasury, and that's just the one here. There's a Treasury in every Citadel."

Gadsden's assurance faltered for a moment, then he sneered again. "Richer than any human alive, then."

"That I believe," Thea said. "So, did you help Kendrick escape as well?"

Gadsden's lip curled. "No. He managed that on his own." He sounded disgusted.

Thea's brows rose, startled by the direct and blunt answer. "But you spoke to him at the guild. You knew he was free." That was a guess. Her memory still was not clear.

"He thought he could just come back," Gadsden said, lip curling.

"But you had other plans," Thea said. And the means to get rid of his rivals. Hannaford. Paulin. Kendrick. "So, you wanted their wealth. Was that all it was? All this just for money?"

"Such a limited imagination," he said, with an undertone that told Thea she had struck a nerve. She had accused him of being petty. Of just being after money. And that had stung.

"So, there's more to it," she said slowly. "I know that you're part of the Hand. That you worked with Mage Waters and Apprentice Sisley to create a copy of the goddess Alayla." She saw his eyes widen slightly. Surprised she knew so much? "What? Did you think I wouldn't remember a woman made of gold? Or a new gang in the city calling themselves the Hand of the goddess? Kendrick was part of it, too. What are you planning?"

"You couldn't possibly understand," he said, grinning, all his arrogance and assurance back in place. His human eyes were oddly shaded, bits of dark and light mixed together.

"I'd still like to know," she said, trying to break away from him. His fingers tightened around hers, far beyond what he should have been able to manage, until she could feel her bones grind together. He was stronger than any human should be. "Let me guess. You're going to challenge the Ageless?"

His eyes widened, grin slipping a little. "How did-" He shook his head. "It doesn't matter. You can't stop us. We're stronger than you know."

"You certainly have a firm grip," Thea acknowledged, mind spinning on what he had admitted. Whoever was behind the Hand of the goddess was setting themselves up to challenge the Ageless. "Do you realise how many people could get hurt in your stupid challenge?"

The grin was back in place again, and she had an urge to violence just to make that expression disappear.

"Cattle. All of them. They'll soon come around when they see the better life we can offer."

"Better life? How? What do you mean?" Thea asked, trying to focus through the pain. He had not let her go. She could barely feel her fingers, the back of her hand a mass of white-hot pain.

"Freedom from the Ageless," he said, still grinning. "Freedom to make our own choices. To have a human nation once again."

"Oh, for goodness' sake," Thea snapped, pain and irritation spiking together. "You really think a human nation will be better? Do you even realise what that means? Driving hundreds of people out of this city, for one."

"A small price to pay for living our lives," Gadsden said.

"I think I've heard enough," she said, and twisted her arm, ignoring the renewed pain shooting up her wrist.

He had not been expecting her to try and break free, his own grip slipping until she was able to pull herself away, bringing her staff up, aiming for his head. He ducked, clumsy and slow but just fast enough to miss the strike, then tripped over his feet, falling backwards, scrambling away on his heels and hands.

"No. You can't stop me," he said. "You can't." He pulled something out from under his collar. A chain with a vial at the end.

Before Thea could react, he had opened the vial and swallowed its contents. He vanished before her eyes, a backlash of cold magic sending her spinning back, off her own feet, tumbling onto the plain wooden floor, trying to catch herself on her hands and crying out in agony as her injured hand gave way so that she sprawled onto the floor, staff clattering against the wood and rolling away.

"Thea."

It took her a moment to place the voice, which was bad. She turned her head and found Niath kneeling beside her, face halfway between human and hiandar, expression full of concern.

"Are you alright?" he asked.

She made a non-committal sound and tried to sit up, putting pressure on her hands and falling back again as her injured hand refused to hold any weight. She rolled onto her back and then sat up, cradling her injured hand to her chest.

"Mostly alright," she told him. "He's gone, hasn't he?"

"Some spell I don't recognise. Did you see what he did?" Niath asked.

"He had a vial on a chain around his neck. He swallowed it and there was this ... I don't know ... explosion of sorts. He vanished."

"A transportation spell," Niath said, eyes wide. "I've heard of them in theory. I didn't think anyone had managed to make any."

"Well, he didn't make it," Thea said, with confidence. "We know he didn't have any magic of his own."

"What happened to your hand?"

"He crushed it," she said, glancing down and then wishing she hadn't. Her fingers were swollen and purple, the back of her hand a mess of bruising. "I think he might have broken bones. He was a lot stronger than he should have been."

"A strength spell is easy enough," Niath said. "Although it doesn't last for long. Here. This is another of Mage Fisk's potions. It should help."

"Just how many of those did you get from him?" Thea asked, taking the open vial from Niath.

"A few," he answered, smiling. "We seem to encounter a lot of trouble. It seemed wise to be prepared."

Thea wished she could disagree, but could not, and was simply grateful he had planned ahead. She swallowed the foul-tasting mixture, eyes watering from the taste, and then doubled over as agony shot through her hand, the bones grinding together as they realigned themselves. Even as she watched, the purple and bruising faded back to something close to her normal, pale skin tone.

When she could breathe again, a stinging sensation running across her hand, she looked back at Niath. "How much did you hear?"

"When he had you in the spell? I couldn't hear anything."

"It was a spell?" Thea asked, then shook her head. "Of course it was. How did he get hold of that?"

"I don't know. It was activated when he touched you. It's old magic. I came across a reference to it in the papers," Niath said.

"Was there a transportation spell there as well?" Thea asked, glaring at the spot where Gadsden had been. Now that she was not in pain, she had time to be truly annoyed that the Master Merchant had escaped.

"Possibly. We haven't had time to go through all of the papers yet."

Thea was distracted as her eyes travelled around the room, realising that it was a meeting place of sorts. Too small for an Ageless' wings, but plenty big enough for a half dozen seats around the low table. The ornate chair that Gadsden had been sitting in looked like it belonged to the person in charge. And it was in Gadsden's house. She shivered, remembering what he had said about the Hand challenging the Ageless. With the spells in this house and the oppressive darkness they had encountered, it was easy to imagine the organisers of the Hand sitting around this table, plotting their next move.

"I suspect Kendrick sat around this table with Gadsden. I wonder who else?" she speculated. "Paulin? Hannaford? Mage Waters to bring the goddess back to life?"

"Those seem like good bets," Niath said, looking around the room as well. "There are seven seats in all. I wonder if they were all occupied."

Thea's blood ran cold, looking around the empty spaces. All too easy to imagine the conspirators gathered here, however reluctantly they had begun. There was plenty of space between the chairs for other people, too, she realised. Somehow, she doubted that Mage Waters would have been in this room without his apprentice.

"Well, Gadsden seemed to think that the Hand would continue without the dead merchants, so I'm guessing that all the seats were taken, and perhaps there were more involved, too," Thea said, glaring at the empty chair that Gadsden had been sitting in. "I'd like to ask him, though. Can we track him?" she asked.

"Not without knowing the spell." Niath frowned at the empty spot as well. "Although, he would have needed a specific destination in mind."

"So he couldn't just trigger the spell at random?" Thea asked, absently massaging her now-healing hand. "That's useful. There can't be that many places he'd feel comfortable going to. He'd need to know it was safe."

"It will still take a while to hunt for him, though," Niath said, his own irritation clear. "We had him. Right here. What did he say to you?"

Thea told him as they made their way out of the room and back through the house, making sure that the mercenaries were still tied up. Niath could not sense anyone else in the building, so they went to the front door to find the welcome sight of Sutter and a half-dozen Watchmen and women, all armed with cudgels and determined expressions.

Thea told Sutter where to find the mercenaries, and he sent the Watch in, with instructions to search the house first before bringing the mercenaries out. Sutter nodded at Niath. "I don't doubt you can't sense any other people in there, but there might be bodies."

"That's true." Niath said.

As the Watch moved into the building, Thea spotted movement around the corner of a nearby building. Leaving Niath to brief Sutter on what had happened, she made her way across the street to meet Matthew and Iva, a body on the ground between them.

"She died rather than be questioned," Matthew said, face and voice tight.

"The death is my responsibility, if the Watch wants to make something of it." Iva said, staring at Thea. The fiandar was holding herself stiff and still, but Thea could still tell she was injured, one arm pressed tightly to her side.

"I doubt it," Thea said, crouching down next to Kady's body. The only obvious injury she could see was to the side of her head. It looked as if she had been hit with something hard. Or fallen against it. "She killed three people. I am sure you were just defending yourself."

"She was," Matthew said. "She came at us with knives. We resisted. She fell against a gatepost."

"She died here?" Thea asked.

"No. A few streets away. We can show you," he answered. He looked past her shoulder to the house. "Is it over?"

"Not nearly," Thea said, getting to her feet, abruptly exhausted. "Gadsden got away. But he admitted to being part of the Hand. He said they are going to challenge the Ageless."

"Idiots," Matthew said. He did not seem at all surprised, instead smiling at Thea's expression. "I've lived far longer than you might think, Investigator March. The Hand are not the first who want to challenge the Ageless."

"They are still dangerous," Iva said. She moved, restless, and hissed a breath, pressing her hand to her side. Thea saw a dark stain on her clothing.

"You're badly injured," Thea said. "Let me-"

"I'll live," Iva said, voice sharp. "As long as we don't stand here talking all day."

Thea found herself smiling. "Fair enough. I'll need to get a Watchman to keep an eye on the body, but if you can show me where she died, that's all I need for now."

Sutter came across the street at Thea's raised hand, Niath with him, and promised to keep an eye on the body while she and Niath went with the fiandar to see where Kady had died.

The anonymous bit of street where the fiandar had died tied in with the description that Matthew and Iva gave. They offered to show Thea how it had happened, but she believed them.

It was not the ending that Thea had wanted. Not at all. The killer was dead. But the person who had hired her had vanished, escaped in front of her eyes using magic he should not have been able to wield. It did not sit well with her at all. Hannaford, Paulin and Kendrick might not have been good people. For one, she would not mourn Kendrick's death. But they deserved an accounting and reckoning for their murders, just like everyone else. And they would not get it.

Chapter Twenty-Eight

It was mid-morning by the time Thea had finished writing her reports, eyes burning with lack of sleep, hand aching with writer's cramp. But she had wanted to get it all done, set it all out, before she forgot.

While she had been writing her reports, she had also started a list of loose ends and questions. Gadsden's whereabouts, for one. Who else was in the Hand, and where they were. Understanding the contents of the papers found at Bordan Hannaford's house. The list covered two full sides of parchment, and she was sure there were more questions to be considered.

The threat of the Hand was real. She remembered Mage Waters, mad and filthy, corrupted by blood magic, confessing to helping them. The Hand wasn't some fanatical group dedicated to the ancient goddess. They were far more dangerous. Their organisers had included some of the most ruthless and wealthiest citizens of Accanter. Gadsden had seemed certain that they would challenge the Ageless, and Thea could not see that going well for anyone in the city. Not the Hand, and not the general population. More than that, the Hand seemed to want to create a human-only city. She was both disgusted and amused by that. The humans in the city were mostly completely blind to the fact that a lot of their neighbours were not human. They would be shocked to find just how many non-humans lived among them, and how dependent they were on the non-human population. The nairiad who provided fresh fish through the year. The fiandar, and the forest dwellers, who provided fresh produce even in the hottest or coldest weather. The other night kind who lent their strength to some of the hardest manual jobs in the city.

Everyone in the city had grown used to the idea of going to the market and finding what they wanted. Or that the industries would just run and run, providing jobs to pay wages and necessary items to buy from furniture to clothing. Thea was not sure that some of the industries would survive if the non-human population was banned from the city's limits.

And that was before she considered the Ageless-born and the mages. Mages were usually human through and through, but non-magical humans often didn't think so. And Ageless-born were despised, when they were recognised.

If the Hand had their way, there would be chaos. And a lot of people would be hurt.

She sat back in her chair and stretched, feeling the tension in her muscles, and the heaviness that came from lack of sleep.

Sutter appeared in her office doorway, as if somehow knowing it was the perfect time to interrupt before her thoughts could spiral down further.

"Mistress Hannaford left this for you," he said, putting a very large box on the side of her desk. "I suggest you take it home with you as soon as you can. It smells delicious."

Thea blinked, staring at the box that looked like the sort of light construction that a bakery would use. "Oh," she said. "Did she say why?"

"She said it was on behalf of her niece, if that makes sense," Sutter said.

"It does. Sort of." Thea remembered Neda, practically skipping away along the street, going to see her aunt to tell her what she considered to be the good news of Kendrick's death. Thea could not help but wonder how Megan Hannaford felt. She had lost her husband and her brother within a few days of each other.

"So, are you going home now? Most of us managed a bit of sleep last night, but you've been here the whole time."

Thea was about to protest that she was fine to stay on duty, but had to stop as a huge yawn took her over. "Well, perhaps it is time I go home," she agreed, glancing at her desk. There was a neat stack of reports to one side, and her list of questions to the other. She put the list of questions into a drawer and got up, handing the stack of reports to Sutter. "My reports."

Sutter grinned. He was the only person Thea had ever met who seemed happy to be handed paperwork. "Thank you. I am sure these will be interesting reading."

"There's still just one thing I don't understand," Thea said, picking up the box as she made her way out of the office.

"Just one thing?" Sutter said. "You're much further along than the rest of us, then."

"Well, there are lots of open questions. But one thing I don't get about the killings. We know that Kady could influence people one at a time. So she could probably get each of the victims to stand and let her kill them. But then she got out of two rooms with a locked door, the key on the inside."

"Ah, you'll want to follow me, then," Sutter said. He turned along the corridor towards the captain's office. The door was locked, and Dina was standing outside it, a lit candle in one hand.

"Are you ready?" Dina called through the door.

Thea heard a muffled reply from Ware, which must have been an affirmative. Dina moved her free hand, as if pulling something.

Interested, Thea moved closer and saw a thin thread in Dina's hand, which seemed to have been fed through the keyhole. The examiner pulled the thread until there was an audible click of the door lock, then set the naked flame to the thread and stepped back.

Before Thea could react, or protest at the examiner trying to burn down the Watch Station, she saw a thin line of flame course up the length of the thread and through the keyhole.

A moment later and the door handle turned and Ware opened the door, staring at the key in the lock on his side of the door. The inside of the door.

"That's ingenious," he said. "How did you work that out?"

"Well," Dina said, eyes gleaming.

Sutter cleared his throat.

Dina glanced at him, lips pursing together. "Alright. The short version. I remembered a few years back we had a burglar that seemed to manage to get into locked houses. Only it turned out they weren't locked. He somehow put the keys back in the locks when he left." She blew out the candle and held up a spool of thread with her other hand. "Waxed thread. It's an absolute pest to make, but once done it's a bit tougher than normal thread, more than strong enough to pull a key under a door and up to the keyhole. So, you tie the key onto the thread, and feed it under the door and then pull it up into the lock," Dina said, eyes bright. "Of course, it only works if there's a gap for the key under the door."

"But most doors have a small gap at least," Thea said slowly, nodding her head. Room enough to slide a key under. "Very clever," Thea said. "So, now we know how Kady apparently escaped a room locked from the inside."

"And not one bit of magic involved," Dina said, grinning. She was clearly delighted with herself and Thea found herself smiling back. Not one bit of magic, or any Ageless or other natured creature involved. Just a bit of ingenuity. "Is that a box from Megan Hannaford?" Dina asked, eyes straying to the package Thea was carrying.

"We have a prior appointment," Sutter said, before Dina could demand a share of whatever was in the box.

"So we do. Well, you're buying dessert," Dina said cheerfully. It was only then that Thea realised Dina was looking tidier than normal. She was dressed differently, too, in wide-legged trousers and a plain shirt that were not rumpled or covered in stains. She had also brushed her hair within the past day.

"It really is ingenious," Ware said, staring at the key in his door lock. "Is there a way of protecting against such interference?" he asked.

"Oh, now, there's a good question," Dina said, narrowing her eyes at the key in the lock. "Let me think about that and get back to you."

"Tomorrow," Sutter said.

"Oh, alright," Dina said.

The two of them descended the stairs in perfect harmony, leaving Thea standing next to Ware.

"Reports finished?" he asked.

"Yes, sir. I was going to head home for a few hours."

"Two days," he said. "No, not a request. You've not had any time off for a while. We're all taking the afternoon off, and then I don't want to see you back here for another two days."

Thea had her mouth open to argue when Ware turned and looked at her.

"No arguments, and no excuses. We all need a rest some time."

Niath was outside the station as she left. He was just waiting there as she came down the steps. She should be getting used to him just turning up, but she found herself surprised and pleased to see him, as usual.

"Is that a gift from Megan Hannaford?" he asked, eyes on the box Thea was carrying.

"It is. Would you like to share it?" Thea asked.

"Oh, yes, please," he said, and fell into step beside her. "Where are we going?"

"Well, it's a nice day, so I thought I would go and sit in my mother's garden for a bit," Thea said. "I've been told to take the next two days off, and I've got no idea what to do with them."

"Don't you like having time off?" Niath asked.

"Normally, yes," Thea said, and shook her head. "It's just. Well. I would normally do chores around the house. Spend time with my mother. But-"

"You have been keeping secrets from each other," Niath said, with perfect understanding. "I have an alternate idea, if I may?"

"Please."

"There's a festival in Fallowfield over the next few days. Jugglers and acrobats and players. We could go out of uniform," Niath suggested, a hint of mischief in his face when Thea looked across at him.

"Pretend to be ordinary people for a while," she said, and felt a surge of longing rise up in her. Be ordinary. Not have to think about her unwanted wings, or the Hand, or the Ageless, or the missing merchant, or what any of it might mean for her city and the people she cared about. Instead, she could put on plain clothes and just be another citizen, gasping at the feats of the festival players. "That sounds lovely," she said.

"Good. I will come and get you tomorrow morning," Niath said.

They took a longer route back to her mother's house, talking about nothing in particular, and it was only when they reached her mother's house that Thea wondered if he meant anything more by the invitation than simply friends.

By then, it was too late to ask. They were at the side gate, and Thea could hear the murmur of conversation drifting out into the street, along with laughter. She had not heard laughter in her mother's house for a long time.

She pushed open the gate and she and Niath went through to find her mother, Trymian and Ware settled in chairs in the garden, a low table between them holding a bottle of wine, glasses, and plates with what looked like the remains of a meal.

Thea's brows lifted, and not just at Trymian's presence. Ware had said he was taking the afternoon off. Apparently, he was spending it with her mother.

"Thea. Look who found us," her mother said, smiling.

"Thea?" Trymian rose to his feet, looking faintly shocked. "You're Elise's daughter."

"I am," Thea said, stopping just outside the circle.

"The same young thing who fell after her brother at Kellto," Trymian said, face as serious as she had ever seen it.

"Yes," Thea confirmed, a lump in her throat, a flash of memory surfacing, of Theo's body too still on the ground below.

"I am so glad to see you grown, and making such a good life for yourself," Trymian said, face breaking into a smile.

"Trymian came looking for some ingredients," her mother said, and patted the chair next to her. "Ware's only just got here. I was just about to make some tea. Do come and sit. You too, Niath."

Thea took the seat, Niath settling next to her, and set the box on the only spare space on the table. "We should share these," Thea said.

"What's in there?" her mother asked, intrigued.

"A gift. From Megan Hannaford," Thea said, and untied the string that was holding the box together. The top and sides lifted away to reveal tiers of small, fancy cakes.

"Oh, my," her mother said. "This calls for something better than tea."

"Do not worry, I have more wine," Trymian said.

"I'll get more glasses, plates and forks from the kitchen," Ware said, and disappeared into the house, leaving Thea to wonder just when and how he had become so familiar with the kitchen that he knew where things were.

It didn't take long for the plates and glasses to be filled and passed around. Mistress Hannaford's cakes were as delicious as Thea remembered them, and Trymian seemed to have brought an endless supply of fine wine.

So the afternoon passed with Thea sitting in the sunshine in her mother's garden, surrounded by lively chatter and laughter, the frustrations and worries of the investigation slowly seeping away along with the lingering tension at her mother's lies. She understood her mother's reasons.

There would be time enough to find Gadsden, and work out what the Hand were doing. And time enough for Thea to look past the lies her mother had told and work out the truth of the Ageless for herself.

For now, she had some of her favourite people in the world around her, and the prospect of a day out with Niath the next day. A day of pure enjoyment. She could not remember the last time that had happened. She laughed along with the others, her heart lifting.

THANK YOU

Thank you very much for reading *Assassin's Noon*, Ageless Mysteries - Book 4. I do hope that you've enjoyed continuing Thea's story.

It would be great, if you have five minutes, if you could leave an honest review at the store you got it from. Reviews are really helpful for other readers to decide whether the book is for them, and also help me get visibility for my books - thank you.

Thea's story will continue in *Flightless Afternoon*, Ageless Mysteries - Book 5, also available at Amazon.

If you want to know what I'm working on and when the next book will be available, you can contact me and sign up for my newsletter at the website: www.taellaneth.com.

CHARACTER LIST

(Note: to avoid spoilers, some names may have been missed, and some details changed)

Alayla - goddess of war and fire (from the time before the Ageless)

Aldric - Ageless, Edris' son

Algar Hobbs - human, Watchman, minds the desk at the Captain's Watch Station

Bordan Hannaford - human, merchant, Master Merchant and head of the merchants' guild in Accanter

Caroline March - human, skilled apothecary, Thea's mother

Cedd Trant - human, merchant, Odilia's oldest brother

Dalston Paulin - human, Master Merchant and member of the council of the merchants' guild in Accanter

Dina Soter - human, in charge of the forensics team

Edris - Ageless, Archon of the known worlds

Everson - human, Watchman

Fionn - Ageless-born, steward at The Summer House

Gaderian - Ageless (deceased) - a renowned magical scholar and creator of spells

Gilbert - cat, lives with Thea and her mother

Gordie Trant - human, merchant, Odilia's brother

Hern - horse borrowed by Thea

Iason Pallas - human, doctor in charge of the city morgue

Iva - night kind, warrior, a friend of Mathew Shand's

Jilt Fisk - human, mage for hire in Accanter

Kady - night kind living in Accanter

Kendrick - human, Master Merchant with business interests in Brightfield

Laurelle - Ageless - archivist of the Citadel

Lucan - Ageless, wing commander in the Citadel's garrison

Matthew Shand - night kind, leader of the fiandar clan in Accanter

Megan Hannaford - human, Bordan Hannaford's wife

Mort - Ageless-born, owns a bookshop in Brightfield

Neda - human, living in Lowcroft

Niath - mage, based at the Citadel

Odilia Trant - part-human, mage assigned to the city watch

Reardon - Ageless, one of the garrison commanders at the Citadel

Richard - human, younger son of the family that used to live in Brightfield House

Roe Gadsden - human, Master Merchant, and member of the council of the merchants' guild in Accanter

Sisley - human, Apprentice Mage at the Citadel

Sutter - human, Senior Sergeant of the Watch

Thea (Althea) March - junior law officer, Caroline's daughter

Trymian - Ageless, Mort's father

Ware Handerson - captain of the Watch

Waters - human, Mage, senior Mage of the Citadel

PLACES

Accanter - city where Thea and her mother live, home to the Archon

Brightfield - former village, now part of Accanter - one of the Watch districts

Brightfield House - former home of the lord of Brightfield, now headquarters for the Watch's physician and scientific examiner

Citadel - houses the Ageless and their soldiers, in the case of Accanter

Cross Keys Tavern - tavern in Brightfield

Fallowfield - former village, now part of Accanter - one of the Watch districts

Highfield - former village, now part of Accanter - one of the Watch districts

Institute of Scientific Enquiry - also known as the institute, part of Accanter, in the Watch district of Northcroft

Lowcroft - former village, now part of Accanter - where Thea and her mother live

Meadowcroft - former village, now part of Accanter - one of the Watch districts, borders the Citadel

Middlefield - former village, now part of Accanter - one of the Watch districts, between Brightfield and Fallowfield - where the Watch Captain is based

Northcroft - former village, now part of Accanter - one of the Watch districts, borders the Citadel

Summer House - grand old house outside Accanter

Threshers Street - part of the Watch district of Wheatcroft

Wheatcroft - former village, now part of the city of Accanter - one of the Watch districts

ALSO BY THE AUTHOR

(as at February 2024)

Fractured Conclave
A Usual Suspect, Book 1
A Broken Contract, Book 2 – expected to release October 2024

The Grey Gates (complete)
Outcast, Book 1
Called, Book 2
Hunted, Book 3
Forged, Book 4
Chosen, Book 5

Ageless Mysteries (complete)
Deadly Night, Book 1
False Dawn, Book 2
Morning Trap, Book 3
Assassin's Noon, Book 4
Flightless Afternoon, Book 5
Ascension Day, Book 6

The Hundred series (complete)
The Gathering, Book 1

The Sundering, Book 2
The Reckoning, Book 3
The Rending, Book 4
The Searching, Book 5
The Rising, Book 6

The Taellaneth series (complete)
Concealed, Book 1
Revealed, Book 2
Betrayed, Book 3
Tainted, Book 4
Cloaked, Book 5

Taellaneth Box Set (all five books in one e-book)
Taellaneth Complete Series (Books 1–5)

ABOUT THE AUTHOR

Vanessa Nelson is a fantasy author who lives in Scotland, United Kingdom and spends her days juggling the demands of an elderly spoiled cat, two giant dogs and her fictional characters.

As far as the cat is concerned, she is in charge and should always come first. The older dog lets her know when he isn't getting enough attention by chewing up the house. The younger dog's favourite method of getting her attention is a gentle nudge with his head. At least, he would say it's gentle.

You can find out more information online at the following places:

Website: www.taellaneth.com

Facebook: www.facebook.com/taellaneth

Made in the USA
Monee, IL
15 November 2024